Penguin

THE BLOODING

His lawyer tells Col to write it all down: from the time the protesters arrive in the tiny Australian town to halt the logging to the moment when his father drives the bulldozer into the tree and puts him in hospital.

Torn between his attraction for Jade, the student protester, and loyalty towards his family and friends, who depend so completely on logging for their livelihoods, Col finds even his deepest secret threatened. For while he drinks with the gang, boxes, plays football and expects one day to work in the mill, the forest and the place it hides are precious to him.

Thus with a foot in both camps, he eventually becomes, in his confusion, the centre of a dramatic and violent confrontation.

This powerful novel, brimming with energy, charts with immense passion Col's personal dilemma and the political issues he faces in a world of compromise and contradiction.

Nadia Wheatley is a highly acclaimed writer of books for young people in her native Australia. She has lived in inner-city Sydney as well as spending ten years in Greece. She now lives on a farm in Australia.

▸▸▸ THE BLOODING

Nadia Wheatley

Penguin Books

PENGUIN BOOKS

Published by the Penguin Group
27 Wrights Lane, London W8 5TZ, England
Viking Penguin Inc., 40 West 23rd Street, New York, New York 10010, USA
Penguin Books Australia Ltd, Ringwood, Victoria, Australia
Penguin Books Canada Ltd, 2801 John Street, Markham, Ontario, Canada L3R 1B4
Penguin Books (NZ) Ltd, 182–190 Wairau Road, Auckland 10, New Zealand

Penguin Books Ltd, Registered Offices: Harmondsworth, Middlesex, England

First published in Australia by Viking Penguin 1987
First published in Great Britain by Viking Kestrel 1988
Published in Penguin Books 1989
1 3 5 7 9 10 8 6 4 2

Printed and bound in Great Britain by
Cox & Wyman Ltd, Reading

This book is for Simon

Acknowledgement

I wish to thank Mick Price, Jackie Fewster, Martin Johnston, Meredith Burgmann, Simon Whithear, and Ken Searle, for helpful suggestions and general support. Thanks too to Kay Ronai for editing. This book was written with the financial assistance of the Literature Board of the Australia Council.

Acknowledgement is also due to Methuen, London, for permission to quote 'The Old Triangle', from *The Quare Fellow,* by Brendan Behan; to Castle Music Pty Ltd for permission to quote 'It Might As Well Rain Until September', by Carol King and Jerry Griffin, and to Les A. Murray and Angus and Robertson for permission to quote 'The Princes' Land', from *The Vernacular Republic, Poems 1961-1981.*

An idle prince, with a cembalo sings to
the golden afternoon.
Les A. Murray, *The Prince's Land.*

▶ ▶ ▶

The Lawyer said to write down what happened.

'Everything?' I said.

'Everything,' he said. 'The whole sequence of events.'

'About both things?' I said.

He got a bit of a funny look on his face. 'About ... both things.'

I guess it is funny. I don't mean funny ha-ha, but funny peculiar (as my Mum says).

To be arrested for being a greenie, and arrested at the same time for being against the greenies. It's Offensive Behaviour and Trespass for one thing, but for the other thing it might be going to turn into Manslaughter. It depends how the bloke makes out. He's still in a coma.

So anyway, that's my both things.

'Two bob each way, I guess you could say,' the Lawyer reckoned, when he explained the charges. (I still don't understand them.)

'And put down why you did it,' he said. 'We'll try to get you off under First Offenders. We'll stress your age and ... inexperience ...' (he looked like he meant stupidity) 'and try to show that you were just regrettably led astray by older people.' He paused, then added, 'In ... both cases.' He looked as if he didn't think it was a real good argument.

'I'm not going to dob.' I told him that flat.

He ignored me. 'Just write down what happened. This is between you and me. And I'll be the judge of what we say in court.'

Judge. Court. Mostly I don't think about it. He reckons I'll probably just get a fine or something for the first two charges so that's OK (not that I've got any money), but the manslaughter stuff gets me. Specially as I didn't even do it. Or not much. Not as much as – don't put their names down.

I must have been looking blank or something – I sometimes do that – cut off completely and get into some place in my head and don't even hear people – it's like being alone in the forest. (My Grandad used to say I was one of the 'dreaming Ferrises'.) Then I saw the lawyer's hand on my pyjama sleeve, like a big white cabbage moth, waiting.

'Just begin at the beginning,' he said very patiently, 'and work through to the middle, and end at the end. Pretend you're just telling a story. You'll find it's easy, once you start. I'll ask the Sister to give you a pen and some paper.'

'No worries,' I said, meaning about the paper. Squirt had got Mum to send in my bag of school stuff and I could use some of that. It's not as if I'll be going back. I won't even be able to go back to Cornwall. Get my head kicked in.

'Good, then.' The Lawyer nodded, as if everything was settled. 'Take your time. And just post it to me when you finish. There's nothing really for us to discuss till I've read it.' He seemed glad to be going. He's a free one, from Legal Aid, so I suppose he's not as good as one you pay for. The old man always reckons: 'You get nothing for nothing in this world.' But I don't have any choice. Just see the old man coughing up for a fancy mouthpiece for me. Even if he could afford it. Even if he – stop it.

Anyway, the Lawyer said ta-ta or whatever, had a quick flirt with Baby Nurse at the door, and was off.

And here I am, back on my Paddy Malone, as Mum says. It's the waiting that gets me. I just wish it could all be over and done with. The Lawyer said the cases won't come up for a while, and I'm out on bail. (The greenies put up the dough.) He reckoned it wasn't much, 'under the circumstances'.

What a joke. Both legs in plaster, I can't even get out of bed to go to the dunny. And where'd I escape to, anyway? The only place I know in the world is home. And it's not that any more.

Anyway. That was an hour ago, he left. And I got out my Communication Skills folder and opened a packet of new paper.

'Begin at the beginning,' he reckoned. That's not so easy. But writing it down will be something to do, anyhow. (I've already filled three pages!) So here goes.

▷ ▷ ▷ ————————————

The first day, if it was the first day, I lay behind a blackberry bush, having a bit of a feed as I waited. The berries were black and full, warm from the sun, staining my T-shirt red where I wiped my fingers on it. Mum would look at it and sigh when I got home. Wouldn't say anything, but. She never did. Men are meant to be dirty, in my family.

The rabbits were just starting to come out, on the slope. The forest was behind me, the shadows of the trees creeping down towards me, autumn night-time on its way. 'Just *bang-bang,*' I thought, 'then *home James and don't spare the horses.*' That was one of Mum's sayings too. Mum was always coming out with sayings that other kids' mums didn't say. Made Scott and them laugh at me, when I was little.

They didn't laugh any more. I was the second-best bowler on the cricket team, the sharpest kicker in the B-grade footie team. I was one of the boys. Drank with them after the games, even if I was a bit younger than the gang at seventeen. But you don't get barred for being under-age in Cornwall. Half the time old Golden Gloves (he's the sergeant) would be shouting me. I was the best boxer he'd ever taught, he sometimes said.

(The Lawyer reckons, it'll go against me on the Manslaughter or whatever it is, the fact I won the district cup for my age group.)

Where was I?

Yeah, about how I was one of the gang, even though I was different too in being the only one still at school. That was Mum's idea, but I didn't really mind. There was nothing else to do while I waited for a job to come up. I didn't want to go on the dole, hang around all day watching the midday movies like Scott and Terry and Danny and Sean. And the old man reckoned the dole was wrong.

I remember, I was thinking about jobs that day on the hill. How maybe, when the old man retired, I'd get his job. He'd like that, I thought. And hate it. Still, it'd be a few years yet before the old man went. Unless the greenies stopped the logging. Then there'd be no jobs for any of us.

(See, the mill and the logging are the only things going in Cornwall. And already there's too many blokes for the work.)

'Bastards,' I thought. On the News the night before, they'd shown the greenies coming into town, because of the new coup.

Bang.

As I fired, I imagined the rabbit was a greenie's head, and got it. The other rabbits hopped into their burrows, but my rabbit was red.

'Bugger it,' I thought. 'I should've got two.' I started to get up, but I saw a rabbit all by itself, real close, waiting, too scared to move. I lined it up.

And then, as I looked at it down along the barrel, I felt as if I could see right into its brain.

(I don't know why I'm putting this stuff in, except the Lawyer said to put in everything, and somehow this about the rabbit is part of the story.)

My finger waited on the trigger. 'Take it easy,' I thought, 'Plenty of time.' The rabbit was stuck there by my watching. It was mesmerised or hypnotised or whatever you call it. And I knew that it knew that whichever way it jumped, it was a goner. There was no way out.

'Come on,' I kind of urged myself. The old man always said, 'It's you or the other bugger. It's a dog-eat-dog world.'

But the funny thing was, as I saw into the rabbit's head, it felt as if it was my own head, and I had the feeling that I was inside a narrow tunnel, no way to turn, and something blocking me at either end.

'Stop it,' I thought, meaning *stop the feeling*, and – this sounds a bit weird, but anyway – now I hated the rabbit for making me feel like that. If I killed it, my own scariness would go away.

'Here we go mate.' I moved my finger onto the trigger, and something like a great soft rock landed on my back. The gun went off, right next to my ear, making a scream.

'I'm dead,' I thought. The colours were muddled up green and black, like being in the forest, free and floaty. 'This is nice. Now I won't have to live in the tunnel any more.' But as I remembered it, the tunnel closed in again, and I knew I was alive. Face down in the blackberry bush.

I bucked the weight off my back and, turning, grabbed it, so now it was me on the top. I looked at what it was.

A girl. And a greenie. Long black hair, a 'Save The Trees' sweatshirt, jeans, city-type gumboots, crying. Well, nearly.

'Does she think I'm going to rape her?' I thought. 'Serve her right. Something to tell Scott and the boys.'

She was bony, her tits hardly there beneath the picture of trees. 'Please,' she said, 'let me go.' Her eyes were big and this incredible green with no make-up, and she scratched at the ground with little soft hands. Her voice was posh.

Made me sick. I rolled off her and shoved her hard into the blackberries. 'Flash-jack people coming from the city,' I thought, 'telling us what to do with our bit of bush. If she had her way, the old man would lose his job, I'd never get one, and what would she care?'

When her face came back out of the bush there was blood on it. A deep scratch ran right down her left cheek. I picked my gun up. She had the nerve to smile.

'What you go and do that for?' I said.

'You were going to kill it,' she said.

'Yeah, and eat it.' My stomach turned over with hunger, as if to remind me to be angry with her. It was hard. She made me feel sorry for her, then sorry for myself, like the rabbit had. And then I did something funny. With the back of my hand I wiped the blood off her cheek, and then I automatically licked my hand clean, as if it was my own blood.

I didn't realise what I was doing till I'd done it. Then I think I probably went a bit red. It seemed a sort of personal thing to do.

'The blooding,' she seemed to say.

'Huh?'

'Nothing.' She squirmed, as if she wished she hadn't said anything. 'Just something Mike says.'

'Mike?' I said. I hate people who talk about people you've never met.

'This guy. Mike Marchant.'

I had him now. I'd seen him on TV the night before. The News lady had announced something about how 'Conservationist Mike Marchant today led his supporters into the Settlement Creek area, near the small town of Cornwall . . .' Then the TV had shown this real smart aleck, 'Save The Trees' T-shirt, mouthing on in front of a bunch of greenies with backpacks. Then the old man had turned the set off. 'Bunch of bludgers,' he'd reckoned. 'Yeah,' I'd said. But now I thought: 'I wonder if I saw this girl.'

'What's he say?' I asked. I don't know why. I didn't want to know what a greenie had said.

'Just that it's a kind of blooding,' she said. 'For the ones like me. Who're new to it. Who haven't been in anything before, I mean.' (I'm writing it down like this because she spoke in little sort of half-sentences, like as if she was shy underneath, or something. Of course, these aren't her exact words, but it's what she said.)

'He reckons, Mike I mean, that it's like in England, when kids go foxhunting for the first time, and the Master of the Hunt bloods them by making them touch the dead fox's tail. I mean, not that Mike believes in hunting of course.' She gave my gun a dirty look. 'We don't eat dead animals.'

'Yeah, well I don't eat live ones,' I muttered, but she gabbled on over me.

'But anyway, he reckons it's like that, the first time you're in a struggle, well, you'll be sick and scared. But it's just a kind of political blooding. A sort of initiation rite, like black kids have, to make them grown-up members of the tribe. And after that, Mike says, it gets easier.'

Professional demonstrators, that's what the old man called them. Live on the dole, travel round the country, stopping workers from having jobs. 'The old man's right,' I thought. And yet . . .

I may as well say this bit now. I know it'll sound stupid, but it sort of explains a bit of what happened.

See, I had this sort of a game. I mean, when I was little. You know how kids play King of the Castle? Well, that was me. But I was a prince, and the forest was my land. And right at its heart, where no one ever went, I had a palace. I used to go there all the time, on weekends and holidays.

Of course, I don't play it any more. It was like a kind of fairytale. But still, the logging made scars in my head, where the green was.

Of course, I'd never told Scott or anyone, not even Mum. If you said something like that in my town, you'd get your head punched in. Or worse. No one would like you. But it meant I sort of half agreed with what the greenies said. Probably the real reason I was still at school was I didn't want a job in the logging anyway. Though I did, because it was the only job I'd ever get.

(Here I go again, two bob each way. But do you see now what I meant about the rabbit? I felt like I was stuck in the middle, no way to jump. I guess I'm putting this in because I didn't like what the Lawyer said about being led astray. It makes me seem like a silly kid, without my own ideas.)

Anyway, I thought the old man was right about the greenies, but I secretly agreed with the greenies about the trees.

'Are you scared?' I said.

'Not really.' She shrugged. 'I suppose I'll get arrested. My parents will be shitty. Probably throw me out of home. Their darling daughter, having her name in the paper.' She spoke the last bit real sarcastic, as if she'd like to bring them down. But underneath it all she did sound a bit frightened.

I'd never thought of greenies having mums and dads and homes and hassles before. Didn't they just live in tents and old vans and stuff, or those squatting houses you sometimes saw them getting thrown out of on the News, with graffiti on the walls and piles of mouldy mattresses on the floor? It always made me think of head-lice. 'Where do you live?'

She named a suburb. It didn't mean anything. I'd only been to the city twice, on school excursions. (This is my third time. What a joke. I haven't even got a window bed.) But I knew for sure she'd come from a posh place.

'It's really boring – you know, nothing to do. But it's close to uni.'

'You go to uni?' I felt disappointed, or something. It made her seem old. Well, older than me.

'Yeah, first year Arts. English, Psych and Politics.' She sighed. 'I don't know why. Dad raves on about qualifications. But there aren't any jobs.'

'Funny to think of her having the same hassles as me,' I thought. 'No work and a heavy old man.' But what's really funny, now I come to think of it, is that it wasn't till then that I thought of my old man as being heavy. We got on real well. ('Like father, like son,' Mum used to say when I left my dirty clothes all over the bathroom floor and didn't hang the wet towel up. 'You're a chip off the old block all right.') It was only after this first day that the old man got heavy. Only when I stopped saying 'Yeah' to everything he said. Though now I come to think about it even more, I reckon this wasn't really the first day, the trouble had been coming for a long time, and the trees were only the excuse.

'I really want to move out of home,' she said, 'but I don't have any money.'

'Join the club,' I said, though till that minute the thought of moving had never occurred to me. In Cornwall, you lived at home till you got married. Then you moved down the caravan park on the rec reserve. 'I thought there was something students got,' I said, 'like the dole.'

'TEAS,' she said flatly. 'But Dad earns too much for me to get it.'

Stiff. The old man was right. These greenies were just a pack of flash-jack city wankers.

The shadows of the trees covered the hillside now and I suddenly noticed I was cold.

'What do you do?' she asked.

'Bit of this and a bit of that. There's not much work around here.' I said it real heavy, but she just fiddled at her hair. 'Look, I've got to go.'

She went like she was Cinderella and it was a minute off midnight. 'Geez, is it that late? I've got to get back to camp or it'll be dark, blah blah blah.' Her posh voice got me. I thought, 'Soon she'll say it was nice meeting me, or something.'

'Look, it's been nice talking to you,' she said. 'Why don't you drop over to the camp some time? If you're not busy.' She was so up herself, she didn't even realise I was on the other side.

(Was I? Well. I wasn't on her side.)

'Have a cup of tea or something,' she went on. 'It's not far.' She turned like she was going to give me directions.

'I know where it is.' As if I hadn't lived here all my life. As if it wasn't the old man who'd dozed the track in. (As if the forest wasn't mine.)

'OK then, I'll see you later.' She was off. But she turned back and yelled, 'Sorry about your rabbit.' It almost sounded as if she meant it.

I got my gun, and crossed the hillside for my kill. It was cold and skinny, reminded me of me somehow. Or this kitten I brought home as a kid, that the old man wouldn't let me keep.

I can't explain this next thing either, but when I got to where my bike was parked, at the edge of the trees, I slung the body high over my head and into the forest, like (this sounds dumb) a kind of sacrifice. As if its death could stop the trouble that felt now as if it had been coming since the very beginning.

▷ ▷ ▷ ———————————

I'll stop now. One of the blue women is wheeling in the tea trolley. I've been going since eleven o'clock this morning. Squirt'd be pleased. 'You could *write*, Colum,' he always reckoned, 'if only you'd stop being so macho and let yourself.'

Let yourself
Wet yourself

My poem for the day.

I hate asking for a bedpan. Specially if it's Baby Nurse on duty. That, and the nurses washing me, that's what gets me down here. And the food. (White fish with white sauce and mashed potato has just arrived.) And the boringness. (No one to talk to, one telly for the ward and it's up the main end. I'm in the middle.) And the not knowing what's going to happen. And the waiting. I reckon, if it does turn out to be manslaughter, and I go to prison, it won't be any worse than this. At least there, I'll know. Though come to think of it, they reckon you get raped there, so it would be worse. Just my luck, never get to do it with a girl, and then have a bloke do it.

Stop it.

▷ ▷ ▷ ———————————

The next morning.

Reading that last bit – not the rape bit, the stuff about Squirt and writing – and thinking about the forest, and then thinking about how yesterday wasn't as bad as the day before, I got this funny idea that writing is a bit like being in among the trees. Both things kind of make you lose yourself inside your head, so you wander, and it's free and floaty. Kind of dark green. If I was explaining it to Scott and them, I'd say it's a bit like being stoned. Not that I'd ever tell Scott and them. Sean maybe wouldn't laugh, but the other three would.

Anyway, I've decided to keep on with this. I can see already it's not really for the Lawyer. It can't be, because I want to put it all down, and there's stuff I can't let him know about. When I read yesterday's bit, I saw how I'm kind of explaining everything to someone called 'you'.

So HI! there, whoever you are! Here we go again.

▷ ▷ ▷ ———————————

When I came home that night, Mum had my tea keeping hot over a saucepan of boiling veggie water. The kitchen smelled of cauliflower and the damp tea towels drying on the oven rail. Plus woodsmoke from the crack in the top of the stove, the old man's tobacco, and Mum's green hand-soap that she uses all the time so her knitting doesn't get dirty.

'And what's my smell?' I thought as I came in.

I remember thinking that. It was like I was seeing and smelling the kitchen as if it was new, or someone else's place, or something. That greenie whingeing about her home had kind of made me wonder if I really liked my mine.

So 'What's my smell?' I thought. 'Where do I fit in, what track do I leave here?' The whole house was full of their signs, their business. And Grandad's. Though in a way he was kind of a ghost, you could still feel him all the time. Even the sleep-out at the back that was meant to be my bit, all it had was a bed and a cupboard and my trunk under the bed. And Mum made it really neat all the time. As if the Queen was about to visit. Well, not the Queen. Maybe the Pope.

I put the old man's gun up in the old man's gun rack, with the other two. The rack was on the kitchen wall, next to one of Mum's Jesus pictures. The bleeding heart of our Lord. (Underneath it was written a kind of motto, about Him Dying to Save Us.) Anyway, you know how your mind can do funny jumps? Well, for a moment it made me think of her blood on my hand.

'Yeah,' I thought, maybe to get my mind off that, 'where's my place? I could die or something and there'd be no sign I'd ever lived here. Mum would bundle up my clothes for the Morlong St V de P, and that'd be that.' Deep down of course, I knew that wasn't true. Mum would say prayers for my soul. (Fat lot of good that'd do me. I don't think I've got one.)

'You're late,' the old man said, real heavy.

I nodded. Since when had being late been a crime in this family? The old man and me, and Grandad too when he was up and about, we always just came in whenever we liked and Mum had our tea waiting. Sometimes on pay night the old man didn't come home till the pub shut.

'Don't just nod your head. Answer when you're spoken to!'

'Yeah,' I said. Yeah, I'm late, yeah I'll answer, get off my back.

I'm putting this down because it wasn't normal. As I said,

the old man wouldn't usually give a flying fart when I came in. And neither would he care about me just nodding. We often didn't talk much, me and the old man. Mum rattled on, but she was a woman, and she was Irish too. 'The gift of the gab,' she called it. But for us men, it was like speaking because you were spoken to, just for manners, was sissy or something. (Grandad sometimes used to talk a lot, when he was telling yarns, but he hasn't done that much for a few years now.)

But if I'm saying the old man wasn't quite normal, I'd better be fair and say I wasn't too. I'd said 'Yeah' in a kind of way I'd never spoken to him before. Mum must've noticed, because she cut in real smart.

'Get anything, dear?'

I washed my hands under the kitchen tap. Why answer? If I had, I'd have brought it in. I was shitty at myself suddenly, for throwing the one I'd got away, and shitty at the greenie, for making me miss the other one. Mum really liked it when I brought her a couple of bunnies. And it made me feel as if at least I put in something. At seventeen, I should be earning money and paying board. I was as much a bludger as the bloody greenie.

The old man blew his top. 'Answer your mother!'

'He did,' Mum said quickly. 'You just didn't hear, with that thing blaring.' The old man always had the TV on loud, and sat at the bit of table closest to the set. The weather was on.

'Shush!' the old man suddenly said, as the capital-city temperatures were replaced by the contours of the weather map. There were squiggles and lines heading our way that didn't look good. The old man was tapping his teeth with his index finger, a kind of habit he has when he's worried.

The weather man pointed at our bit of Australia now with his teacher-cane, and said the long-range forecast suggested the possibility of storms developing in the south. The old man tapped more heavily, and I saw Mum watching him. She looked as worried about the old man as the old man did about the squiggles on the map.

If it rained heavily over the next couple of weeks, then the logging would be cut short. In our area, there's only a few months of the year when the blokes can get into the forest. It's a condition, see, of the logging permits that there's no logging during or after heavy rainfall. It'd been a real bad-luck summer anyway, so the work was behind – rain right through

January, and then when it cleared it was a couple of weeks before the company got the go-ahead to cut the track into the new coup. That was the old man's job – he drove the big dozer – but a couple of days after he started, there was trouble with it.

You should've heard him then – night after night, he'd come home whingeing – they couldn't get the part they needed, had to order it from Italy or somewhere, then there was a wharf strike, and when the part finally arrived it was the wrong one and they had to get one made up for them after all. Right through it, the old man reckoned they should've just hired another bulldozer. 'Mean as catshit!' he reckoned Cornwall Milling was. 'Wasting a fortune to save two bob! City bloody bosses!' (The company was based in the city, just had a manager in Cornwall, and it was like the big brass just didn't understand about time and weather and that. Cornwall Milling was just a subsidiary or whatever you call it anyway of some big outfit that made biscuits and drilled oil and did a heap of other stuff, and you could tell that the old man's dozer wasn't exactly first on their list of Things To Worry About.)

'Be patient,' Mum reckoned. 'You'll get there in the end.'

Well of course he did in the end, but it was March by then. And now the greenies were here, and they'd stop everything till the cops got them out. And if it rained over the next few weeks, well, that'd put an end to logging till next summer, and there wouldn't be enough logs cut to keep the mill going full pace over the winter. That'd mean blokes laid off. See, the blokes who worked in the forest in the logging season worked in the mill in the off season. If there was enough work, I mean.

If there wasn't enough, the old man would sit around the house belly-aching and Mum would have to put up with that as well as dipping into the savings account for the mortgage payments and the HP on the lounge and the freezer. It'd been like that three years ago, and it was a winter you wouldn't want to go through again. That's why Mum was watching the old man watching the weather and tapping his dentures.

'It'll be all right, darl,' she told him. 'You know the weather man's always wrong. There wasn't a cloud in the sky today, and it's only March and besides, my ants aren't out.'

Mum's ants lived next to the stove and told her lots of things. They hid when it was dry and they came out and ran up and down the wall beside the oven when it was going to rain, and the one time it snowed Mum reckoned she'd known because her ants had gone berserk.

'You and your ants!' the old man mocked, but at least it made him stop tapping, as I reckon Mum knew it would.

Besides, the weather was gone now. Mum put my plate down in front of me. Two chops and peas and mashed spud and cauliflower-cheese and that tomato thing she does with the breadcrumbs on the top. (Makes me hungry, just to write it.) One thing about Mum was, no matter when you got home, your tea was never dried out. I'd been back to Scott's place after footie training, and seen him take a tea out of the oven that looked like a collection of old tyre patches.

'Ta,' I said, and Mum smiled, but it was the old man's good mood she was smiling at. Or better mood, should I say. He'd been in a real doozie when I'd come in, that was for sure.

And then that changed again. It was *News Report* now, with that baldy-headed guy that's the introducer. Of course, I can't remember word-for word what he said, but I'll make it up like a broadcast. (Squirt sometimes got us to write pretend TV stuff in Communication, and it was something I seemed to do pretty easily). So the guy said something like:

'Well, trees or jobs? It's a thorny problem. In 1982 we saw the issue mobilise thousands of people over the issue of the Franklin Dam. Public pressure in that case was one of the factors behind the Labor Party's victory in the federal elections, and in return the Hawke Government declared for the conservationists. A couple of years ago, we witnessed the Battle of Farmhouse Creek, where the loggers took matters into their own hands, and police stood by as the environmentalist campers were evicted . . .'

There was half a minute of pictures of a dozer going through the water and screaming greenies scrambling out of the way. I could feel the old man silently cheering in his seat. Then it was back to the baldy guy.

'Now another creek is becoming the subject of debate. Earlier, in our News coverage, we showed you the scene today at Settlement Creek, near the small timber town of Cornwall . . .'

This next cut made my stomach kind of turn over. It showed the clearing on the creek bank, at the end of the new track. (It's weird, seeing something you know, on television. Like when you come round a corner in the clothes bit of Target, and suddenly see yourself in a mirror, or something.) The clearing's a natural one, about eighty metres across, with a huge old blackwood tree towards one side. Behind it, to the south-west, was the area marked off for the new logging coup. I felt my stomach turn over again, as I thought of all those trees going. All that changing.

But it was already changed. There were bright spots of tents there and little coloured blobs of people sitting around a fire, boiling a billy, talking, laughing. One bloke was playing a guitar. That Mike Marchant guy was holding up a placard. There was something about him, got my goat. I felt sick at the whole thing. It was *my* forest. Before the new logging track, no one but me ever went to that clearing. I looked for the girl, but the baldy guy was back on the screen.

'So far, things are peaceful. But for how long? With logging scheduled to start tomorrow, tension is mounting. Each day, more conservationists arrive at the town. And extra police have been directed to the area. Local timberworkers claim that if logging stops, there will be a hundred jobs lost to the town.'

That mightn't sound like many, but there only *are* a hundred jobs in Cornwall, and there's no other work around. There was also the pine plantation, where the native hardwood trees had been completely logged out, but the mill manager had said that without the hardwood, it wouldn't be worthwhile keeping the mill open. Of course, there weren't actually a hundred blokes employed by Cornwall Milling; but if the mill closed, it'd do one of those multiplier things we learned in Commerce, till the whole town closed down.

'... Conservationists, however, claim that jobs are ultimately replaceable, while our forests are not. They state that of the original forest of which the Settlement Creek area is part, more than sixty per cent has been destroyed to make way for farmland, and that much of the remaining forest has been depleted for timber. They also claim that every day, thirty hectares of virgin forest are logged on our planet.'

Again my stomach went on me. I pushed my plate away, though there was still quite a bit of cauliflower and tomato left. I found myself almost panicking for a moment about how I would be if I couldn't go into the forest when I needed to.

'... To put the conservationists' case, here tonight in our studio we have Dr Brian MacBride, from the World Heritage Commission ...'

Now the screen showed a bloke in an armchair next to the baldy guy. He immediately reminded me of a picture of Brendan Behan, that Squirt had up on our class notice-board along with Jane Austen and Charles Dickens and William Shakespeare and about fifty others. (It was meant to make you write better, if you had them round you.) Anyway, this guy was fat, in a comfy beery slobby sort of way, with a face that looked as if someone had sat on it, and a healthy drinking colour to the nose and cheeks. His hair was curly and still mostly black though he must've been as old as the old man, and his eyes and mouth were grinning. He had a wrinkled dark suit on, white shirt, and no tie.

'Dr MacBride . . . Welcome to Australia . . .'

'Thanks . . . It's grand to be here . . .'

I won't try to write the way he talked, but I'll just say it was so Irish you could have cut it with a knife. I saw Mum's eyes brighten. Any sound of the language reminds her of her old Da.

Talking of old men, mine snapped the set off. 'Bloody greenie!'

And blow me down if Mum didn't answer back. ('Must be the Irish in her, sort of brought up to the surface,' I thought at the time.)

'He's not dear, not really, he's a professor, or a doctor or something. And World Heritage . . . isn't that the United Nations? He's not like a greenie. Greenies are . . .' Mum searched for a description. 'Well, they're young people. Silly. Still wet behind the ears. There was two of them come into the store today. You could pick them a mile off. You should've heard what Ev said to them . . .'

Ev was Terry and Danny's mum. With a husband killed by a tree and two boys out of work and a third forced to leave town and get a job in the army, I could imagine what Mrs Bail had said to them.

' "I bet yous don't mind trees being turned into paper when your dole form comes on it," she told them. I could've died laughing! And then . . .' Mum chattered on, after a while changing the subject to what Ev had gone on to say after the greenies had left about what her eldest boy Solly had written in his letter from the army that week, until she bored the old man into forgetting the Irishman and greenies and the news and the weather, and he pushed away his empty pie-and-custard plate and got his pub coat from the nail.

'Well I'm off.'

I followed him out the back to take my leftovers to Max.

'Yum yum!' I called, and he came. Scratched himself along my leg. My mate. I'd raised him since he was six weeks old, and now he was nearly grown up. 'Like me,' I thought, sending myself up. 'But you don't have to hang about,' I told him, 'waiting for a job in the logging you don't want anyway. Just guzzle guzzle, and lie in the sun . . .' He made the wheezing sound that always made me laugh. 'You'd miss me, wouldn't you, if I was to go?'

'Yeah, Col, go where?' I thought. Kids did sometimes leave for the city, but it was hard to find work there if you didn't know anyone. They were usually back again in a couple of years. And I wouldn't know where to live. End up in a slum with graffiti on the walls and nothing to eat but raw head-lice. 'No thanks', I thought. Besides, I couldn't leave my land.

Mum was calling. '*Col*-um. *Col*-um.' Though she was born in Australia her voice had a trace of her Dad's Irish in it, that made it different from how everyone else in Cornwall talked. Scott and the Bail boys used to copy it and jeer in the old days. '*Col*-um. *Col*-um.' Banging their suitcases to make a song of it as they followed me home through the fog. Sometimes Scott would slip ahead, and jump me. (Have you ever felt something coming to get you?) But Scott was my mate now. Funny how things change. Now I was in the top gang. And if you were going to live in my town, that was the only place to be.

Inside, Mum wanted my dirty plate.

'Maxi's already washed it.'

'Oh Colum, I wish you wouldn't.'

It doesn't sound much, but coming from Mum a criticism like that was a pretty big deal.

▷ ▷ ▷ ————————————

I've maybe got a bit long-winded, putting down every little thing the old man and Mum and me and the baldy guy on TV said that night. Like Mum's last comment, it all mightn't seem like much, but looking back on it I can see how it sort of set the mood for how home was going to be after that. The old man stormy, Mum edgy, and me . . . well, fed up with everything. And I put in the *News Report* stuff because that didn't seem important at the time, but it does now. The instant

I saw that Dr MacBride, I felt some sort of thing. I don't want to get spooky, talking like something out of *The Twilight Zone* on late-night ABC, but it was as if I felt there was this kind of bond or link or, like I said, *thing* between us. A vibe, as Jade would probably say. At the time, maybe it was the Irish of his talk and the sloppiness of his suit that made me feel I liked him. And I thought that was all the feeling was. But now I wonder if it wasn't one of those ESP numbers. Because he's the bloke I've maybe manslaughtered.

▷ ▷ ▷ ———

Monday, 25 March, 7 a.m. (They sure get you up early here, seeing as how there's nothing to do.)

Couldn't write anything yesterday. After writing that about Dr MacBride, Saturday night, I just felt like nothing I can describe. Maybe I seem real cool about it to you, but that's probably just what Squirt calls my 'macho veneer'. I don't really understand what he means (it always makes me think of furniture, like when he sometimes calls me a closet thinker) but it's sort of about the way I talk and act tough – or try to. It's all very well for Squirt to criticise, but it took me years to learn. Squirt didn't have to grow up in Cornwall. Didn't have Scott and them jeering all the time at him for being a sook and a mummy's boy, and the old man too.

Maybe I should explain this a bit.

Well, it was Mum's fault really. She didn't have me till she was forty, and before me she had all these miscarriages, which were specially bad because she's Catholic and she wanted to have a whole heap of kids, and she worried too about where the dead babies' souls went. (Not that they were babies yet, but still.) And of course the old man really wanted a son, to keep on the tradition. We're one of the oldest families in the area – my Grandad's Grandad was one of the first settlers – and all the men have been timberworkers. Anyway, when Mum finally had me she saw it as a kind of miracle because she'd been making special novenas and all that stuff for years, and so I guess she spoiled me a bit. It wasn't any big deal, but it meant that I looked different.

See, all the other kids had other kids in their family, and they wore hand-me-downs and things. But my Mum's always been a great knitter, she even does Fair Isle – you know, real fancy patterns in all different coloured wool. Anyway, she was always knitting me these jumpers that she copied from what city kids wear in the *Women's Weekly*, and I had beanies and mittens and looked a right little gig. I even had knitted singlets, she was so hard up for things to knit. And because there was only the one of me to worry about, Mum washed my clothes more and made me change my boots when they got wet, and she used to pin a square of clean old sheet inside my shirt pocket, so I'd always have a hanky. (The other boys wiped their snot on their sleeve.)

So I looked like a snob or something, though of course the old man's pay was as bad as everyone else's and our house was the same old two-bedroom weatherboard as the rest of Cornwall.

And then my Mum spoke a bit different, and she was the only Catholic in town – well, the only one who bothered about it enough to drive into Morlong on Sunday mornings, and she used to take me too. Up until about three years ago, that is, when I stopped being a Catholic.

All that was enough to set me apart from Scott and them, and even my old man used to complain that Mum was making me into a pansy. (You can see why I worry about gaol.)

▷ ▷ ▷ ———————————

Can't hang on any longer. Ring the buzzer. Baby Nurse comes. I mutter what I want. Back she comes with it, and helps me onto it. I hate it I hate it I hate it.

I won't tell you those bits any more.

▷ ▷ ▷ ———————————

Anyway, it sort of became a vicious circle. Because Scott and them called me names, I hung around quite a bit by myself.

I don't want to make this sound as if I was lonely and miserable. Mum always used to say *'Sticks and stones may break my bones but names will never hurt me.'* And that was pretty much how I felt. I was happy by myself. And anyway, I had Grandad.

He lived with us – he still does – and though he was seventy-something, he often used to take me into the forest. He knew it like the back of his hand. And then, when I turned seven, he showed me the palace – his dad had taken him there when *he* was little. From the minute he took me there – well, it became *my* place.

I'd got a bike for that birthday too, and after that I'd ride to the forest of an afternoon, after school, and explore by myself. Not every afternoon, but pretty often. And so I wasn't down the recreation reserve, playing with the other kids. And that set me apart even more.

On weekends I'd go to the palace and spend the whole day, sometimes alone, sometimes with Grandad. He'd make up stories about the olden days there, and we'd fossick around, looking for treasure – and finding it too. I've got broken bits of plates and bottles and all sorts of stuff in the trunk under my bed. And once I even found a little knife, with a fancy silver handle, and I used to play that it was magic. That was my best treasure. And Grandad made a sheath for it, of black leather.

Anyway, that's how things were. The only thing I really minded was the old man calling me a sissy.

And then, that winter when the work was real short, I was feeling so down that I took to carrying the silver knife around with me, like a good-luck thing. And one lunchtime it fell out of my pocket.

'What's that?' Scott dived to pick it up, but I grabbed it.

'Nothing,' I said. 'Just something Grandad gave me.'

'Give us a look.'

'No!'

Luckily the bell rang, but on the way home, Scott jumped me and said I had to give him the knife. (Terry and Danny and Sean were there, and about half a dozen other kids.)

Scott was a good fighter – still is – and I'd never really fought before. But it was as if he was trying to take a part of me. So I just punched and kicked and punched and kicked and never even noticed what he was doing. And then he slipped in the mud. He was down, and couldn't get up, and I still kept on at him. Till suddenly I found myself hauled off and dumped aside.

It was old Golden Gloves that grabbed me. Scott was lying there groaning, covered in mud and blood, and I was thinking: 'Now I'm for it!' But Golden Gloves just grinned and said, 'That was pretty good, son. But you could do with a few pointers. Why don't you come down the hall, Friday night?'

(I should explain there's a sort of boxing club in the

Uniting Church hall on Fridays, 6.30 to 8.30, and Golden Gloves runs it. Some of the young blokes from the mill go – it's meant to keep the fighters out of the pub. Fat chance. Just makes them better at it, and even thirstier when they get there.)

Then Golden Gloves turned to Scott and said, 'You'll get piles you know, sitting around on the wet ground.'

I ran home, before Scott could get up, and told Mum I'd fallen over. But when the old man came home from the pub, Golden Gloves had told him about it. The old man was pleased as anything. Being in a brawl that a cop had to break up – well, that was something! And winning as well!

For the first time in my life, I felt as if the old man thought I was good enough to be his son. Mum wasn't too happy of course, but I think she was so pleased that the old man was pleased that she didn't really mind.

I was too scared about what would happen when I got to school the next day to get the most out of my victory. I just knew Scott would get me.

But he didn't do a thing. Just sort of looked at me sideways through the first lessons, and when the elevenses break came, Sean asked if he could borrow my geography homework to copy. At lunchtime, Terry asked if I'd like to swap sandwiches. And when the last bell went, Danny said, 'Coming down the reserve?' as if it was normal for me to spend the afternoon kicking a footie with them.

Soon it was. By the end of term, I was part of the gang. And after I was in it, I wondered how ever I could have survived outside it. I mean, it's the only place to be.

▷ ▷ ▷ ————————————

The Head Doc's just been. It's a lady one, and she's Chinese as well. Asked me how I was feeling and everything, now the first week's over. I hadn't really realised till then, but it was last Monday they brought me in. Tuesday was the operation, setting my legs and that. Wednesday I was really woozy. Thursday I was bored out of my tree. (Very funny, Col, I don't think!) Friday the Lawyer came and I started writing this . . . And now it's now.

Sometimes I feel as if I got here about a minute ago. Other times I feel I've been here for ever.

Afternoon visiting's starting. That gets me down a bit. Everyone else gets visitors. Of course, there's no one who'd come for me. I don't know anyone in the city, and it's too far away for anyone from home to come. Not that anyone from home would want to come. I'll be branded as a greenie down there. Scott and them won't have me any more. (I sometimes wonder what they're up to, if they're scared I'll dob. But they'd know I wouldn't.) Mum's rung a couple of times, and they've brought the phone to my bed, but there's nothing to say.

'Hello, son.'

'Hello, Mum.'

'How are you?'

'Fine. How're you?'

'Oh . . . getting by . . .' Sigh. 'Are you in any pain?'

'No.'

'That's good, love. The Sister says you're not sleeping real well. Are you sure you . . .'

'Is it still raining?'

'Don't even ask!'

'How's Grandad?'

Pause. 'Oh . . . you know. Here, there and everywhere. I told him you're off on a school trip, but he knows something's up. If I don't keep my eye on him, he gets out in the rain, stands at the gate as if he's waiting for you, or something. You know how he gets, when something's bothering him.'

(Yes.)

'Yeah, well I'd better be going.'

'Do you need anything?'

'Not really.' She sent pyjamas and a dressing gown and a jumper and a pack of playing cards and my school bag when I first came in.

'Would you like a fruit cake? I could make one and post it . . .'

'I'm fine, really.'

'Oh well, I guess I'd better be going too. I'm running out of twenty cents.'

Neither of us mention the old man.

I guess Mum would probably catch the train up from Morlong and come to see me, except for Grandad. Though the old man would never let her hear the end of it.

It's funny, until now I haven't really thought about him. I

mean, I've thought about him in the past, as I've been writing down the story, but I haven't thought about how I feel about him. Do I still hate him? I know I want to. But it seems less real in this place, with all the white sheets and the strangers. I've just realised: this week is the longest time I've ever spent away from my Mum and him.

Don't want to think about what I think about the old man, so I'll get on with the story.

▷ ▷ ▷ ————————

The next day was Friday. Things were a bit tense at breakfast, because that was the day the logging at the new coup was meant to start. Maybe it seems a bit funny, starting a job on a Friday, but as I said the work was behind and it was a race against time to get the logs out while this dry spell lasted.

The old man stared into his porridge, as if it was a crystal ball, and finally pushed it away after about two mouthfuls. Mum didn't say anything – just took the bowl and put his bacon and eggs and tomato in front of him. Normally the radio would be on for the News but that morning the kitchen was so quiet you could have heard a pin drop. The old man started staring again.

'It's not going to help, dear,' Mum sighed, 'not eating. You can't work on an empty stomach.'

'Work!' the old man said. 'Do you think they're going to let us?'

There was silence for a while, and I ate my porridge. The old man had one of his eggs and a bit of toast, left the rest.

Mum spoke sort of soothingly and nervously at the same time, like how you speak to a wounded dog that might bite your hand off. 'The coppers will be there, dear. They'll get the greenies out, and then you'll be able to start.'

The old man snorted. 'Coppers! Bunch of jumped-up johnnies from the city, what do they care! You've seen them on TV, they're bloody soft on greenies. Scared of treading on their civil liberties, or whatever they call it.' He put on a pooncey voice. *'Excuse me please sir, would you mind if I arrested you?'* He swore inside his dentures – he never used bad language in front of a woman, not even Mum. 'Golden Gloves is OK, even Wee Willie Winkie . . .' (He was the local constable – twenty-one and baby-faced. His proper name was Wilkinson.) 'But it's not them in charge. They've sent some bloody inspector, meant to be an expert in crowd control, or something. Crowd control! If they'd just left Golden Gloves to it . . .'

Mum popped the old man's bacon onto my plate, scraped the rest of his breakfast into Max's bucket. (She knew I didn't like him having bacon.) 'Well, someone's scored out of this, anyway,' I thought.

'But how could Sergeant Henderson cope, dear, just him and Wee Willie . . .?'

The old man shot her a look like 'Trust a woman.' I knew what he meant. If it was just Golden Gloves, he'd stand aside and let the blokes go in and get the greenies, like they did at Farmhouse Creek. But with one difference. Golden Gloves wouldn't let the TV film it. He'd have the reporters out of town before they could say a word. I'd heard him boast about it, down at boxing.

'Well I'm off.' The old man took his work coat from the nail.

'Good luck, dear,' Mum murmured like she did if I was having end-of-term tests.

'I wouldn't bet on it.'

I did my morning chores – let the chooks out, fed Max, brought in the wood for the day – then took Grandad in his second cuppa. He doesn't usually get out of bed much these days. That bad winter, three years ago, when the only good thing to happen was me getting in with Scott and them, Grandad had a stroke. I sometimes wonder if I would've spent so much time down the rec reserve, mucking round with the gang, if Grandad hadn't been so bad I couldn't stand seeing him, and Mum flat off her feet nursing him, and the old man sitting around the house. (But come to think of it, I wouldn't have been carrying the knife if Grandad hadn't had his stroke.) He was a lot better now, but he couldn't move much and his mind wandered. Sometimes, when he was really off his kadoover, he called me Sam. Like he thought I was the old man, when *he* was young. That spooked me.

That morning but, he was OK. Said 'Hello young-feller-me-lad, would you roll me a smoke?' He's only got power now in his right hand, and all us Ferris men are left-handers. Besides, he lost three fingers off his right in a mill accident, so even that one's not much use to the poor old bugger.

When I came back into the kitchen, Mum was back from the store with the newspaper. She was all in a tizz, her cheeks pink with excitement.

'You'll never guess who I saw!'

'No Mum, I'll never guess.' I started looking through the paper. We had to cut out what we thought was the 'most significant' news item each morning and take it in for our Communication Skills class. It was Squirt's idea of Show and Tell. (The old man got dirty because I usually took the sports page and forgot to bring it home again.)

'Oh go on.'

I pretended to think as I read the headlines. 'Mrs Woolcott.' She was the woman who ran the store.

'Yeah, but . . .'

'Mr Woolcott.' On page five there was an item about the greenies being around town. I reached for the scissors.

'Oh Colum!'

I screwed up my face with concentration. 'The Pope.'

'Don't be silly'

'Dr Brian MacBride.'

'How did you know!' Mum looked real disappointed.

'ESP,' I said. (It seems funny now, me saying that. As if I knew even then that there was something pulling us together.)

'No, really . . .'

I took pity on her. 'Elementary, my dear Colleen.' (Grandad used to get me to read him Sherlock Holmes.) 'It says here that he's going to come to Cornwall today to make a report on the forest for the World Whatsummy. And so when I see you bouncing in all bright-eyed and bushy-tailed, I know you've seen your boyfriend.'

'Get on with you! My boyfriend!'

'Come on Ma, admit it, you do fancy him. It was love at first sight.'

She really bristled then. I was casting nasturtiums on her Catholic virtue. 'You know the only man that's ever been for me is your father. And a better man I couldn't wish for. Blah blah blah . . .' I flicked back and started looking at page three, even though it was all the political stuff I'd usually skip over. 'You must admit but,' she added, 'he's got a lovely voice.'

'The old man? Yeah, you're right there.'

She gave me an exasperated look. 'Brian MacBride.'

'Oh, it's "Brian" now is it?' I clasped my hands over my head as she grabbed for the scissors. 'Help! Grandad!!!'

'Shush, boy. Don't you go stirring up your grandad. Poor old codger. Doesn't know if he's Arthur or Martha half the time as it is . . .' She put the scissors down and looked her normal slightly anxious self. It'd been good to have a game with her. We hadn't played much, the last few years. Not since I'd graduated to being the old man's boy.

'Come on, Mum,' I said. 'Tell me all about it.'

But I'd taken the fun out of it and she just said that *Doctor* MacBride had come into the store to buy a packet of fags, three loaves of sliced wholemeal and six litres of milk, then he'd gone out again and got into a little Vee-Double-You and headed off in the direction of the new coup. And the reason why she was interested in him, she'd have me know, was his voice reminded her of her old Da, and there was nothing wrong with that, even if he *was* a greenie.

'Your old Da?' I said. 'A greenie?'

'Shouldn't you be at school by now?'

'Yeah, in a minute.' I could hear the bell ringing, but something on page three had kind of grabbed my attention. It was a boring political thing, about a by-election coming up, but I noticed it because it said that one of the people standing was 'the Independent Green Candidate, Mr Michael Marchant'. There was something about that guy, got my goat. It seemed like you couldn't turn on the TV or open the paper without coming across him. He already had his name in the other item I'd cut out. Wasn't that enough for him? Besides, if he was standing for election or whatever it was, what was he doing down here in my neck of the woods? I cut out that item too, and pronged it into my Communication folder, along with the first one. They're both still in it, so you might as well read them, while I have my tea.

▷ ▷ ▷ ———————————

The Argus
Friday 15 March

MATESHIP AND MALEVOLENCE

Dr Brian MacBride, of the World Heritage Commission, arrived in Australia yesterday to get a first-hand impression of the effect of logging on the country's native forests.

A man renowned for his high energy level and infectious enthusiasm, Dr MacBride announced that he would be leaving at dawn this morning for the Settlement Creek area, near the small timber town of Cornwall, where logging is scheduled to start today.

Dr MacBride, or Brian as he prefers to be called, describes himself as being part of 'the Fighting Wing of the W.H.C.'

Earlier this week, conservation leader Mike Marchant led a small group of his forces into the threatened forest, where they have set up camp, promising to block the bulldozers and stop the logging. But have they taken on more than they will be able to cope with?

It seems that greenies risk their skins when they go to this town, where the old frontier values hold sway. JERRY DENNING tried mixing with the locals, and had some anxious moments.

The first thing I noticed when I arrived in Cornwall was that nearly every car bears a 'Doze in a Greenie' sticker.

But it was when the young police constable warned me against walking down the main street of town after dark that I began seriously to question the wisdom of coming here.

Already, signs of hostility had been evident.

In the town's one hotel, a place where serious drinking is done standing up – and every night of the week – a question touching on the presence of the conservationists who have been drifting into the area over the last few days, set off a round of: 'Why don't you f--k off?'

No one, it seemed, wanted to talk to this outsider. Nevertheless, there were a considerable number who wanted to jeer and whistle at him as he left the pub and walked through the town towards the police station for some advice on just what was acceptable conversation.

Cornwall, an isolated timber town, is a very strange place.

For a start, you can walk around it in five minutes.

In the main street there is the general store cum service station, post office and Commonwealth Bank agency, the takeway, the Uniting Church (services every fourth Sunday) and its hall, the Church of England Church (closed), the Consolidated Primary-Secondary School, the mill manager's almost imposing residence, a sprawl of tiny weatherboard cottages, and the End of the Road Hotel.

In the back street that runs parallel to this there are more cottages, the mill, and the recreation reserve, which doubles as a van-site for the thirty-odd caravans that house the town's single and poorer workers. In the two side streets there are some more cottages, and the police and fire stations.

And that's all.

There is no library, no picture theatre, no swimming pool, no CYSS centre for the town's unemployed youth, no senior citizens' centre, no baby health centre, no hospital – indeed, no doctor – and the list could go on. Indeed, I was unable even to locate a public lavatory.

Though the seaside resort of Baytown is only 30 or so kilometres south as the crow flies, a trip to the sea involves a roundabout route over near-impossible roads.

'So what do people do here?' I asked local police Sergeant Jack 'Golden Gloves' Henderson.

His answer was short. 'They work.'

However part of the reason for the tension in town since the arrival of the greenies is that many of the townsfolk don't work.

There are already a couple of dozen ex-timberworkers here – men who have been laid off because the government has reduced the number of hectares of state land which can be logged each year.

There is also about the same number of youths who have left school and are unable to find work in the town.

Already, the locals argue, the greenies have caused these workers and potential workers to be thrown on the industrial scrap-heap.

And if the mill were to close and the millworkers left the town – then there would be no work for those who provide services both to the mill itself and to the logging families.

As I felt the brunt of the sergeant's hostility, I thought: 'And so everyone would leave, and then there wouldn't even be any work for the police!'

'So what do people do when they don't work?' I tried again with Sergeant Henderson.

'They drink.'

It was then that the young constable warned me that when the serious drinking starts, after dark, it is the wise outsider who does not show himself on the streets.

'Is it really that bad?' I asked.

The Sergeant – himself the son of a local timberworker – quickly leaped to the town's defence. 'Bad? Look. Over the last century or more, Cornwall has developed a wild west mentality. It's something the locals are proud of.

'It's pretty remote here. Morlong (the closest town) is only 30 kays away, but the road's real bad, and in the rainy season it's often impassable. We're in a backwater, on a road to nowhere. The blokes work hard. And we have a long hard winter, when there's often not much else to do but drink.

'And when the blokes drink, they're liable to fight. It's only natural.'

'So you have quite a problem here,' I suggested.

The Sergeant looked at me as if it were me that was strange. 'No problem at all, mate. Except when jumped-up johnnies from the city come nosing around, asked too many f--king questions.'

I beat a hasty retreat. The Constable had also proudly told me that Sergeant Henderson had acquired his nickname 'Golden Gloves' by being the best fighter in town.

Back on the main street, I was again the target for jeers and whistles. There may only be a handful of unemployed youths here, but they seem to dominate the town.

One can only put up with the heckles for so long. There comes a time either to pack up and leave, or try to answer the attacks.

If a challenge is mounted with something like 'Hey, what's the matter? Is it something I'm wearing?' there is at first embarrassed silence. If that is followed up with 'Can I buy you a beer?' there is almost instant mateship.

Scott Robinson, 18, unemployed, was one of those who took the beer. Over the second round, it was he who raised the dangerous subject of greenies.

'They should bloody let us at them,' he declared. 'I'd split their f--king heads open with a crowbar.'

'Why's that?'

'I'd have a job, wouldn't I, if it wasn't for them?'

Another youth explained: 'The people of this area have been here for generations, and they don't like all these flash-jack bludgers from the city telling them what to do with their own bit of bush. This is a frontier town. People here take care of whatever happens themselves.'

Being seen drinking beer with some of the locals in Cornwall changes everything. Almost instantly you are accepted by people who had earlier ignored or abused you. After a couple of rounds it was the local youths shouting me, out of their dole cheques.

When I finally said I had to be going, I was looked at with pity. 'Back to the city? You poor bugger.'

'Here you go, mate,' Scott said. 'A souvenir of Cornwall.' He pulled a 'Doze in a Greenie' sticker from his pocket and stuck it across my briefcase.

There were backslaps, drunken kisses, and numerous offers of a bed on the lounge for the night. 'You can't drive back now.' The friendliness and mateship was like nothing one encounters from strangers in the city.

There is a lesson to be learned at Cornwall.

This is a place where mateship is available to anyone who knows the rules. If you argue, then you are in trouble; if you agree, you become one of them.

As I drove out of town, along the severely potholed road that ultimately joins the highway, I passed the beginning of the track to the new logging coup.

At the end of that track, the greenies are camped, waiting.

Waiting for what?

I thought of the shiny new sticker on my briefcase, and decided that I wouldn't want to be Mike Marchant or one of his supporters.

Not for all the trees in the world.

Page 5: Labor Fears Green Vote.

▷ ▷ ▷ ———————————————

The Argus
Friday, 15 March

LABOR FEARS GREEN VOTE

by Jill Philps, political correspondent

The Labor Party opened its campaign yesterday for the state seat of Hadley, which faces a by-election on Saturday, 30 March, with expressions of great confidence.

'We won it last time, and we'll win it this time!' announced the retiring member, Ms Anne Greaves, in a speech to local party volunteers.

Ms Greaves, whose sudden retirement owing to ill-health is the reason for the by-election, was looking decidedly frail. And many local party activists secretly believe that Labor's chance of retaining the seat is also less than healthy.

In the last state election Ms Greaves, who has been the member for Hadley for the last ten years, retained her seat by only a slim majority.

Though traditionally a Labor seat, Hadley has undergone a social and economic change over the last decade. Many of the older working-class members of the electorate have been forced out to the western suburbs by rising rents and house prices, and the young middle class have moved in.

This is in line with the overall pattern of the inner-city suburbs, to which business persons have been moving in order to commute easily to work.

The change is physically apparent in Hadley. Old terrace houses have been expensively restored, and many a local pub has turned into a bistro or an art gallery.

As the university is close by, there is also the odd student bar or coffee shop, but while the students make their presence felt, not many can afford to live there.

A typical Hadley household now consists of a business couple in their mid to late thirties, both working, with one or two young children, attending a community play-centre or private prep school.

The economic interests of such members of the electorate would definitely incline them towards the Liberal Party.

Many of these new inhabitants of the seat however are what the old residents call 'trendies'.

In the seventies, they would have marched in the moratoriums and voted for Gough Whitlam. A decade and a half later, they have cast off the socialism of their youth but they retain an allegiance to certain radical beliefs, such as nuclear disarmament and conservation.

In the last election, it is believed that it was the Labor Party's pledge to halt logging in state forests that won Ms Greaves a considerable portion of her vote.

The vital question which faces Labor Party headquarters now is: will they still vote the same way?

Firstly, it seems that Ms Greaves had a great following among the business women of Hadley because she had initiated a large network of creches and play-centres at which these mothers could leave their children.

The new Labor candidate, Mr Morris Simpson, is not only a man, but a man whose image is cast in the old-style Labor mould. (His opposition to state aid for private schools will win him little popularity in a seat where many parents pay school fees.)

Secondly, and most importantly however, certain members of the Labor Party fear that the Party's recent record on conservation will turn many of these voters away from the Party.

Since the last election, the Labor Party has failed to honour its pledge to halt logging in state forests. There has been a reduction, but the bulk of the logging continues.

This issue has been highlighted by the candidature of

well-known conservationist, Mr Michael Marchant. Mr Marchant, 31, full-time activist for the Save The Trees Society, is standing as an Independent Green candidate.

His platform is simple: 'Stop Logging Now', his leaflet declares.

Mr Marchant, of course, has no hope of winning. Yet his aim is not a seat in Parliament, but the exertion of pressure on the Labor Party to implement its conservation pledge.

His tactic is simple too. He is directing those who vote for him not to allocate their preferences to the Labor Party.

He is also, however, directing them not to vote for any of what he calls 'the anti-tree parties'.

In short, he is asking his supporters to vote (1) Independent Green, and leave the rest of the ballot sheet blank.

According to the electoral procedures of this state, that of course will mean that these votes will be Informal.

Will they make any difference to the outcome in Hadley?

Organisers of both the established parties believe they could be vital.

Labor fears that Mr Marchant could win away enough former Labor voters to cause the party to lose the seat.

The Liberal Party, of course, is quietly smiling at this turmoil. It believes it will win, thanks to Mr Marchant.

There is more at stake than just a seat. In the present state Lower House, the Labor Party holds 51 seats to the Liberal Party's 40, and National Party's 8. With Hadley gone, the situation would be Labor 50, Liberal/National Party Coalition 49.

This would be a most uncomfortable position for the Labor Party, for it would then need the loss of only one more Labor member in one more swinging seat and the government might lose power.

What could be done to hold Hadley?

Mr Marchant's answer is again simple: 'If the Minister for Conservation, Forests and Tourism were to announce the immediate end to the logging of state forests, beginning with a halt to the logging of the Settlement Creek area, I would direct my preferences to Labor, and Labor would win.'

The Labor Party's official response to this ultimatum is to throw it back in Mr Marchant's face.

'We will not be blackmailed, we will not be threatened,' the Premier announced yesterday.

'Logging will end, as we have promised. What people like Mr Marchant don't understand is that the government has contracts with certain logging companies – contracts made by the previous Liberal government – which nevertheless must be honoured.

'If we don't honour our contracts with business, then we cannot expect business to honour its contracts with us.

'There is also the question of workers' jobs to be considered. As a Labor government, we are committed to full employment, and a halt to logging in the Settlement Creek area alone would mean the retrenchment of the entire workforce of that town.

'That is a sacrifice we are not prepared to make, unless we can assure ourselves of providing alternative employment for those workers.'

The Premier added that he did not believe that Mr Marchant's ultimatum carried any real weight. 'These trendy alternative candidates only ever attract the lunatic vote. We will win Hadley, and we will win it by ourselves.'

They were fighting words, but they failed to convince many at the Party's Head Office.

In an effort to capitalise upon what is left of the working-class vote, the Labor Party has taken the much-criticised step of holding the by-election on Easter Saturday, in the belief that the working-class voters will stay home while the more affluent constituents go on holiday.

Though this will of course mean a large number of postal votes, the ALP pundits hope that the holiday makers will simply take the easiest course, and vote as they did last time.

This however, is a political long-short.

All over Hadley, green stickers are sprouting like mushrooms.

Green supporters are making the most of their candidate's current stand at Settlement Creek, near the small timber town of Cornwall. If Mike Marchant is arrested – as he is certain to be – his popularity will increase.

The issue that faces the swinging voters of Hadley is: are trees more important than political parties?

They will make their choice on Saturday, 30 March, just two weeks from tomorrow.

And until that choice is made, the Labor Party machine will be wondering whether business contracts and workers' jobs are worth the risk of holding power by only one seat.

Page 5: Mateship and Malevolence
Page 11: Easter poll ungodly, declares Archbishop

▷ ▷ ▷ ————————————

Are you bored?

Yeah? Well now you know how I feel. Stuck here with my legs in plaster, not even a window bed and too far up the ward for the TV. A pack of cards and sick of playing Patience. (I mean, there is a limit, as Mum says.) No visitors. (I remember this old docco Squirt showed us, about this black African woman who'd been in solitary and exile and stuff. She reckoned it had been a good day when an ant came into her cell. I thought that was crazy at the time, but now I think it'd be really neat if, say, one of Mum's ants came trucking around my table-thingummy, talking about what the weather's like and all that. Just had a funny thought. Maybe Mum had her ants at home because she felt kind of in solitary, in a house with three blokes who went about their business and didn't talk to her much . . . Another funny thought. You who I'm writing to – maybe you're my ant.) Anyway, apart from the cards I've got nothing to do but write like a maniac, and I don't even know who I'm writing to.

And now you reckon you're bored.

I bet you didn't read them properly anyhow. I know I didn't, that Friday morning when I was mucking around with Mum and putting off going to school. It's funny, though. I read them through while I was having my tea, and the second one made a bit more sense. The first one just made me dead homesick. The way that Jerry Denning guy described the streets of the town, even old Golden Gloves talking, it was *home.* A home I'll never have again. And Scottie giving the reporter-bloke a souvenir. That's Scottie. He might be a bit of a bastard, but he's my mate. Or he was. There was a bit of it though, made me sick. Where the reporter said about 'drunken kisses.' Yeah, sometimes when we're pissed we do kiss I suppose you'd call it sometimes, but we're not poofs or anything. And it's not kisses. Not like you'd do with a girl. Just like footballers do, when they're proud of each other, and mates. Mucking around. Not like that poofter that came down from the Ministry, that hung around with Kathy Dolan. What I reckon is, poofs should at least just stick with poofs. Not hang around with girls.

Tea, in case you're interested, was white chook in white sauce with white cauliflower and white mashed potato with yellowy-white beans on a white plate on a white paper table-mat on a white tray on a white table thingummy on a white bed. Just to make everything match right (white), my two legs that I'm not allowed to walk on are white too. (So's this paper. Sometimes I feel as if this pen and my hand are the only things real in the universe.) For afters there was white ice cream. That was better than the rest, and I spooned it down like I was a little kid.

'You like, eh?' a voice said. 'One thing you like. So maybe you like to have mine too. It hurt my enemy.'

At first I didn't think the voice was talking to me. I mean, why should I? No one had talked to me since I'd been here. Except the nurses and the blue women and the Chinese lady doctor and the lawyer and Mum on the phone.

'Eh, mate?' said the voice.

I looked over at the bed on my right. (The one on the other side is empty.) The bloke there was (is) about seventy-something, I guess, and a migrant or whatever you call them. (Squirt is always on about how you can't say 'wogs'. Not that you get much call to in Cornwall. As a practising Catholic with a bit of an Irish accent, my mum was the foreignest thing in town, until the Dolans moved in last winter. Or till Dr Brian MacBride. Stop it.)

Anyway, this guy, when he said 'Mate', really said 'Mite', so you could tell he was from somewhere. But just as I can't write Irish, I can't properly do Nick's Greek.

That's his name, Nick, and he's from somewhere called Thessalonika, or something, in Greece. He gave me his ice cream and now he reckons we're mites. He's got an enemy in his gut, whatever that means, and he's got six kids and seventeen grandchildren and one great-grandson (I saw all the photos) and he's a member of something called 'Koo-koo-eh'. Or he was, back in Greece. They don't have it here, he reckons.

'You know Koo-koo-eh mate?' he asked, real hopeful.

'No mate.'

Nick waved at the air, tried to explain. Leaned way over from his bed towards my bed so he could speak soft. 'Communist Party,' he said.

'They got one of them here all right mate,' I said. 'You know, all those Labor bludgers, bunch of city wankers . . .' I think, reading that article about home, made me talk like I would down the pub at Cornwall. Really, I couldn't give a stuff about politics. But Nick wasn't listening anyway.

'I tell you,' he said, 'only you, because you are comrade. Understand?' He gave me a wink like someone in a spy movie.

'The little nurse,' he said, 'she tells me you break your legs in what you call it? Demonstration. Against the government. Very good.' He threw his arms out, like Jesus on one of Mum's crucifixes, about to save us all. 'The young peoples! I say to my sons this: "My time is over. Your time is nearly over. But the time of my grandchildren is beginning. And perhaps my great-grandson will live in a good world! But only if we all struggle and fight, struggle and fight, never give up, never give up." You understand?'

'Sure mate,' I said. Thinking: 'Trust me to get a bed next to the ward loonie.'

'Sure you do,' Nick agreed. 'You good boy, I know it.'

Then one of the Blue Women came back for our plates.

Then the bell rang for night-time visiting. The ward doors opened and about a million and a half children and grand-children and even the famous great-grandson flooded down like a tidal wave to Nick's bed, and thank Christ I was left alone at last to get back to this.

It's taken me nearly all of visiting to get down just what's happened since tea. It's funny. The story I'm simply trying to tell about what happened in Cornwall in that little bit of time from the Thursday afternoon when I met Jade when I was hunting, till the Monday morning when the old man ran me down with the bulldozer, all seems to get gobbled up by talking about the hospital or how I got into the gang with Scott or how I used to get on best with Mum till I won the old man to me with fighting and sport or how the happiest times of my life have been in my land. Plus there's the stuff about Grandad too. (There's less about him, because since the stroke I haven't liked to think about him much.)

Anyway, I'm sick of this raving on. What I need to tell you now is to go back to that Friday morning.

The bell's rung, and I've got my two newspaper thingummies in my Communication folder, and I've given Mum the shits, so I grab my bag and just GO!

School. How do I describe it? Like the reporter bloke said, it's a Consolidated Primary-Secondary. All up, there's maybe 150 kids, mostly town kids (timberworkers' kids) but some farm kids get bussed in. Almost everyone leaves at Year 10. Then the boys hang around town, waiting for jobs at the mill, and the girls hang around town, waiting for their boyfriends to get jobs at the mill and marry them. If they're lucky, that happens before the first kid. If they're not, they just get married anyway, and live in the caravan park down the rec reserve and keep waiting.

So in Year 11-and-12 there were only four besides me: Helen Tayler, the daughter of the Uniting Church minister who only did services once a month because he moonlighted in other hick towns the other three weeks; Monica Ward, the daughter of one of the local cockies, who rode a horse to school and was Helen Tayler's mate; Janice Henderson, old Golden Gloves's kid and the town moll; and Kathy Dolan, from the pub, who dances in costume on St Patrick's Day and hangs around with poofters from the Ministry on other days, who has red hair and serves in the bar of a Friday and Saturday night, who goes and talks to my own Grandad, who goes and gets into my secrets, who utterly gives me the shits.

And then there was Squirt. We had him mostly. For all our

unreal subjects like Communication Skills and Personal Development and Local History and the rest of the bullshit that was just meant to keep us off the dole. (Did I say, we don't have HSC in Cornwall?)

Maybe Squirt's name sets you wrong. That was a Cornwall idea of a joke, calling a bloke who's six foot six and built like a meat-axe and the toughest guy in a football team of timberworkers a name like that. I tell you, if he didn't look like that, Squirt would've been done the minute he set foot in town. Because as you may have gathered, some of his ideas were pretty greenie. Or commie, or whatever they were.

So that was our little troop, as Squirt liked to say. A teacher, two deadshits, a slut, Kathy Dolan, and me.

▷ ▷ ▷ ————————————

Night-time visiting's over. The bell's just rung and the Greeks un-invade around me. Give me back my chair with lots of 'Thank you, Excuse, Thank you'.

'Keep it,' I say. 'I don't need it anyway.'

An old lady in black shakes her head at my buried lump of legs and goes 'Popopopopopopop!' like that's the Greek way of saying 'Tut tut'. 'Never mind, love,' she adds, 'you get out of bed soon, eh? You walk. Go home. See your mum, dad, brothers, sisters, even your girlfriend, eh love? Nice boy like you, going to have a girlfriend.'

'Don't rub it in,' I think. I have nothing. I have no one.

She rattles on: 'Nick, he says you nice boy. Good boy, he says, very good boy. Nick, he's always right.' She flashes a gob of gold teeth at me, and is gone.

Then Nick leans over again. 'Oh no,' I think. 'He's whispering. More kookoodoodledoo.'

The nurses are all busy up the end, saying tata to the visitors. 'Give me your glass,' he whispers.

I pass over my water glass. It comes back half full of something that looks like water.

It doesn't taste like water.

'Raki,' Nick says. 'We call it ----------' (he says a word I can't write down) 'but in your language, you say raki.'

'Not in my language, mate,' I think. I've never come across anything like this in my life. It's like drinking jet-aeroplane fuel. Not that I've ever drunk jet-aeroplane fuel. But you know what I mean. But it's nice.

The next thing that comes is a great hunk of crusty bread and kind of salty white cheese, skewered on a knife.

Then there's a Winfield cigarette, that we pass back and forth as if it was a joint.

I take another sip.

Have another drag.

This time when I pass the fag back I get a fistful of olives. I've never eaten them before. But they're tasty, full of juice, and not white.

It takes the nurses ages to do the night rounds. By the time they're up to us, we've had our second cigarette and Nick's put more in my glass. Plus I've had some salami. The first real meat I've eaten in a week.

The Night Sister sniffs. 'Has someone here been smoking?'

Nick rolls his eyes. Spreads his hands in an apologetic gesture. 'One of my visitings. I'm sorry. But you know, love. Greeks. They bad peoples. Never obey laws.'

I ask her if I can please have the death curtains put round my bed and the little night light on, as it's still only 9.30 and please, Miss, I have to do my schoolwork. HSC, you know, and all that.

'They're not death curtains,' she says. 'What a horrible name.' But the magic initials of the HSC get her, and so here I am, the only person in the ward allowed to stay up late. The only person in the ward, getting pissed.

Except for Nick. He's outside the curtains now. But he's my mate. The only one in the world, come to think of it.

▷ ▷ ▷ ———————————

That day at school, to cut a long story short, we had Show and Tell time, first up. We all opened our Communication Skills folders to our little news clippings. It was like a competition, because Squirt had always already decided what was the 'most significant' item of news for that day, and the trick was to pick the same one as he did. Kathy Dolan got it right about half of the time. The rest of us got it right about none of the time. I usually got it more wrong than anyone else. But once I'd got it right by picking an item about footballers not going to South

Africa, so I'd mostly gone for sport after that. My theory was like that old Mortein ad: 'If you're on a good thing, stick to it.' Plus it meant I had something to read in class while Squirt discussed the state of the world. Plus it gave Squirt the shits. And it added to my macho veneer.

Anyway, that day, I was sure I couldn't lose. I had the big item about Cornwall, and that just had to be the most significant thing in the world. And for once in my life I had a second item, to show I had what Squirt called broader interests. I knew too that everyone else would have the Cornwall item, but what the hell? At least today I didn't have anything that interested me, so it had to be good.

'Show and Tell time,' Squirt said. (He'd picked up the slogan from me. A typical teacher trick. Steal a kid's joke and make it not funny any more.) 'Helen, you can lead off.'

'Well, I think this is most significant,' said Helen Tayler, and she produced of course the Cornwall item.

'Why?' said Squirt.

'Because it's about here.'

'Pass it around the class please, Helen.'

That's what we always did with our items. But that day, everyone groaned.

'Come on.' 'Piss off.' 'Piss off.' 'Boring.' (That was Monica, Janice, me and Kathy.)

'OK Monica,' Squirt cut in, 'what's your item?'

'This,' said Monica, and she un-pronged the Cornwall item as if it was something new.

'Why?' said Squirt.

Monica went red. 'Because like Helen says, it's about here.' She looked wildly at the noticeboards, as if for inspiration. 'And the greenies,' she added. 'And everything.'

'Great!' said Squirt. 'And what about you, Jan?'

Janice pulled out the same thing.

'Why's this significant to you, Janice?'

Jan smiled. 'Because my boyfriend's in it. That's Scott.'

I sort of laughed to myself. Boyfriend! He might root her sometimes, but Danny had done it with her last year, and Terry the year before.

'What's that, Colum?' Squirt said.

'Nothing.'

'And what little gem from the sports section do you have for us today, Colum? Is it a footballer getting a half-a-million-dollar transfer or a boxer getting his brains knocked down to his balls?'

'No . . . Sir. Just this . . . Sir,' I said, and pulled out the second thing, about the boring by-election. I couldn't show my Cornwall piece, because it was clear Squirt didn't think it was significant.

Squirt slowly read it. I could tell he'd missed it when he'd skimmed through the paper to get his answer to the quiz.

'Clever, Colum,' he said. Then he repeated, 'Clever Colum', but how you'd talk to a parrot or something. 'Clever, clever Colum.' He shook his head in mock wonder. 'I always said there was something more to you, my old mate, than your macho veneer.'

See what I mean? You couldn't understand the bastard. But I sort of silently went *nyer nyer* to Kathy Dolan: Here's me finding something significant.

Then Squirt turned to her. 'And what about you?'

Kathy of course had to be different again. She had an item about the American President and Star Wars and how this was all going to mean that we might be going to be so blown up in the near future that Cornwall and logging and even my by-election were going to be irrelevant.

'Go to the top of the class, Kathy Dolan.' That's the sort of look Squirt gave her.

'But as far as the local news goes . . .' Kathy said. She sort of blushed, and looked apologetically at the other girls, as if she was letting them down by not having the Cornwall item. 'I think this is most important,' she said. And she pulled out a weather map.

It had those contours on it, that had made my old man tap his teeth the night before. The lines moving in on us, like the ants around the stove.

Except that the ants weren't moving round the stove. I'd checked, that morning.

Then – does your mind ever say something, that you didn't tell it to say? Well, mine said a kind of prayer then, real loud inside my head.

'Save us!'

It was like I was talking to the ants, urging them like the old man will urge a horse race that he's backed, that's running on TV – *'Come on, come on, come on will you! Get back, stay back there why don't you!'* – though of course the horses don't know the old man's yelling at them, and wouldn't care if they did. All they know are the natural laws of their world – the joy of galloping, the fear of the whip. They know nothing of the ten bucks the old man's invested. And whether the old man wins or loses, it means nothing to the horses.

Well, the ants of course were like that. Rain or fine, they just obeyed the laws of their world.

And yet my mind prayed to them, as if they actually *made* the weather happen to the map – as if by running their circles they made the storms come in threatening squiggles, as if by staying in the wall they made the loops nice and calm.

So *'Save us!'* my mind prayed.

But save us how?

(Come on, come on, come out and stop the logging. Make my green land safe till next year. Stop the movement of the scars towards the palace.)

(Get back, get back, stay back there will you, or the old man will be home, half the winter. No money, for the mortgage and the HP. Mum frazzled to a bone. And then the rows will start, and Grandad will get worse.)

So *save us save us.* Save us how?

Oh my shit, oh Christ. No matter which way I turned, there was no way out. Just the long darkness of a tunnel, and both ends blocked.

'And so,' Squirt was saying, 'the greenies may turn out to be irrelevant.'

Something in me screamed. It was all relevant to me.

Then to get my head out of the tunnel, I started thinking about the girl I'd met the afternoon before.

Long black hair. *Green* eyes. Small white hands . . . I was remembering her in little sections, like you might pick up a few jigsaw pieces, a bit of sky, a bit of cloud, a bit of tree, a bit of castle, each piece only a clue to the picture and nothing fitting together. It's a bit like that again now as I try to make a picture of her. I must be a bit pissed or I wouldn't be writing like this. Because of course I hate her too. Her and the old man. If it wasn't for them, I wouldn't be here. Them, and of course MacBride. It was him who started it, the craziness that seized my brain that Sunday night and whirled me up and up till I was down on the ground again, you might say, with a bang. Down on the ground, lying like *he* was when he sent me crazy. Stop it. But it was my fault he was down there. So it was *me* that started it. No, stop it.

. . . But long black hair (I was thinking then). Green green eyes. Her bones fine, frail-looking, like a bird's. But like a bird too there was something strong about her, as if she had some power or ability that I didn't. Like a bird can seem small and weak, sitting on a branch, but when it wants to it can fly and you can't. (I can't. Can't even walk now.) Her posh voice. Her university. Her 'Dad earns too much'. That was her difference. She could wear dirty jeans and no make-up, she could get arrested and be a greenie, because if she wanted to she could fly off above the world and me. Why?

I saw her for a moment, way up in a cloudless sky, a tiny speck, playing on the air currents, her hair streaming back, black. I didn't even know her name.

Then it was my name I heard.

'Colum?'

'Huh?'

'I said, what do you think, Colum?'

'About what, Sir?' I called him 'Sir' to nark him. We were meant to call him John. It was supposed to be grown-up and informal in our little troop.

'About Kathy Dolan's proposal.'

'It's not *my* idea,' she cut in quickly, as if I might think she was up herself for having one. 'Just something this bloke Garry, who's staying at the pub, said.'

I'm starting to get tired at last, so I'll cut this bit short and just give you the gist of it, without too many 'I saids' and 'Squirt saids'. (Hopefully. But I do get carried away. Must be Mum's gift of the gab in me, after all.)

Anyway, Kathy explained that this guy Garry Lazlo was from the Ministry of Conservation, Forests and Tourism, and he'd been staying in the pub for a couple of days. (Have I said that Kathy's old man ran the pub?) He (Garry, I mean) was meant to be doing an investigation, to see if there was any possible alternative work that could be started in the area. Kathy said that Garry said that the Ministry would be willing to spend bulk money setting up a new industry, because then it could stop the logging and keep jobs and therefore keep both the govenment's election promises.

Squirt cut in to say, 'But what alternative work could there be around Cornwall, Col?'

I was buggered if I knew. See, the farmers didn't need workers, and Morlong was just a farm centre – it had the sale yards and lots of shops selling hay and fence posts and tractor parts and that sort of stuff, but it didn't have any industries, and it was three hours away from the city so you couldn't have factories there. And anyhow, factories for what?

'What does Cornwall have to sell?' Squirt urged me. He was leading me up to the idea of this Garry bloke, that Kathy had explained when I wasn't listening, and he was using what he calls his Socratic method. (There was some old Greek, evidently, who used to pester his students like this. I must ask Nick if he had it at his school.)

'So what does Cornwall have to sell?' Squirt repeated.

'Timber, Sir.'

'But what does timber come from?'

'Trees, Sir.'

'And what are trees good for, apart from timber, Colum?'

He had me there. What *are* trees good for, apart from timber? Brainwave! 'Growing things on, Sir! Like apples and oranges and peaches and nectarines and quinces and plums and bananas and coconuts and . . .' I was prepared to go on for a long time.

'Don't be smart, mate. What are *forest* trees good for, apart from timber?'

'I don't know, Sir.'

'*Beauty*, Colum, if that's not a word which will unduly embarrass you. There is a very famous poem which goes: *"I think that I will never see a poem as lovely as a tree."* 'Squirt quickly scribbled the words on the board. Honestly! That's what I mean about his greenie ideas. Sometimes you wouldn't think that Squirt was the dirtiest footballer on the Cornwall team.

He turned back to me. 'Trees, Col, are good to look at, and walk amongst, and sit under.'

'Yes, Sir,' I said, in an anything-you-say-sir sort of voice. I'd never heard of Squirt going walking in the forest. I was the only person in Cornwall who did that.

'And so how could Cornwall sell its trees for beauty, and not for timber?'

I was sick of the game. I just stared.

'By establishing a tourist industry!' Squirt announced as if it was his own idea. 'Kathy, will you explain it once more please.'

Again I'll cut the next bit short. (The Night Sister just popped in to see if I wanted a sleeping tablet. 'I don't take drugs,' I told her. She was so fazed she popped out again and didn't tell me to turn the light off. And it's 12.30.)

Then Kathy said that Garry said that if he could find some special thing to interest tourists in the area, such as enormous waterfalls or caves or Aboriginal art or endangered flora or fauna, then he might be able to convince the Ministry (which is in charge of tourism as well as forests and conservation) that it should spend its bulk money investing in a new road to Baytown and brochures and stuff encouraging the Baytown holiday makers to come up to Cornwall when the surf was bad or the weather cold or something.

(See, Baytown's only 25-30 kays south, down on the coast, but to get there now you've got to head north virtually to Morlong, then cut down through the east side of the peninsula along old logging tracks that are so bad that you mostly need a four-wheel drive, till you join up to the Coast Road and get into Baytown that way. Of course, Scott and us did it sometimes in the Jet, but often as not there'd be a tree across the track, or we'd get bogged, or the surf would be lousy when we got there.)

Anyway, the idea was that tourists could go for walks in the forest, and instead of cutting down the trees the people of Cornwall could build the new road and make forest trails and car parks and barbecue spots and that, and lead tours and sell postcards and Devonshire Teas and perhaps even handicrafts.

'Great!' I said. I could just see the old man leading a bunch of city wankers through the forest, pointing out the koalas and caves. (Not that we had any.)

I mean, of all the lame-brained schemes! As if city people would come to Cornwall! And as if anyone in their right mind would want them to! But the rest of the troop was going buzz-buzz about it. Except for Jan. She was taking the paint off her nails.

'You know what I think?' said Helen Tayler. She didn't usually think much, but when she did it was always good for a laugh. 'I think we should help him.'

'What?' said Squirt.

'Help him find something. Then the greenies will go away and there won't be any violence, like they say is going to happen.' I suppose, being a Christian, she had to think like that.

'Yes,' said Monica. 'We could do it on the weekend. All go for a walk with him, and find something.'

Honestly, even Kathy was pissing herself! Squirt politely said that it was a nice idea, but 'Realistically speaking, Rome wasn't built in a day, and neither could the man from the Ministry expect to find an item of significant tourist interest in a weekend, even with the help of our little troop.

'After all,' he added, 'if there was something significant in the forest, we'd all know about it already, wouldn't we Jan? . . . Janice?' (Jan used to cut off nearly as much as I did.) 'What do you think, Janice?'

Jan looked up from her nails. She was repainting them now, the same colour they just had been.

'That Garry Whatsit's a poofter.'

'How do you know?' I said. I was kind of interested, because I wasn't sure I'd ever seen one in real life. Not that I'd seen this bloke either, but still.

'Scott says.'

'They're not poofters, Jan, Colum,' Squirt said. 'They're gays. And besides, it's got nothing to do with it if he is. And you don't even know he is, anyway.'

'Scott says he is,' Jan repeated.

So Squirt got off trees and onto Prejudice, and that was the end of that lesson. Kathy Dolan had been the winner by even more than usual.

Nothing else much happened at school that day. For homework we were reminded to get on with our Local-History projects. That was a thing we did because we weren't meant to be brainy enough to do the whole of Australia, like HSC kids. We just had to interview someone old who lived in the town and wasn't a member of our own family. We had to ask them questions on the school's tape recorder, like 'What did you do when you were a little boy?' and then copy the answers into a book and stick in old photos if we had any. We had all year to do it in. And Scott and us had decided to do some extra footie training, because Golden Gloves had called off the boxing that Friday.

So when the last bell rang I headed off to the Greasy Spoon to buy some afternoon tea.

▷ ▷ ▷ ————————————

Nick just muttered someting like 'Karlei maira.'

'Same to you with knobs on,' I agreed.

I don't think either of us feel real bright. It's now the next morning (Tuesday). I mean, in real life. If you could call this that.

In my story it's still Friday afternoon. I've had a Chiko Roll with sauce and Scott's just come in.

▷ ▷ ▷ ———————————————

'Hey, come down the cop shop!' he reckoned.

It was in the side street down from the Greasy Spoon, so in a sec we were there. So was the rest of town.

There were about twenty cops, unloading greenies from four paddy waggons. Golden Gloves was on the edge of the cops, looking real dark, because the city inspector was being just like the old man had said. 'Would you mind coming this way please, Sir? Mind the step.' Or that's what it looked like. The greenies were walking out of the waggons, no handcuffs or anything, and up the path and into the cop shop. Two sets of guys with TV news cameras were filming them, as if they were heroes or something.

All the blokes from town were there, as well as the blokes who'd been in the forest that day. All booing and yelling. And then the police started getting heavy with guess who? Us! They formed a chain (Golden Gloves and Wee Willie weren't in it) and kept shoving us back so we couldn't get close to the greenies. Scott picked up a bit of gravel and threw it at Mike Marchant, and a cop grabbed his arm and twisted it right round behind his back. If it wasn't for Golden Gloves coming up, Terry and Danny and Sean and I would've been on top of that cop.

'Leave the kid alone,' old Golden Gloves growled, and the city cop got such a shock he let go.

By that time, the greenies were all inside. Because I'd got distracted, I'd missed my chance to see her. I was shitty. Shitty at the greenies and the cop and at Scott too though it wasn't his fault and why did I want to see a fucking greenie anyway?

The old man had seen me nearly go for the cop that had Scott, and he came up and slapped me on the back. 'That's it, son, stand up for your mates.'

He told me what had happened out at the coup. The blokes had got there about nine, with two dozers and all the works, ready to start. The greenies were lined up on the forest side of the creek, in front of their tents and stuff which were all over the clearing.

'They talk about protecting the environment or whatever they call it!' the old man reckoned. 'Then they go and sleep and eat and shit all over it, hang flags on the trees and banners too, bits of cardboard placards everywhere, sleeping bags draped out over the bushes, a rope strung up with – listen to this – *tea towels* on it!' The closest the old man's ever got to a tea towel is to hand one to Mum. I could see how he'd object to them being in his workplace.

Anyway, the cops were there already, plus the two news crews and some other notepad-type reporters. About the news crews – get this! Sean told me they had two helicopters, waiting for them down the rec reserve, so that when they'd finished filming they could get back to the city in time for the evening news. Helicopters! That's how important they reckoned the greenies were.

'But as I said,' the old man said, 'the cops were lined up on one side of the creek and the greenies on the other, and the cops wouldn't let *us* cross the creek! The inspector had a loud-hailer . . .' (Not that he would've needed it. The creek's only a few metres across at that spot.) '. . . And he yelled out how the greenies were trespassing on state land or something and he *"requested"* them to leave immediately. But of course the greenies all linked arms and sat down.'

You've probably seen them on TV, talking about how they train themselves in non-violence or something. Well, evidently they did some of that. The old man said they sung that song they always sing, you know, 'We Shall Not Be Moved'.

The old man went on: 'By then it was morning tea time, and us blokes had a fire going of course and a billy brewed, and all the bludging cops got out of line and asked to borrow our mugs and had a sit-down and a smoke for a while.

'Then they lined up again and the inspector read about a hundred pages of some Act that says how if you trespass on State Land you can be arrested under section something something of the Something Something Act.' (That's one of the charges I've got against me now.)

'Then bugger me,' the old man reckoned, 'if this lawyer in a suit and gumboots didn't appear out of nowhere and go up to the inspector and ask to have a look at the Act. He read away at it for a while, and then he said something to the inspector and there was a lot of buzzing around and it finally turned out that the inspector had brought the wrong Act. He had the one for Commonwealth land, and not state land, or something.

'Anyway, Wee Willie was sent back to the station to get a different Act from the inspector's briefcase. Evidently the briefcase wasn't where the inspector had reckoned, or something, because it was lunchtime by the time he got back.'

'Then this special sort of canteen came, for the cops, with hot soup in big thermoses and sandwiches thick as your arm and fruit cake and apples, all taxpayers' money, and this time there was no talk of going shares, not on your nellie! Course, we had our own tucker like we always do, but still a bit of soup would've eased the pain. Meanwhile of course the greenies were chewing into their nuts or whatever it is they eat.'

'Next they all lined up again on either side of the creek and the inspector read the right Act this time, and the greenies sang again about how they wouldn't be moved – out of tune, I might add, even if they did have a guitar and that.'

'And then at long bloody last the inspector finally said: "As you continue to trespass under the Something Something Act, you will now be arrested and charged with trespass. Any acts of resistance could lead to further charges of blah blah or blah blah.' "

'Of course, the bludgers were sitting with their arms linked, so the coppers waded across the creek and pulled them apart, but so gentle, like your mum might untangle her knitting, and then the bludgers wouldn't walk, so get this will you! The coppers picked up the bludging greenies and carried them across the creek and up the track and into the paddy waggons! Carried them! Two coppers to a greenie, or more in some cases. It took four to get that beer-gutted Irishman across the creek.'

'So he was there,' I thought. I hadn't seem him get out of a paddy waggon either.

'And your mum reckoning he's a professor! Professor of sitting down on his bleeding arsehole!'

If that seems like a long speech for the old man to stand there and make, after I've said how he didn't talk much, I should say that it came out more in dribs and drabs, as we walked up to the pub. There was him and a few of his mates, and me and my mates, and while he told me, the others put in bits like 'Yeah!' and 'Too bloody right, mate'. (Scott and them had been out at the coup, though of course they didn't have work there. Just went along to help the blokes if they needed it, but the cops wouldn't let the blokes do anything.)

Anyway, that was how come it took all day to get the greenies out of the forest, and how the blokes didn't even make a start on the work.

'Well, that's it, then,' I said. We were in the pub by now, though Scott and us were just having squashes because we had training in a minute. 'But at least they're gone now, and you'll be able to start work, Monday morning.' I spoke kind of quiet and low-key, like Mum does when she tries to cheer the old man up. Actually, I had a bit of disappointment myself, to think that girl was gone and I'd never see her again.

The old man snarled at me. 'You're as green as a greenie. They'll be back in there by tomorrow lunchtime, you see if they're not.'

The blokes explained it to me, like Wee Willie had explained it to them. Though the greenies were arrested, all they needed was for someone to bail them out and they'd be free. Free to go where they liked, including back into the forest. It seemed the greenies always had someone on the scene with enough bail money – probably the lawyer bloke, everyone reckoned. Golden Gloves was still in charge of the station, so he was going to take as long as he could to hold up the bail, but he couldn't refuse it, so they'd probably all be out by the morning. And back at the camp by lunchtime.

Now I haven't got all this legal stuff right, but there was something about how they could only be arrested between nine and five, Monday to Friday, according to the Act. Or maybe it was that they had to be actually obstructing something, such as the loggers, for them to be arrested. (The blokes said different things about what the law was.) But anyway, it meant the police wouldn't go in to get them again till work was due to start on Monday morning. Maybe it was just that the coppers wanted the weekend off, I don't know.

'I know what we should do, next time,' the old man's mate Bluey Waters reckoned.

Scott and the rest of us went off to training, down the rec reserve. (The helicopters had already left, so I didn't get to see them. I was a bit disappointed about that too, because I'd never seen one close up.)

After we finished our laps and push-ups and everything, Scott and the others went back to the pub for a proper drink. I said I'd meet them later at Scott's place, and went home, even though it was a Friday. I just didn't feel like a drink. For a start, because I didn't get the dole, I only had the fifteen bucks each week I earned for picking up glasses in the pub on Sunday nights. (That was Kathy's night off, thank Christ.) Mr Dolan and his missus were always pretty good about giving me a free drink or two when I did go in, and my mates always reckoned no worries, they didn't mind shouting me, but I hated to be a bludger. And because it was nearly the end of the week, I'd just spent my last cash on the Chiko Roll. All I had in the world was the ten cents in my pocket.

The other reason I didn't feel like a drink was because I felt kind of low. I wasn't really admitting it to myself, but it had something to do with the fact I'd missed seeing that girl. And another even worse bit of it was that I kept seeing her sitting in a police cell. Now, I knew what the cells at Cornwall cop shop looked like – old Golden Gloves threw Scott and me in one last New Year, to cool us off a bit. (He didn't charge us or anything. Just gave us steak and eggs courtesy of the taxpayer and Mrs Hendo the next morning, plus a hair of the dog.) Anyway, there were two Cornwall cells and they were a bit basic, but nothing gruesome. But in the picture in my head this cell was something dark in a dungeon out of convict times, and the girl was all by herself, with chains on, in a long white raggedy dress, crying and eating a crust and water. The scratch on her cheek had grown into a great welt. Stupid, eh? (The good thing about not knowing who I'm writing to is I can say these things.)

And the *other* other reason I didn't feel like a drink was that Friday was one of Kathy Dolan's nights behind the bar, and I didn't feel like seeing her.

But when I got home (it was about 5.30), who should be there of course but Kathy Dolan, sitting in the kitchen with the school tape-recorder, interviewing my own Grandad for her Local History project!

'Speak of the devil!' Mum said. 'We were just talking about you.'

▷ ▷ ▷ ————————————

When you've got a hangover you feel real hungry don't you?

Or don't you?

Yeah, that's you I'm talking to.

The Lone Reader.

Who are you, behind your mask?

Maybe you don't get hangovers. Maybe you don't even drink. Like Helen Tayler, or Monica Ward. A Wowser. At least even Kathy Dolan drinks. Though she'd have to, being Irish and brought up in dozens of pubs. Once, in the time when I used to talk to her, she told me how she'd never been at the same school for a whole year. Her Dad, old Dom Dolan, he's one of what my Mum calls the Itchy-Footed Irish. The Dolans have had pubs all over Australia. Of course he doesn't buy them, just rents them for a while, then moves on. Anyway, Kathy said the thing she wanted more than anything in the world was just to stay put in the one place for ever. 'Even a hole like Cornwall?' I asked. 'This would do me fine,' she said.

. . . Just mucking around with this now, filling in time till lunch. The trolley is nearly here. What I'd like is steak and eggs and bacon and onion and chips and tomato and beetroot and a cob of fresh sweet corn. With a can of Coke.

. . . What I got was white soup with white bread, a bowl of coleslaw (all limp and sour), four jatz and cheese, weak lukewarm tea and a floury apple. But there was a visitor floating in my tea. I wonder who it will be!!!

Maybe you, L.R.

Maybe not.

Eureka! Nick just slipped me a hunk of salami and a real tomato. 'Grown from my own hands,' he said.

'Cheers!' I said, and toasted him with the last dreg of my tea.

'Ya sou, comrade!' he toasted me back with his. He didn't eat any of his lunch, I noticed. I don't blame him.

'You don't mind if I don't talk now, go back to sleep?' he said.

'No mate, go for your life. Feeling a bit crook on it, eh?' I nodded towards his water glass, to show what I meant.

He looked like I'd insulted him – or the drink. 'Is not that!' he said. 'Is the enemy. In my gut. He fight me today. The fascist. But he won't win. No fascist ever going to beat this old comrade.' He turned his face aside, and shut his eyes.

But the old comrade has *me* beat, all right. Fascists were something in the war, weren't they, like Nazis or something? So how could one be inside Nick? But he really spoke as if there was a little man in there.

Suddenly now I think I get it. It must be something like a tapeworm, and 'fascist' is the slang name for it in Greek. He's a funny bloke, all right. Hard to understand. I don't just mean his words and his accent. His ideas, like. No, not his ideas, because ideas can be all separate different things. It's more like Nick has a whole way of looking at everything, that I've never met before.

He's asleep now. His hands are outside the white quilt. They're good hands, brown, callousy, with deep wrinkles. I lean right over to get a good look. People's hands always interest me. You can just see them, growing the tomato. They don't have those horrible spots that old men's hands sometimes get. And the knuckles are a bit big, swollen, not as if it's from arthritis, but as if he's done a lot of fighting in his time. Even now, while he sleeps, they're clenched tight, to make a fist. Two fists.

Maybe though he's not asleep. Maybe he's fighting the fascist. Hanging on through the pain.

I tell you one thing, but. There's no way Nick would let something get the better of him in a struggle.

Yeah, he's a winner, Nick.

The opposite of me.

Maybe that's why I like him. But also, his hands remind me of something.

▷ ▷ ▷ ————————————

Where was I?

Oh yeah, speaking of the devil. Kathy Dolan. Her sitting in my kitchen when I came home cold and tired and hungry and generally pissed off and wanting my own peace and quiet.

Grandad was in his dressing gown with the teapot in front of him, and there were the crumbs of fruit cake and anzac biscuits and chocolate royals on one of the Good Plates. Mum was pink-cheeked and happy as Larry (whoever he is) as she shelled the peas. Kathy had her folder out, but I'd noticed her switch the tape recorder off when I came in.

The hide of it! Not just talking about me, but talking about me on tape. The tapes from the projects were going to go into what Squirt called the Cornwall School Oral History Archive. I just knew Mum had been gabbling on about what Colum had been like as a little boy (that's her idea of history), and to think of all that going to the school, for Squirt to listen to, or even Janice Henderson!

But I didn't say anything. What was the point? I couldn't ask her to wipe it. I'd be as likely to ask her to wipe my arse. I wouldn't ask Kathy Dolan to do anything. (I once asked her to do something and she wouldn't. So that was it.)

I just walked to the fridge and got myself out a can of beer. Mum raised her eyes. The cans were the old man's. He sometimes offered me one, but I never just took one. Besides, I hardly ever drank at home, even when he did offer. Drinking's something you do with your mates. And the old man was hardly that. (Even when I didn't hate him.)

'Well you mob have been having a right old party.' I stupidly went and defended myself.

Mum raised her eyebrows again. 'Well, if you'd have come home for afternoon tea instead of eating grease with your mates. Especially as Kathy was here . . .'

'I never do, Fridays. You know that.'

'*I* know that,' Kathy cut in. 'That's why I came today, honestly Mrs Ferris, I didn't want Colum here.'

And so now she could decide whether she wanted me to be in my own house or not!

'But Col could've been a real help, dear. Jogging Grandad's memory, and that. Col heard all the stories when Grandad was himself. I'm sure he knows half of them by heart, Col does. He used to be with his Grandad all the time, except when he was swinging on the gate, waiting for his Dad to come home, or playing by himself up in the forest. He didn't use to hang around with that Scott Robinson and Danny and Terry Bail in them days . . .'

I slammed out of the kitchen and into the sleep-out and hurled myself down on the bed with my boots on. Not that it was any more private. The sleep-out was half the old back verandah, closed in with fibro, so the back kitchen window looked right onto my bed. The window didn't shut properly, so I could hear every word that was said. And I could see Kathy watching me lying there, pretending not to listen as I rolled a one-handed Drum. (I was practising for when I had a stroke.)

'Honestly, Mrs Dolan, I just want Grandad's – I mean old Mr Ferris's – memories, I don't want them all *interpreted*, like, by Colum, and mucked up.' (That was another thing I had against Kathy Dolan. She was the only person in the world to call me Colum, except Mum and Grandad, and Squirt when he was being narky.)

Mum gave up. She was miffed, I could see. Kathy had said I might muck something up, and in Mum's eyes even Kathy Dolan wasn't good enough to think that. Plus Kathy had said she hadn't wanted me there, and that had set back Mum's wedding-bell plans a bit. (Kathy was technically a Catholic, see, so as far as Mum was concerned she was the one for me.)

'Well, go *on*, Grandad,' Mum said. 'Tell the girl something.'

'Hang on,' Kathy muttered, 'I'll just turn the tape back on.'

'I don't know what she wants to know,' Grandad complained. 'I already done told her about when I saw that . . . that Hailey's Comet. That was in nineteen . . . nineteen . . . nineteen . . .'

'1986!' I yelled through the window, then I could have cut my tongue out for letting on I was listening. But I hadn't been able to help it.

'Probably,' Grandad agreed. 'You see, Sis, he *does* know more about it than what I do myself.'

Kathy looked fed up, then made herself be gentle again for Grandad. 'Perhaps, Mr Ferris, you might remember what year it was you were born. And we could start from there . . . Not for Halley's Comet,' she added quickly, 'but for other things.'

'What other things?'

'Whatever you like,' Kathy sighed.

'Just tell her when you were *born*, Grandad.' Mum was getting impatient. She was onto the spuds, and glancing at the wall clock. Six o'clock. They should've been on the boil by now, really. The old man was sometimes home at 6.30, and he liked his tea ready on the table by the time he got his coat off.

'1901!' Grandad said quickly. 'I remember the date, because it's easy to remember. And something else happened that year too, besides. Something famous, I seem to recollect.'

'Federation?' Kathy suggested.

'*Yes,*' he said. '*That's* what I remember. We had a party. For the Federation. I danced with Molly . . . Molly . . . Molly someone . . . *Big* girlie. Beef to the heels and mutton through the brain . . . Asked her to marry me, I seem to remember . . . Don t think she ever did but.'

I shot a quick sideways look through the window. Grandad had to be bunging it on. Didn't he? But his eyes were glazed and fixed upon the teapot, no little fold at the edge of them like he always used to have when he put one over on me. It'd taken me a long time to learn that look. And he'd got away with an awful lot of whoppers before I did.

For instance, in the beginning he told me that my palace had really been a palace, built by a Prince for his Lady. The Prince came to the forest, see, all by himself, one springtime, and discovered the place where the two arms of the creek meet. He looked around and said to himself: 'This place is good as gold. Or better, really, because it's mine.' Then he cut the trees in the junction with a little silver knife (my little silver knife, of course), for it was then a magical knife that could cut through a mighty mountainash trunk quick as you could say 'mashed pertater'. And then he built the palace, and he planted the magnolias and the camellias and the orchard of apples and pears and plums and quinces, and the climbing roses, and the jasmine, and the spring bulbs, and the herbs. And then he waited for his Lady to come.

He waited and waited, and waited and waited, but still she didn't come. Meanwhile, the fruit trees grew, and the flowers and herbs, and the bulbs multiplied like a secret inside the dark earth, and he never gave up hope.

And while he waited, and while the things grew, he grew up too. For he'd only been a lad when he'd first come there.

'How old?' I used to ask.

'Oh . . . seventeen.' It'd sounded old to me at the time, for I was only seven.

And then one spring, when the daffodils were thick through the grass, making the whole place look good as gold, or better really, for daffodils are live and gold is cold (Grandad used to say), she just just walked in from the forest all by herself one day, plonked herself down as if she was home, and there she was.

'How old was he then?' I used to ask.

'As old as his eyes and a little older than his smile,' Grandad would say.

'And then what happened?'

'They lived happily ever after. Or as long as they lived. And that's all there is to say about it,' Grandad would end up.

'Oh go on, Grandad,' I'd nag him. We'd be sitting outside the palace, when he told me this story. 'Tell me about the long rooms at the back, and who lived in them.'

'Them big rooms,' Grandad would say, 'they were the guest-rooms, where the Prince's friends stayed. You see, while the Prince waited for his Lady, he gave parties, to while the time away, parties with a heap of drink and whole roasted sheep, and blokes had to stay for years at a time to eat all the tucker. It was only blokes, you see, because there were no women there, not till the Prince's Lady . . . And talking of tucker,' he'd add, 'we'd best be getting home to ours. It's a long road home from the palace, and a hard one. And you don't ever want to get off the track in the forest of a night.'

'Why not?'

Grandad would clam up. 'Because I say so.'

Anyway, that's the sort of story Grandad used to tell me when his eyes had that edge to them. He told it much better than me, of course, so it was more believable, but even with that you no doubt think me really stupid to have fallen for it.

Maybe I just believed because I wanted to. But you see, I knew the palace really was a palace. And besides, there was an extra bit to the story, that made the palace special, and me special. Grandad used to say that my name showed I was descended from the Prince. (That kind of made me feel better, about being called Colum.) And perhaps one day, Grandad always said, I would inherit the palace.

'When?' I'd nag.

'Oh . . . when you're grown up.'

'But when'll *that* be?'

His answer was always the same, and always strange. 'When you've learned the truth of fairytales.'

'But when'll *that* be?'

'Maybe when you're seventeen. Maybe when you're seventy. Maybe never. It's up to you.'

. . . 'Don't be silly,' Mum told Grandad now. 'You can't have danced at a Federation party with Molly Anyone. You'd have been a baby in nappies. If they had nappies then. I'm sure I don't know, I'm no good at history . . . I'm sorry, Kathy-love, his mind is really too far gone today, over the hills and far away I'm afraid, you'd best come back another time. Oh heavens, now the custard's gone and caught!'

A sour scorched smell was wafting through the window. Mum pulled the pot off the fire.

'Gee I'm sorry, Mrs Ferris, that's *my* fault, I've got to go anyway. Shit! (Sorry Mrs Ferris!) Is that the time? I'm meant to be serving by now. And all the extra coppers in the pub, no doubt, and Friday night.' Kathy grabbed her folder, but Grandad slammed his fist down on the table.

'I was so born in 1901. I remember it well. Colum, get the Bible out and prove it to her! Thinks she knows better than me, this lass.'

I had to laugh. Then I lied, 'Sorry Grandad, don't know where the Bible is.' Let the bitch go, now she was starting to. And about bloody time.

'Bull,' said Grandad. The grumpiness was bringing him back to himself. 'It's in the tin trunk under your bed, where you're lying now, and with your boots on. Get it out. And roll me a smoke while you're about it.'

OK, OK. Show her the Bible, and that'll be it.

I opened my treasure trunk (but under the bed, in case Kathy saw anything) and got out the big Bible that had been in the old man's family since they all were in the Ark. I took it in, dumped it on the table, and rolled a Drum for the poor old bugger.

Grandad opened to the pages at the back where all the dates and stuff were written down. The handwriting had been done by a number of different people, and the early things were in old-fashioned spider-scrawl.

Funnily enough, I've got a list of the main dates with me here, because Kathy quickly copied them out that day and then left them behind. (I'll explain why later.) Anyway, this is what she noted down:

1836 **Samuel Ferris** *born (illegible)*
1850 **Samuel Ferris** *arrives Australia*
1853 **Samuel Ferris** *discovers the junction.*
1869 **Samuel Ferris** *marries (illegible. Lady . . .???)*
1870 **Samuel Ferris** *born at The Settlement. April 10*
1870 **Samuel Ferris** *dies in Act of God. April 10*
1897 **Samuel Ferris** *marries Ann Winslow at Cornwall*
1901 **Samuel Ferris** *born Cornwall*
1928 **Samuel Ferris** *marries Jane Hart at Cornwall*
1930 **Samuel Ferris** *born Cornwall*
1954 **Samuel Ferris** *marries Colleen Cafferty*

That isn't the full list of all the stuff in the Bible – it went back before 1836, and after 1901 there were names of girls born too, and other boys, and the names of who they married, and who their kids were, plus stuff such as so and so dying in the war and so and so moving to the city. But Kathy was fascinated with how all the first sons were called Samuel, and she copied them out.

'Do you think I could come back and borrow this, but, Mrs Ferris, and copy the full list on the school photocopier? It'd be a good thing to put in my project, a record of one family that's been here from just about the beginning, and I'll be really careful with it.'

('Goody-goody,' I thought. 'Fancy caring about a bloody school project.' I mean, Kathy had once told me she really liked history because it seemed somehow permanent, compared to her life of moving round all the time and losing friends as soon as she made them, but she didn't have to go this far.)

'Sure, Kathy-love.' Mum was fascinated herself now, the custard and the rest of the tea forgotten. 'You know, it'd quite slipped my mind that we had it. I know Grandad wrote in it, when Colum was born, but I haven't seen it since then. It's not a Catholic Bible, see,' she explained.

'What do you mean Sis,' Grandad cut in, *' "been here since just about the beginning"?* I'll have you know it was my grandad, Samuel Ferris, discovered the creek. Moved in by himself, except for a cat and a team of bullocks, and felled the first trees that ever come down in this area. It was him too, planned out the first mill. Then the other blokes come, of course, and they all lived there. And after a while, a long while of waiting, his missus come too. The first woman in the forest, she was. And he was the first, the very very first white man.'

Kathy stared. 'You mean Settlement Creek, your Grandad discovered that? And he kind of founded Cornwall? And he started up the Cornwall mill?'

'Yes and no, Sis,' Grandad said. His eyes were completely unglazed now, he'd moved right back into what Mum called himself again. He'd been like that since the stroke – gone one minute, here the next. 'You're getting the *history* arse over elbow, because you haven't got a hold of the geography! Now look here Sis . . .' He took Kathy's pencil and started to scribble a tiny map onto a cigarette paper that he flattened out lengthwise in front of him.

'Uh-uh,' I thought, 'this is getting dangerous.'

'Won't your Dad be getting hostile?' I said to Kathy. 'The pub was packed even at four.'

But Kathy utterly ignored me. 'Go on,' she urged Grandad. (The tape was still running, of course.)

'Now this . . .' Grandad pointed to a squiggle that ran down the bottom half of the paper, 'this is the creek. It's like a "Y" see, with a very long tail, heading south, and here where the tail runs off the paper, that's where the forest stops. Then the creek turns south-east, and heads on to Baytown – that's this, see Sis.' He popped a pea out of a pod and carefully positioned it about six centimetres to the bottom right of the paper, ate the rest of the little green towns then angled the pod underneath Baytown to show the coastline.

He picked up the pencil again. (You've got to remember of course that he was doing this with his right hand, which was his left hand so to speak, and minus a couple of fingers as well, so it was all pretty rough. 'Thank Christ,' I thought at the time.) Now he did a tiny scrawl up at the top edge of the paper. 'And this "C", see Sis, this is Cornwall. In most people's minds, it's in the middle of nowhere, but it's where we live, so I've done it nice and important, up here at the top.' He draped a twirl of potato peel down to it from the north, and plonked the match box at the end of the peel. 'Them matches, they're Morlong, and course that's the Morlong road, all twisty as a corkscrew and dirty as hell.'

Now he scribbled a line down from the 'C' towards the middle of the 'Y', then made it turn left (west) at a right angle before it got there. 'This here, Sis, is the Farm Road, leastways that's what we call it, though on the signpost it's the Mulvers Hill Road because that's where it ends up at. Course, the Mulvers Hill folk think it ends up here, just like the Morlong people think the other road does, and of course that's why your pub is called the End of the Road. Which is a stupid bloody name if ever I heard one, cause no road ever ends. Leastways not if you've got legs. Or a good bike even, like the one I gave to Col here. You can still ride down the old Bay track, least a bit of the way, if you know where to find it, and then shanks pony it the rest of the way to Baytown . . .'

His pencil started hovering down from the place where the Farm Road did its right angle.

'Grandad . . .' I said, 'Why don't you go and watch your own little telly, eh? Kathy's running late for the pub, and it's time for *Dr Who*.' (*Dr Who* was his favourite.)

'Why don't you shut up?' Grandad said.

'Yeah, Colum,' Kathy muttered under her breath.

I was scared the old bugger was going to go on till he'd spilled the full bag of beans, so I reached into the fridge for another beer to calm my nerves. This time Mum didn't even notice, she was so intrigued with the little map.

'I'll have one of them, while you're shouting,' Grandad said. 'And another smoke.'

'Where was I?' he went on. 'Oh yeah, here in the centre of the "Y", where the west branch and the east branch of Settlement Creek meet. The way they say it on the telly, you wouldn't know there's two arms, but rightly speaking they should say them groupies or whatever they call themselves is camped at the top of the west branch, at the end of this new little line that Col's dad cut in from the Farm Road . . . Turn that flaming thing off!'

I'd switched the TV on, to try to lure him with Daleks, but Mum gave me a filthy look and jabbed the power switch.

Grandad was holding his pencil like a flagpole now, up from the centre of the 'Y'.

'And this here's the junction, see Sis, that it says here in the Bible. *"1853, Samuel Ferris . . ."* (that's my Grandad, see) *"Samuel Ferris discovers the junction."* All by himself he was, as I said, and just a lad of seventeen, like my Colum here. But bigger, I don't doubt, sturdier like, he must've been, because he set to and cut some of the trees all by himself, and he started building. He did have his bullocks to help him, but that was all. Except for Moggie, his cat.

'Then after a bit, he persuaded some blokes from Morlong to come and join him. Morlong was already there, see, but not Cornwall. There was no Cornwall in them days. No road either. It was my grandad and the Morlong blokes and their bullocks, cleared the track up to Morlong, then ran it on down to this pea here that's Baytown. Course, it was Baytown, not Morlong, that was the main town for the Settlement . . .'

'That's what he called it, see Sis, the little settlement he started at the junction of the creeks. He just called it the Settlement, like it says here when little Sam was born at the Settlement. There wasn't much time in them days to go thinking of fancy names for places.'

Grandad stubbed out his butt and had a long swig from his can. 'So there it is,' he concluded, 'and that's all there is to say about it.'

'But it isn't!' Kathy's voice was kind of desperate. Despite how I was feeling, I was almost a bit sorry for her. I knew how frustrating Grandad's endings always were.

'What happened to it, the Settlement? Where is it now and what about Cornwall, and. how come in 1897' (she was looking at her date list) 'Samuel Ferris was at Cornwall?'

'Different Samuel,' Grandad said. 'The first Sam, see Sis, he died, 1870, in the Act of God. That's when the Settlement died too, you might say. That same night – oh a terrible night it was, a storm they say like near as bad as Noah's time – that same night Samuel Number Two was born, him that grew up to become my old man. It was him of course got married at Cornwall, 1897. And then here's me . . .' He pointed back at the Bible. *"1901 Samuel Ferris born . . ."* just like I told you!'

Mum was floundering still among the Samuels, but I could see Kathy starting to swim her way out.

'This Act of God, when the Settlement died, and Sam One . . .'

'It's got another name too of course, the Act of God,' Grandad said. 'Some things got more than one name, like people. Seems wasteful to me. Plain Samuel Ferris was good enough for all of us, no messing around with second names, till this young feller-me-lad come along. One name wasn't good enough for him, oh no . . . Had to be Samuel *Colum*, this one did, and then his mother made it even worse and called him by the middle, reckoned there was too many Sams what with his dad and me and it got confusing. "Confusing!" I said. "Makes it simple!" Might as well say it's confusing to all be Ferrises. And we've been being Ferrises since the name was thought up, and Samuel Ferris for a long time too, leastways till this Colum here . . .'

'That's enough, Grandad,' Mum snapped. She turned to Kathy. 'You'd think the Ferrises were the kings of the land, the way he tells it. Now "Colum," that was my old Da's name, and a Cafferty name to way back . . .'

'Yes well . . .' Kathy was fidgeting and giving me 'Help! Help!' looks.

I reached into the fridge.

Grandad made a performance of squinting down the opening of his can, then shook it next to his ear and listened to the silence. 'Don't mind if I do,' he nodded at me.

'If only people didn't keep interrupting, I'd know where I was getting to . . .'

'The Act of God,' Kathy prompted. 'What was it's other name?'

'Easy!' Grandad jumped in as if this was a quiz show. 'The Big Slide! Not a slippery slide, like down the rec reserve – though it must've been awful slippery, to tell you the truth – but a landslide, see Sis, an almighty big one, that come whoompf, in the Wet Winter. And that was the end of the Settlement, and old Sam too.'

I gathered up Kathy's cup and plate, to try to end the account there, but there was no stopping her. Mum was knitting now, the collar of my new Fair Isle jumper, as if this was going to go on for what she calls the Duration.

'So the Big Slide buried the Settlement,' Kathy said. 'But how come little Sam Two survived?'

'Not a bit of it!' Grandad disagreed. 'Missed the Settlement by a long shot. Do you think old Sam would've settled a Settlement onto slippy ground? Not a bit of it, Sis. No, it was the track that went, the track down to Baytown. Some of the bottom bit of the Morlong track too, but that was less important. But sheer three mile of the old Bay track, it was there one minute, gone the next. And just as bad, all the creek work the men had done, that was ruined too. See, there was two ways to get the timber out – first, the easy way, they rafted it down the creek when the water was running high enough. Course, it was never real deep or wide, but they'd hauled a lot of rocks out, made it like a kind of little canal so they could shunt the milled logs down, no sweat, and when the timber got to Baytown it went by boat to the city. The track was for getting supplies like, in from Baytown, but also for getting the timber out with bullocks when the creek was too low . . .'

Grandad stared at his can. Then he started to look as if he might drift away from himself again, and Kathy nudged him back.

'So the track went . . .'

'Yeah, wiped out, completely buried, and Sam with it, for he was on the track that night, riding to Baytown for the midwife to come and help little Sammy Two get born. Leastways, he was on it and off it. For when the Big Slide come, the track itself was off the track, so to speak. And Sam with it. Yes, and Sam with it, Sis.'

'That was sad.' The way Grandad tells a tale, he really gets you in, and Kathy was no exception. It was as if old Sam was one of her heroes now, like he was one of mine. (I hated her for it. I still do. Taking over my own ancestors. Still, it's typical.)

'But couldn't they just rebuild the track? Why did the Settlement die?'

Grandad looked at her as if she was a bit thick. 'Like I said Sis, it was called the *Big* Slide. Whole ridge shifted, went in on itself, buckled up the middle, tossed itself around. After it was finished its rock and roll, it was too steep for the bullocks, plus the whole caboodle was so soft and dangerous that no one in their right mind would build a new track on it. Took years, they reckon, for all the land to completely make up its mind where it wanted to be. And by that time, of course, the forest had growed over it all again . . .

I could see Grandad getting into the greenness, and I was glad. Maybe I was safe still. If only he'd lose himself in what he called the Moving Country.

But Kathy interrupted the drifting. *'So . . . .'*

'So . . . to cut a long story short, when at last the Wet Winter ended and the springtime came, they upped stakes, all the blokes and old Sam's missus and little baby Sam (but not Mog the cat – she was the grandaughter of the first Mog, see Sis) and moved themselves to a nice flattish place back towards Morlong about ten mile, and they started all over again, building a new mill. And soon enough, because now there was a woman and a baby and not just a men's camp, these blokes persuaded other women down, and married them, and built houses. And this whole new place, they called it Cornwall, as a kind of memory to Sam, because that was where he was born at, in old England, see Sis?'

Grandad pointed his stub of a right index finger at the couple of words in the Bible after Sam's birth date. And sure enough, now you knew, you could read the second bit of spider-scrawl as Cornwall. (Or more or less.)

I felt proud, somehow, and surprised. Fancy living in Cornwall seventeen years and never knowing it was named for my great-great-grandad. I'd known most of the rest of the story, because Grandad had been telling me it in dribs and drabs ever since he stopped telling me the Prince yarns, but he'd never mentioned that bit before. And he'd never before told it from go to woe, in one piece. Now I understood it all better too.

But Grandad yawned pointedly. 'And this time Sis,' he said, 'that really *is* all there is to say about it.'

I breathed a sigh of relief. He'd told her too much, but at least he'd left me the main thing.

Little Miss Stickybeak finally took the hint. Switched the tape recorder off, and unplugged it. 'Thanks so much, Mr Ferris, that was really great, and thanks for the arvo tea, Mrs Ferris . . .'

'Tea!' Mum flung my new jumper down in the middle of a row. 'I knew there was something I was in the middle of doing! Dad'll be here any minute and I haven't even crumbed the fish!' She went into a flurry. 'And the spuddies sitting here like Lady Muck in cold water! And the peas! I don't know!'

Kathy still hadn't got up, but. Despite how I felt about her, I knew how she felt. (If that makes sense.) It's real hard to come out of one of Grandad's yarns. She was sitting there, sad-looking, twiddling at her fringe. (Did I say she's got red hair? Sort of copper-red, straightish, shortish, just chopped around her face like a helmet.)

'It's sad, isn't it, to think there's nothing left?'

'Nothing left!'

'Oh no,' I thought, 'here we go.' I felt like I'd felt when Scott tried to get the silver knife from me, only worse. And Grandad didn't even give me time to interrupt.

'Why, it's good as gold, girl. Better than gold, matter of fact. Course, the forest has grown back through a lot of it, and over it too, the trees have made like a big green umbrella, but a lot of the building's still there. And the orchard – not the same trees, probably, but ones that've descended down from them. Even a magnolia, couple of camellias, and the roses, and the herbs. Oh, and the daffodils, Sis, you should see it in the springtime. That's what I mean, that it's better than gold.'

Kathy was wide-eyed, her face seeming to glow like Mum's does when she's excited. I suppose it's because they're both Irish, they look a bit the same.

'You get young Col here to take you in some time. Spends half his time in there, Col does. Leastways, he used to, before he got too growed up for himself and stopped believing in the olden days.' He gave me a kind of dirty look, as if it was my bloody job or something to hang about in there by myself, instead of playing sport on weekends and stuff. 'But if you ask him nicely, I'm sure he might stretch a point.'

Mum was muttering into the breadcrumbs: 'Is that what he used to go in the forest for? I always did wonder.' Flurry flurry she slid the fish through the flour and egg. (We had to have fish because it was a Friday in Lent, and Mum was Catholic-er than the Pope on things like that.)

Kathy was looking embarrassed at Grandad's suggestion.

And I was out in the back yard, scratching for comfort at my mate Max. I could've killed Grandad. I could've bashed his brains in. I could've . . . (stop it, stop it.)

And then the old man came through the side gate, his walk rolling, a whiff of rum on him as he pushed past me. The old man holds his beer well, and that's what he normally drinks, but when he gets on the rum, watch out.

I heard the fireworks. 'What, no tea!!! A man comes home from a day of fucking greenies and no . . .' (It was the first time in my life I'd ever heard the old man swear in front of women.) 'And as for you, miss, your Dad's hollering up the residential stairs for you . . .'

Kathy scootted past me, so I went back in. Bad timing. The old man was just opening the fridge.

'Who's drunk my flaming beer!'

There wasn't a can left.

'I think I'll be getting back to my own little telly,' said Grandad. 'Didn't you say it's nearly time for *Dr Who*?'

'I'll run up the pub,' I said, 'and get you some.' I was at the fly-screen door when I remembered I'd spent the last of my week's money on the Chiko Roll. 'Um, Mum . . .'

'Don't bother!' the old man pushed past me again. 'I'll get it myself. And drink it there. And get myself a counter tea while I'm at it.'

Mum's face was set hard, as she whooshed the arvo-tea crumbs off the tablecloth. Kathy's date-list fluttered to the floor, but Mum picked it up.

'You'd better give this to your little girlfriend, when next you see her.'

'How many times do I have to tell you, she's not my girlfriend!'

'You'll patch it up, dear,' Mum murmured, and stuck the list in my school bag, and so it came to the hospital with the stuff that Squirt sent.

'Oh dear,' Mum said as she went back to the stove and plonked the fish (minus the old man's piece) into the frying pan. 'And now my ants are moving.' And she burst into tears.

▷ ▷ ▷ ——————————————

You must be thinking the Blue Women are on strike or something, me writing all this since lunchtime!

'That poor bloke,' I hear you saying, 'lying there, can't get out of bed even to have a leak, his legs maybe in pain though he never mentions it, no one to talk to again now that Nick's sleeping, can't see out the window, doesn't even know what the weather's like, no TV, writing his arm off, and no one even brings him a white plate full of white food on a white tray!'

Or maybe you're not saying that at all. You're maybe down the pub with your mates, saying 'Whose round is it?'

Well, whatever you're saying, I have had my tea. (I won't go into the details this time.) I just didn't want to interrupt writing down Grandad's stories by writing down my boring hospital story.

But, just to keep you up to date, it's now ten past nine on Tuesday night. (I'm like someone on a desert island, aren't I, making scratches on a tree to keep track of the days? Or like someone in a prison movie, no, stop it.)

Nick's been asleep all day, barely opened his eyes when the old woman in black came for night-time visiting. Though I wonder sometimes if he's sleeping, or lying there fighting the fascist. I wonder too now if maybe the fascist isn't a tapeworm, but a cancer. I hope it's not. He'd be a bad bloke, to have die. I mean, he's a good bloke to have next to you. If you were in a fight, I mean, he'd be with you. If you were me, I mean. (I don't know what I mean.)

By the way, I did get the visitor that my tea-cup promised. It wasn't you, or I don't think so. (I guess I'm hoping that you'll be a bit spunkier.)

Her name was Sally Browning, anyway, and she was something that she said is called an Almonder. (When she told me, I said, 'That's OK, I'm a bit of a nutter myself,' but she didn't get it.) She's a type of social worker, I think, because she wanted to know how I felt and all that.

'Not physically, mentally,' she said.

'I told you I was a bit of a nut,' I answered, but it went over even worse the second time.

'Well anyway,' she said, a bit fazed, 'I'm here to cheer you up. The Night Sister said you couldn't sleep,' she said. 'She thought you might be a bit depressed. Or maybe worried over something.'

'Me?' I laughed. 'What've I got to worry about?'

'That's good then.' She looked relieved, and offered me a Mintie. 'Next question. Have you got any money?'

Honestly, I thought she was going to touch me for a loan. 'I've only got ten cents,' I said. It's true. I mean, when everything went crazy and I went up the pole, that's all I happened to have on me. I wasn't planning on a visit to the big city. I'd spent my last money on that Chiko Roll.

Sally looked worried. 'Is that all? But you must have money. For papers and lollies and things.' (A shop trolley comes round at night.) 'My goodness, no wonder you're depressed! I could arrange a withdrawal, if you have your bank book.'

I said I didn't know where my book was, and there was nothing in it anyway.

'If you don't mind me asking, er . . .' (she looked at her folder) '. . . Colin, what do you do for a living?' Much as I hate being called Colum, I hate being called Colin even more. It's a snob's name, I reckon.

'Pick up glasses in the pub, Sunday nights.'

'Goodness, I can't imagine that brings in much. You're not on unemployment benefit? Or any other form of social security?'

I shook my head. Didn't go into my and the old man's views on bludging.

'Well that settles it,' she said brightly, and pulled out a form. 'You're entitled to sickness benefit, you know, now you're here, indeed till you're up and about and on your pins again. That'll take about six weeks to process of course, but in the case of someone destitute like yourself I can apply to the Emergency Assistance Fund to tide you over with thirty dollars a week in the meantime. It's not much, I know, but according to your medical file you'll be in hospital till then, and I don't suppose you'll be running off to discos or pop concerts or whatever it is you young people spend your money on.'

In hospital for six weeks! No one had said that before.

She barely paused to draw breath. 'Have you somewhere nice and quiet to stay when you leave? Somewhere to rest?'

Yeah, I thought, a prison cell.

'I don't know,' I said. I didn't want to go into details.

'Could you go back to wherever you were before the accident, perhaps?'

'No,' I said. (Just see the old man having me. Or me having

him, for that matter. I mean, would *you* live with someone who'd run you down with a bulldozer?)

She looked worried, and checked the file on me again. 'I see you were living at Cornwall. Is that one of the new western suburbs?'

'No,' I said, 'it's in the country. Out Morlong way.'

She looked blank, then worried again. 'But you wouldn't be able to go there anyway. After you've left hopsital, you'll still be an outpatient for about six months, you know. You'll have to come in a few times a week, for physio – you know, dear, exercises to get your muscles going again. And there'll be X-rays, and getting the plaster off first. All sorts of things. You'll have to stay in thc city.'

I felt as if I'd already been judged, and sent to prison. Six weeks in hospital, then six months in the city, trooping back and forth to the hospital, and living where? In a slum with head-lice, no doubt. But how would I find one? I don't know anything, in the city.

I found myself hoping I would go to jail. At lcast it'd be somewhere to go.

Sally must've picked up my mood, because she took hold of my hand for a second. (Her hand was soft like city hands, small and white but not at all like Jade's.) Then she said, 'Don't worry, dear, we'll find you somewhere. There's a couple of church hostels for people in your situation, very clean and not expensive. I'll look into it for you.'

I was so completely down by now that when she asked for all these details for her form, like date of birth and so on, I just gave them to her.

'Any proof of identity?' she murmured. 'Oh well, I guess you wouldn't be in hospital under an alias, so I'll vouch for you.'

Then she got me to sign it. So now I'm a registered bludger.

Just to rub the point in, she pulled ten dollars from her handbag and said. 'Here you are, dear, you won't get your money from the Emergency Fund for a couple of days, so here's something in the meantime.'

When I looked dark she said, 'Well, you can pay me back next week if you feel that way about it. Now cheer *up*!'

And she was off.

I felt so down, after Sally's cheering up, that if I hadn't have had this writing to do, I don't know what I would've done.

(Oh yeah, mate? What would you have done? Haven't even got a window bed to jump from. Besides, I think my jumping days are over. Sometimes, you know, when I sleep, I find myself back in the falling.)

I still feel down, I guess. A church hostel, or gaol, what a choice.

And then what?

I mean, after six months of being an outpatient, or years of being a prisoner, what'll I do then? I won't get a job in Cornwall any more, not after being a greenie. Won't even be able to go back there.

Stop it.

Almost twelve now. I've got the death curtains around me again, and the little light. This Night Sister's all right, really. She says she knows how it is, when you can't sleep, and she thinks it's awful for teenagers not to be able to run off all their energies with exercise. She admires me, for not taking drugs, not even for the pain, and she thinks the hospital should put all the teenagers in the same ward, well, ones of the same sex, so they can play records or whatever at night because she knows teenagers can't sleep in hospital.

So there! I'm allowed to stay up as long as I like.

But a funny thing in me is, if I'm allowed to do something, I want to do the opposite. So having just won that (she was in here a minute ago, and we talked it all out), now I want to go to sleep.

So I'll do that, and you can read this thing that was in the newspaper I bought with Sally's money when the shop trolley came round tonight. (I also got a new packet of writing paper and a Mars Bar.) The newspaper was a morning one, so I got it half-price. I still don't believe I'll get fifty bucks soon for nothing. I don't want it. But I don't believe in it either.

Anyway, sweet dreams! To me, that is. At least, I hope so this time.

▷ ▷ ▷ ————————————

The Argus
Tuesday 26 March

RAIN STOPS PLAY IN THE TREE GAME

by Jerry Denning

After a week of torrential downpours, conservationists yesterday packed up their tents and haversacks and left their camp at Settlement Creek, near the small timber town of Cornwall.

Their leader, Mike Marchant, ordered what he called a strategic withdrawal, because the rain means that logging in the area will not continue this year.

Earlier in the campaign, he had said: 'We will not leave Settlement Creek until the government honours its election pledge and puts a halt to logging in state forests throughout the state, beginning with Settlement Creek.'

Because of this, Settlement Creek is seen as a test case.

Asked if today's move was also a withdrawal from that position, Mike Marchant said: 'By no means, no. It is just that the troops can be better used elsewhere. The logging in the Cornwall area is stopped now, and we have made it stop.

'We haven't backtracked at all. We're going back to the city to fight the battle again, in the Hadley by-election.'

Mr Marchant is standing as the Independent Green candidate, in the by-election for the swinging seat of Hadley, to be held on Saturday, and political punters are tipping that the Green vote might well be vital in the result.

Mr Marchant is urging his supporters to make an informal protest vote, and to not give their preferences to the Labor Party.

This could meant that the Liberal Party will win Hadley.

And without Hadley, the government will hold power by a majority of only one seat.

Reliable sources within the Labor Party's headquarters suggest that many Party organisers are urging the Minister for Conservation, Forests and Tourism, Mr Buckley, to yield to Mr Marchant's demand for an immediate end to logging in state forests, beginning with a promise to end all logging in the Settlement Creek area. They argue that if this demand were met, Mr Marchant would distribute his preferences to the Labor Party, and the Labor Party would be assured of the seat of Hadley.

The Hadley electorate is unusual in having a considerable number of swinging voters who are attracted to issues such as conservation. It is one of those traditional old inner-city working-class areas in which the old corner pub is now an art gallery or a bistro.

In a desperate bid, the government has scheduled the election for Easter Saturday, in the hope that many of these 'trendies' will be on holiday.

The Minister for Conservation, Forests and Tourism, Mr Buckley, however, remains firm against pressures to act fast to save the seat of Hadley, and it is understood that he is taking a low-key approach of not answering questions because it is the Premier himself who is taking the lead on this issue.

'We will not be threatened, we will not be blackmailed,' the Premier replied to Mr Marchant's statement again today. 'We will win Hadley – or lose Hadley – alone.

'We promised an end to logging in state forests, and that will be done. But it may take a few years. Rome wasn't built in a day. The forests didn't grow in a day. And we can't stop the logging in a day.'

Mr Marchant's answer to that is: 'With thirty hectares of virgin forest on the planet being logged every day, we can't afford to wait a few years. We can't even afford to wait a few minutes.'

It is a thorny problem for the Labor Party.

A somewhat dissident source from ALP Head Office who did not wish to be named said: 'The trouble with Mike Marchant is, he isn't a socialist. These middle-class conservationists, they say Save The Trees. That's all very nice. Socialists like trees too. Not that there's many socialists at the top of the Labor Party. But there's still the problem of workers' jobs.'

'In the Settlement Creek area alone, if logging stopped, every worker would lose his job. The Labor Party wouldn't be a Labor Party if it brought in a state of affairs like that.'

The somewhat dissident source added gloomily: 'Not that the Labor Party's a Labor Party anyway.' And wandered across the road in the direction of the Trades Union Hotel.

Meanwhile, back in Cornwall, wet conservationists piled wet tents into wet bags, in order to start the trek back to the city.

At the creek site, there was a desolate feeling.

'I don't want to go,' cried one young girl. 'This forest is a part of me now.' Her long dark hair was sodden with rain, and a deep scratch mark down one cheek bore witness to the dreadful confrontation that occurred only a week ago between the greenies and the local loggers.

She pointed out to me the fallen tree, which a young local greenie activist fell from when his own father, who is a logger, drove a bulldozer into it.

'That shows you how far they'd go,' Mike Marchant explained, 'when they'd be prepared to kill their own kids just so they could kill a few more trees.

'They're the enemy,' he added. 'I'll tell you.'

In the little town of Cornwall, however, it seems there is a different enemy. Every car bears a 'Doze in a Greenie' sticker, and it is a brave man who even admits to coming from the city.

They don't talk much, in Cornwall these days. The drinking in the pub is done quietly, though steadily, and lips are sealed to outsiders.

They don't trust the media.

When asked about recent events, a young boy called Sean who drank with me happily a little more than a week ago said: 'Shut your gob. I'm not going to dob.'

Since the extraordinary and unwarranted attack on World Heritage Commissioner, Dr Brian MacBride, on the night of Sunday, 17 March, the sympathies of the media and the Australian public have swung heavily towards the conservationists.

The subsequent brutal attack upon young local

activist, Colin Ferris, by his own father who bulldozed down a tree in which he was sitting as an act of protest, on the morning of Monday, 18 March, has created even further sympathy for the Settlement Creek cause.

All of this has diminished the Labor Party's chances in this by-election.

In the backblocks of Hadley, I met a voter who said: 'If loggers will try to kill United Nations representatives and their own children, they've got to be stopped.'

She added, 'I've always gone for Labor, but this time it'll be Mike Marchant, and I'll fill in the rest of the ticket however he says.'

But in Cornwall, the rain has set in.

In the backblocks of this little town which you can walk around in five short minutes, a town in which there is no hospital, no library, no centre for the many unemployed youth, not even a public toilet, I met an old man in a rain-sodden dressing-gown, hanging over the gate of a tiny wooden timberworker's cottage. At least he was willing to talk to 'the Press'.

'We haven't had rain like this in March,' he said, 'not since the bad autumn that led up to the wet winter of 1870!'

I asked him what he, as a local, felt about the attacks upon World Heritage Commissioner Dr Brian MacBride, and on the Cornwall boy, Colin Ferris.

'Never heard of them,' he said, and left the gate.

I knew he was an old timberworker, because half the fingers of his right hand were just stubs.

Out at the camp again, they were conscientiously picking up every scrap of placard, every nut shell.

The young girl with the long dark hair, however, was just sitting on the fallen tree, crying. Even after the torrential rains, I could still see the scars where the bulldozer had ploughed through the earth into it.

A bizarre aspect of the attack upon the young local greenie by his own father is the fact that the same youth has apparently been charged with the attack upon the World Heritage Commissioner, Dr Brian MacBride, on the previous night.

'It's all a frame-up,' said Mike Marchant, when I questioned him about this aspect. 'Colin was with us all the way, no risk. He went up that tree, to be a tree-sitter, to stop the dozers.

'He came to our camp, on the Saturday night, and sang songs with us and Brian till dawn. He and Brian, they got on great guns. In fact, I'd say Brian probably liked him even more than he did the rest of us.'

'Colin had no theory, no facts, he didn't know why he wanted to save the trees, he just knew he wanted to, and he also knew more words of the Irish songs that Brian sung than any of the rest of us.

'By the end of the night, he and Brian were in each other's arms.'

'It's ridiculous to say that Colin would've attacked Brian. They loved each other, you know what I mean, as far as two men can without being gay.

'That whole charge against Colin is just typical of how the cops treat conservationists. Frame them, and put them in gaol. And save themselves the trouble of looking for who the real attackers were at the same time.

'I'll tell you who the attackers were. Loggers. Men who kill trees. The sort of men like Colin's father, who was willing to kill his own son to get into the forest.'

Mike Marchant went back to organising his troops to pick up the equipment, so that they can get back to the city and fight the Hadley by-election.

Meanwhile, the rain has stopped play here, until the logging season starts next year.

The loggers are in the pub for the winter, and the bulldozers are nowhere in sight.

A girl sits on a fallen tree, weeping for her wounded boyfriend.

And somewhere in a coma, there lies World Heritage Commissioner, Dr Brian MacBride.

Page 9: Uniting Church joins attack on Easter poll

▷ ▷ ▷ ————————————

2 o'clock Wed morning. Got a couple of hours sleep, and then the night came in. Too scared (yeah, admit it Col) to go back into it just yet, so will write this a while.

Which bit will I do now?

Well, I'd just got up to Friday night tea, the old man leaving, and Mum's ants moving. The next thing that happened that night isn't really important, but I might as well put it in.

▷ ▷ ▷ ————————————

I think I said I'd told the blokes I'd meet them later at Scott's place.

So I walked round there, didn't bother getting the bike out. (Have I said I've got an old Triumph Trophy that used to be Grandad's?)

Tea was over, and Scott was organising Gemma and Kerry into the washing up. Mrs Robinson was at her sewing machine (she does piece work for a little overalls shop at Morlong) and Mark and Ray the bludgers were watching TV. Mr Robinson of course was down the pub. He's a big boozer, even for Cornwall, and that's why Mrs Robbo has to sew and Scott has to keep the other kids in line.

'Come out to the Jet,' Scott said to me. 'Now you kids quit mucking around and get them dishes done. And you two bludgers let them watch what they want when they've done. No fighting! See you later, Mum.'

Mrs Robbo looked anxious. 'You will be home, son, before the pub shuts?'

'Yeah Mum,' Scott sort of sighed, and we went out through the hole in the fly-screen. Scott's old man, when he gets real pissed Friday nights, tends to bash Scott's old lady sometimes when he gets home. So Mrs Robbo likes Scott there, to get between them.

Terry and Danny and Sean were already out in the Jet, having a couple of bongs. Scott and I had a couple, to catch up. A little while back, Scott has found a bit of stuff growing – he wouldn't tell us where – so we had enough to keep us going through the winter.

Anyway, we did that for a while, played a tape or two, then headed.

There was a big chain across the entrance to the new logging track, with a padlock, so we parked the Jet there, next to a few greenie vans. Then I led the way down the track. Not that there was much call for leading, that night, because there was a bit of moon and the fog was only hanging in little snatches. But I think the other blokes felt more comfortable with me in front. I knew the forest, and it can get you kind of spooked if you don't know it, even in daytime. (When I was little, Grandad used to warn me never to get off the track in the forest of a night.)

Anyway, somehow I got myself quite a way out in front. I think being in among the trees, and being a bit out of it, I just wanted to be by myself. It was real good, the dark green of my land mixing with the green of the smoke in my head. I knew the blokes wouldn't get lost, that night, and they'd just catch up to me at the end of the track.

But when I got to the end, and was about to cross the creek, a great light suddenly flashed in my face. It was coming from the camp.

Here's where the stuff about the rabbit on the first day comes into the story again. Because I was mesmerised, or hypnotised or whatever you call it, just like rabbits are when you go out spotlighting.

I didn't know what the Christ was happening. I didn't know which way to jump. I felt trapped there, and I panicked for a moment. I guess the dope didn't help.

Then this voice came: *'Who's there?'*

I was so kind of confused, I didn't think, and I yelled out, 'Col Ferris.'

Then the light moved around me a bit, and a couple more torches came on, and I saw there were three coppers sitting in the greenies' camp. One of them waded across the creek to me now.

'Sergeant Something-or-other,' he introduced himself. 'Col Terrace, was it?'

'Ferris,' I said weakly. I was still so taken aback by surprise. With the greenies all in the lock-up and Golden Gloves going slow on the bail, we were sure no one would be at the greenies' camp. It was a perfect chance to nick the tents and sleeping bags and stuff, so that they wouldn't be able to go on camping there. We'd planned on being the heroes of the town, I guess, planned on running the greenies back to the city so the logging could start on Monday. But there were these coppers there, protecting the greenies' gear. I watched Sergeant Something-or-other scribble my name down in a notebook.

'I was just going for a walk,' I added quickly, thinking 'Act normal and he won't see you're a bit out of it'. Scott had given me a bit of weed, and it was in my pocket. I wanted to get out of there quick-smart, before any bright ideas about body searches. 'Nice night,' I added.

'Yeah well Col Ferris,' said the sergeant, 'you can just walk back through the nice night to where you come from. The inspector doesn't want the situation inflamed by local yahoos setting fire to the greenies' camp, or whatever it was you had in mind. Not that I don't think it wouldn't be what they deserve, myself. But orders are orders.'

'Yeah, sure,' I flustered, and headed back.

I found the others halfway back down the track, sitting under a tree, having a smoke. 'You're back fast,' they said. 'We were just coming along to join you.'

So I told them what the scene was, and we had a smoke and got real mad at the cops and mad at the greenies and disappointed about our brilliant plan not working.

We were there quite a while, and then Scott suddenly looked at his watch and said: 'Shit! The old man'll be home.'

When we got back to the Jet, we let down the tyres on the greenies' vans and stuck some 'Doze in a Greenie' stickers all over them, but we were too kind of pissed off to do much. Plus Scott was saying, 'Come on will you, you guys!'

Scott dropped me off at my place and I went in the back and went to sleep, and never gave a second thought to the cops having my name.

But afterwards, when I got arrested for attacking Brian, that same Sergeant Something-or-other said how I'd been looking for trouble out at the greenie's camp on an earlier occasion.

The Lawyer told me that. And he reckons it'll go against me.

▷ ▷ ▷ ———————————————

4.15 Wed morning. Was about to turn my light off but Nick just poked his head through my death curtains.

'I like you,' he said.

It fazed me a bit, then I realised he meant he's like me.

'I no sleep too,' he said. 'You mind if I come here, we talk, eh mate?'

'Sure,' I said. He's just popped back for something, I've got a bit of an idea what, so I'll stop now.

▷ ▷ ▷ ———————————————

Wed morning after breakfast. Nick stayed till dawn. I turned the light off, and we sat in the dark whispering and having the odd shot of aeroplane fuel. He says it fights the fascist.

I found out what the fascist is too, and it really is a fascist, or a bit of one.

I'll try to explain what Nick told me, though I don't really understand it all, and maybe I dozed off a bit from time to time too, so it's become sort of like a story of my own, that I've dreamed.

In the war, see, Greece was on our side. Mussolini invaded from the north, and Nick helped fight the Italians. Nick had been a farmer before that, on a little scrap of land he worked with his four brothers. It'd been Nick's family's land for generations and generations. (I found that hard to imagine, I mean a family owning land for so long. We owned nothing, except the mortgage on the house we lived in. Maybe that's why I'd been a sucker for Grandad's tale about me owning the palace.)

Anyway, Nick fought, and the Italians were pushed back, and then the Germans came and bombed some places and won. They set up a headquarters in Athens (that's the capital) and they occupied the country. The Greek army had had to give in, but lots of people went underground, and fought in the Resistance. They made raids on Nazi camps and blew up roads and things. Nick was one of them.

When he wasn't fighting, he reckoned, he did a lot of thinking. He thought: 'What are we fighting for? We are fighting for our country, and that's right, but we're also fighting to get our old way of life back. And what was so good about that? The rich were rich and the poor were poor, and the rich people ran the government and the poor people never had a chance.' (I'm putting it into my words, a bit.)

He started thinking that when the war ended, there should be a complete change, and the poor people should get a go. After all, the poor people were the ones who did all the work, and the rich were bludging off them.

In Nick's little fighting group, there were some other blokes who thought the same way, and one of them was a schoolteacher and he had some books by a bloke called Karl Marx.

'You know him?' Nick asked.

I said I'd heard of him.

'Very good man,' Nick said. 'You read him one day, you clever boy, you understand him. Me, I no read, I never have school, but this teacher, he read us Marx every night nearly when we hide in the mountains, and I see this Marx is right.'

Nick explained that Marx was the bloke that started Communism, and anyway, pretty soon Nick and his mates joined something with a name like 'Alas', which was a sort of resistance fighters' branch of the Koo-koo-eh party.

Lots of really horrible things happened in the war. For example, one night this teacher bloke was caught, and the Nazis threatened to shoot him if he didn't tell where the rest of the group was hiding.

But he didn't dob, and he was shot.

The trouble was, because the Nazis knew where he'd taught, they now knew what village the group came from, and so they lined up twenty women from the village, and said they'd shoot them if they didn't say where the hiding place was. One of the women was Nick's mother, and one was his sister.

But the women wouldn't dob either, and they were all killed too.

(I thought of course of me and my mates, and if I'd be willing to be shot to save them. No way.)

Finally, the Allies won the war, and the Pommies came into Greece to clear the Nazis out.

'Now,' thought Nick and his mates, 'now we'll be able to work towards making a new free Greek society, where everyone has a fair go.'

But the Poms put the same old corrupt rich blokes into power that had run things before the war.

And so these blokes who'd been in the Resistance kept fighting, but against the Greek government now. There was a civil war, that went on for about four years. In Nick's area, which was the central and northern bit of the mainland, the Communists had most of the people on their side and they won most of the fighting.

'But you were fighting against you own side,' I said. I was a bit confused. There were two Greek armies in this new war, Nick's army and the other army that supported the Poms and the rich government.

'No,' said Nick, 'I fight always against the fascist.'

'But the Nazis were the fascists,' I said, 'and they'd been kicked out.'

'Yes,' said Nick, 'but every country, every peoples, they all have fascists. Fascists are the few peoples who want to make all the rest of the peoples have nothing. They are the bosses, and the king, peoples like them.'

Anyway, after a lot of fighting, when Nick's side was still winning in lots of places, the Pommies said if everyone gave up their guns there'd be free elections and the people could decide whether they wanted Communists or the old government in power.

'OK,' said Nick's side, and most of them handed in their guns. But the other side kept their guns, and the elections weren't held.

'It is trick, see,' Nick explained.

So Nick's side was beaten, but the fascists were scared they might try to start fighting again, so they just went around shooting Nick's side. One night the soldiers came and rounded up all the blokes in Nick's area, and they put them in the town square and fired off a couple of rounds at them with a machine gun.

Nick was hit, but he didn't die. After the soldiers left, one of the old women took him and dug the bullet out and bandaged him up and looked after him till he was better.

Things sort of quietened down in Greece, because the Communists were too broken to fight, and Nick finally married the old woman's daughter (that's the old black lady that comes to visit him) and had all his kids and finally the kids came to Australia and so Nick did too.

'But I still have, how you say? Souvenir,' he wound up. (The ward was getting light by then, and I could just make out Nick's face.) 'I have it here with me now, I have it always.'

'Oh yeah?' I said, interested. I thought he was going to show me a Nazi helmet or something. But he pointed to his gut.

'Here,' he said, 'Inside me still is this enemy, this fascist. When the old lady, she pull out the bullet, some of him hides inside me. All the time, many years, sometimes he hurt me, this fascist, but never no money to get him cut out. Now last year, this year, I get old and the fascist, he thinks, "Nick weak now, no good fighter, now I fight old Nick hard, and I beat him." So old Nick, he thinks, "I get him cut, once for good." I tell the doctor. "Easy," the doctor say. So here I am. I beat him, this time, once for good. Happy ending, eh?'

'Ya sou,' I said. That's a thing I've learnt to say when we have a drink together.

The light was good on his face now, and I saw it, brown and lined and alive in this place of all the whiteness, and his hand too as he lifted his glass to me.

'Ya sou, paithi mou,' he said. 'Ya sou.'

And I was real happy, knowing it wasn't a cancer and it's just something simple like a bit of metal, because I suddenly remembered what it was his hands reminded me of. It's Grandad's hands. If he just had all his fingers, and if he hadn't had his stroke, his hands would be exactly the same as Nick's.

Then the Day Sister came and took the death curtains away, and roused at both of us for being awake already (!), and sent Nick away so that Baby Nurse could give me a shave and a wash. (I hate that, when the nurses wash me.)

So it's 9 a.m. now and I'll get on with my tale.

I'll start at Saturday morning, after breakfast and my Saturday chores.

▷ ▷ ▷ ————————————

I rode down the Greasy Spoon. That's only a couple of blocks, but I felt like taking the old bike out for a burl. Plus I think I had something in my head about wanting to go to check on the palace, just to kind of make sure no one had been there. You see, no one had ever been there, except Grandad and me. Well, as far as I knew. But I was pretty sure.

Maybe you think that's impossible, so I'll try to explain. See, as Grandad had said, the trees had grown up right around where old Sam had cleared, but as well as that there were the blackberries. There was a great ring of them, maybe thirty metres thick, right round the edge of the Settlement clearing, and they grew out across the creeks, tangling onto each other from side to side, so there wasn't any way in to the Settlement. Well, there was one way of course, but that was our secret.

I should say too that Cornwall people simply didn't go into the forest, just to explore, and the loggers only went into the coups. There was still a bit of a way to go before the logging would get to the Settlement – the Big Slide had made that the hardest bit of the forest for the dozers to get into.

So till now my place had been safe from intruders.

With the greenies around however, and the cops, I had this fear that someone from out of town might somehow have got into it. But mainly, I think, Grandad saying what he'd said to Kathy Dolan the night before had made me feel as if I'd lost a bit of it, and I wanted to go just to kind of say 'G'day' to it.

And I guess too I was deep-down thinking that maybe Grandad had been right, when he'd complained that I didn't spend nearly as much time in there as I used to. But I couldn't, now I was in with Scott and them. I mean, Grandad reckoned I had a duty to the palace, to look after it, but the way I saw it, I had a duty to the town too, to play cricket and footie and that. But Grandad didn't like Scott. And sometimes, since I'd been in the gang, I'd thought maybe he didn't go much on me either. He'd stopped yarning to me, since his stroke.

Anyway, I went down the Spoon but I could see from outside: no Jet. (I'd been thinking of playing a bit of pool before going out to the palace.) So I turned into Scott's street, the one the cop shop's in too, and I saw Kathy Dolan and a bloke heading towards me.

'Hey Col!' She yelled and waved at me, and I was so taken aback I nearly stopped, then I went to go on and the bike cut out on me. I was right next to them by that time.

'Hi!' she said. 'Col, this is Garry, Garry this is Col.'

Garry would be the same height as me, but he looked taller because I was still on my bike. He had dark hair, curly, and he seemed young for some government bloke.

(In case you've forgotten, Garry was the bloke Kathy had been talking about in class, the bloke who was looking for some other industry for Cornwall).

How else do I describe him? Jeans. Gumboots, and not city gumboots, a good pair of Perths. A brown leather jacket, real old and worn, that fitted on him like a skin.

The main thing that got me was, his head was perfect. The bones and that. I don't normally look at faces – hands are my thing to judge people – but his head was so good I never looked at his hands. One time when Squirt had been telling us about this Greek Socrates guy – he was always telling us bits of Greek legends and that – he'd shown us photos of statues, and there was one of this charioteer back in the olden days who looked just like this Garry.

Anyway, head or not, I didn't want to know about him. Kathy was saying something about why didn't we go and have a cup of coffee, and Garry said: 'Yeah, let's have a cappuchino?'

I mean, a cappuchino, in Cornwall! I'd only had two or three of them in my life, up at the Paradise Tea Rooms at Morlong.

Besides, why was Kathy Dolan who'd barely spoken to me for ages suddenly coming on all Hi! and cups of coffee?

'You get nothing for nothing,' my old man always says. 'It's a dog eat dog world.'

I kick-started the bike and luckily it went, so I left in a world of dust before I even had to say anything.

(The trouble with writing is, what happened took ten seconds and it's taken me more than a page to write it down. I guess the real writer people, whose faces Squirt has all over our wall, know what to put in and what to leave out. I'm just trying to get in everything, and I'll leave it up to you to work out what's important.)

Then the bike stalled again. Right opposite from the cop shop. That wouldn't normally matter, me having no licence and no helmet and a bike that isn't registered, but this city cop came up and said 'Hum ho,' and all that.

'What's your name?' he reckoned, and I gave it, and he wrote down 'Colin Ferris' in a book.

'Occupation?' he said.

'None,' I said.

'Troublemaker,' he said, and awarded me the special Defect Notice prize.

'Now you get those lights fixed . . . and the tyres . . . and you get a licence and a helmet before you ride again, sonny-jim,' he reckoned.

'Yeah, well I'll just go home,' I reckoned, and I added, 'Fuck you,' as the cop moved off. (When he was out of hearing.)

And then I saw the girl from the Thursday afternoon, standing there, the scratch still on her face, her eyes that *green* green.

'Pigs!' she said.

'Yeah!' I said.

'Fucking hassling fucking pigs,' she said.

I think I've said the first time I ever heard my old man swear in front of a woman was the night before. And women in

Cornwall don't swear, unless they're like Jan Henderson. In Cornwall, if a girl says it, she does it. It's simple as that.

'Do you want to come for a ride?' I said.

She looked back a bit nervously towards the cop shop. There was a Volvo parked out the front. 'Well, Sharnda will be coming out in a minute. And Jim. He's our lawyer. They've kept the women till last, the bastards, all the rest are out. I'm meant to be getting back to camp . . . '

To tell you the truth, I wasn't paying too much attention. There was a helicopter, real close to us in the sky, as if it was coming in to land, and I thought, 'Well, I'll just go down the rec reserve, and look at a helicopter.' I'd had these funny kind of sentimental thoughts about this girl, after fighting her and that, and what she'd called 'the blooding', and I'd seen her in the long white dress. Then after she'd said 'Fuck', the thought of that too had kind of flashed through my head. But now I was realistic again, and I knew she was too posh for me, and so I'd go and see a helicopter for the first time in my life.

Now she was talking to a guy in a suit, and a fat older girl in jeans.

'Can you give me a lift to the forest?' she asked.

'No worries,' I said, but she just rattled on over me like she knew of course I'd do what she asked. 'There's still five more women for Jim to bail out, so it'll be a lot of hanging around, and there'll be more space in the car if I go back with you. This is Jim, by the way, and Sharnda.'

I picked Jim as the lawyer at once. It was obviously his Volvo. Fucking rich fucking greenies, coming here to steal our jobs.

'Hop on,' I said.

Of course she didn't have a helmet either, but what I liked about her was she wasn't the kind to worry about things like that.

▷ ▷ ▷ ——————————

Speak of the devil, as my mum says.

Speak of the cops hassling you, and here they come.

A minute ago I had a detective inspector here beside my bed. (We don't have morning visiting, but cops and lawyers don't seem to obey rules.)

'I've come to see you about the blah blah and blah blah,' he said. (I never can get the hang of what I'm charged with. One word is assault and another is malicious. But as the Lawyer explained, it could get kind of upgraded into manslaughter if Brian doesn't make it.)

'And now,' he went on, 'I want you to tell me about this.'

He opened a plastic bag, and pulled out my new jumper, the Fair Isle (you know, the fancy one) that Mum was doing the collar of the night Kathy Dolan was round. It was pretty dirty, but it was easy to recognise.

'Yeah, that's mine,' I said.

'When were you last wearing it?' he said.

I tried to think back.

Saturday night, sitting in the forest, having a sing. No. Because I was cold that night, walking back. Besides, Mum was up finishing it when I got home. Sunday morning, she put it in my sports bag to wear when I changed after the game. I had it on in the pub. Then I was hot, and I tied it round my middle. Where was it when I was in the forest? Round my middle still? But later, when I went up the pole, I didn't have it, because I was cold.

'Actually, now I look at it properly, it's like mine, but it's not. Mine, I mean.'

The detective gave me a look, as if to say 'Bullshit!'

'As a matter of fact, sonny-jim, your ownership of it isn't in question. This jumper was at the scene of the crime, half trampled into the mud, when the victim was found. It was identified by Constable Wilkinson, who'd had a discussion about it with you in the pub the previous night. It was subsequently further identified by your mother – who, I might add, thought it was your body that had been found.'

I thought of Mum, crying and thinking it was me bashed up. If only it had've been.

'How else do you think we knew to arrest you?'

(I hadn't thought, actually.) I was looking through the cop, cutting off completely. Stop it stop it stop it.

The cop said something next about how the fact that I'd gone to the greenies' camp on the Friday night was proof of intent, or something, and that that connected in with the malicious stuff. 'But I brought this along,' he went on, 'to show you the weight of the evidence we have against you, in the hope that it would prompt you to give us the names of your companions in crime, so to speak.'

I shook my head. I could see two Blue Men at Nick's bed,

helping him onto a high trolley. He'd told me he had to have tests today. Suddenly I felt so lonely at the thought of being without him, I felt I couldn't stand up to this cop. What with the jumper, I was done like a dinner.

'It will help you in court, son,' the detective said, trying to sound like an uncle or something, 'if you tell us the names of your mates. We'll find them anyway – in fact we know who they were.' He looked down at his notes. 'It was those four lads you always hung about with, wasn't it?'

I looked to Nick, but they were wheeling him off.

'Trouble is, at the moment we haven't got any hard evidence against them. But if you were to give us their names, I'm sure we'd be able to arrange for your charge to be dropped to just "Accessory". After all, you're younger than them, aren't you?'

He'd got me that bamboozled, I was about to say 'Yes.' And then he'd say 'Young than who?' And I'd say . . . It was like a tunnel, closing in around me, and I didn't have the strength to fight my way out.

But then Nick looked back at me from the end of the ward, and his eyes were saying 'Ya sou, comrade!' and he raised his left arm up a bit out of the sheets and made a clenched fist, and then he was out the door. But I was thinking of the school-teacher, and of Nick's sister and mother, and how they died rather than dob. And I thought too of the fascist in Nick's gut, and how he could lie all day and fight it and never say a word.

I clenched my fist beneath the bedclothes, to kind of give me strength. Then I shut my eyes and turned my face away and pretended to go to sleep. I felt the copper shaking me, heard him talking, but I'd so shut him out that I think I really did go to sleep for maybe ten minutes or so, because when I opened my eyes again, he was gone.

Thanks Nick.

Thanks Nick, thanks Nick, thanks Nick.

It's kind of lonely here without you.

But here comes Baby Nurse, carrying a parcel. Mum must've made the fruit cake after all.

▷ ▷ ▷ ———————————

An amazing thing's happened!

I've just got a present from Kathy Dolan. I read her name on the 'From' bit on the postbag, then read my name on the 'To' bit. I just couldn't see how they went together.

I opened it, like it might be a bomb. This is what came out:

A Sony Walkman.

Five cassettes.

A poem.

A letter.

And a big bunch of herbs.

I'll show you the letter first.

End of the Road Hotel,
Cornwall
Sun, 24 March

Dear Colum,

Hi! How are you? (That's probably a stupid question, but still.) Your mum said you can't sleep at night, so I thought if I lent you my Sony Walkman that'd be something to do. Sorry about the tapes. I only got the Walkman a little while ago, so I've hardly got any yet. I made you up one tape from the jukebox – I know they're hardly the latest (!), but thought it might make you feel like home. And another's Irish, I know you like that. Another one's Vivaldi. You probably won't like him, he's classical, but it's how I feel in the forest. Another one's Midnight Oil, so you might like that. And the last one's something Squirt lent me. It's Lawrence Olivier reading John Donne on one side, and T.S. Eliot on the other side. Sorry not to have anything good to lend you, but I thought maybe there might be other people around the hospital that you could borrow tapes from.

Hope you get well soon. Sean says to say hi.

Best wishes,

Kathy Dolan

P.S. There's no hurry about sending the Walkman back, it can wait till you get home. (Your mum says that won't be till September . . . it seems a long time.)

P.P.S. I'm sorry. I wanted to say that, that night in the pub, but somehow I couldn't with all the people.

So that's what the tapes were. I must say, I was a bit rapt to have a way to get through the night. I turned on the Walkman, and just bunged a tape into it. A real posh man's voice, said: *'I gotta use words when I talk to you.'*

That kind of reminded me of this writing, so I turned it over.

'Oh my black soul!' said the voice. *'Now thou art summoned by sickness, Death's herald, and champion.'*

I don't know what it means, but it gives me the shivers. And of course I don't dare play the Irish tape.

'She sure knows how to rub it in,' I thought. And saying sorry: it's too late for that. You can't *un*do something, just by wishing you hadn't done it. (Don't I know it.)

Then I read the poem she sent me, and I hated her all the more. It was a photocopy, done on the school machine, and she'd scribbled on it: 'Squirt made us read this the other day, and it reminded me of Grandad and you. Hope you don't mind. Kathy.'

Hope I don't mind.

Well. Take my grandad, take my place, then give me a piece of paper. But still, you can't take it out on the poem. I don't pretend to understand it, any more than I understood all of what Nick told me last night, but the same as with Nick's story, I can dream away through this, and just get words and pictures. And somehow, despite Kathy Dolan sending it, I do kind of like it.

See, it's called 'The Princes' Land', by a bloke called Les A. Murray, and the first bit reminds me of being at the palace:

Leaves from the ancient forest gleam
in the meadow brook, and dip, and pass.

Then it goes on a bit, about an idle prince with something called a cembalo, singing to a golden afternoon.

A little further on, there's this bit:

The page we've reached is grey with pain.
Some will not hear, some run away,
some go to write books of their own,
some few, as the tale grows cruel, sing Hey

but we who have no other book
spell out the gloomy, blazing text,
page by slow page, wild year by year,
our hope refined to what comes next . . .

That's I suppose how I feel about this writing, this tale, but Les A. Murray says it like I can't. I mean, if I was making up a story, I'd do it different, and have heaps of happy things. But I'm just telling this gloomy blazing text, right, and it has to go page by slow grey page, and if you, Lone Reader, want to get the shits and write your own book, well you can do that, and sing 'Hey' too for all I care.

Anyway, the other thing Kathy Dolan sent me was this bunch of herbs. A bunch as big as the biggest postal bag of rosemary and lavender and thyme and pineapple sage and balm of gilead and comfrey and lemon balm and everything, so that my bed is surrounded by these smells. I know where she got them from. The first Sam planted a herb garden, and it's all self-seeded and gone wild now.

'So she had to go and steal them too,' I thought. (So much for her 'sorry'.)

Then from the middle of them, I pulled out this real nice piece of dried weed. I had a sniff, and I knew it was Scottie's stuff.

I knew too that it was Scott's way of saying: 'Everything's OK, mate. We know you won't dob. We know you're not a greenie. And everything's cool.'

I put it together with Kathy saying Sean said 'Hi', and with the fact that I knew Kathy hated Scottie, and I saw this was how Scott got a message to me, through Sean then through Kathy. I knew Scott was too smart to get in touch with me himself, in case the cops linked him and me together. Plus it was a bit uncool to send a smoke through the post, so why not get Little Miss Prissy Boots to do it?

I saw her too, shit-scared of being busted, and I suppose it was smart, the way she hid it in the herbs. But I've never said Kathy Dolan isn't smart. That's one of the things wrong with her.

It was smart to gatecrash my secret, too. But wrong.

And OK, so she's sent me the Walkman to try to make up for it, but the tapes are deadshit, and I'm not going to crawl up Kathy Dolan's arse for a poem.

The smell of the herbs makes me so homesick, and hate her more. If it wasn't for Kathy, I could run to the palace after hospital and gaol and everything, and hide.

But with Kathy knowing, it isn't my place any more.

Oh well. Back to the gloomy blazing text. The herbs make that Saturday come back even more.

▷ ▷ ▷ ————————————

So this girl hopped on the back of my bike, and we rode south, down the Mulvers Hill road (or the Farm Road, as we call it, because on the west side of it there's paddocks. On the other side there's pines, that were planted when the hardwood was logged out. It's good in there too, but different. Sort of English or German or something, and you can't feel it's part of you. Even the greenies don't seem to mind about the pines being logged.)

As Grandad explained to Kathy, the road does a sudden right angle and turns west. Then the farm land's on the north side, and the forest forms a dense cover up and down the ridges to the south. To get to the new track to the fresh logging coup, you go a couple of kays past the right angle; but pretty soon after the bend I threw the bike down into second, chucked a sudden hard left, and roared up a bank into the forest.

The girl was screaming in my ear, and yanking at my waist as she held on like grim death, as if she could somehow push me and the bike into turning back. But I crouched forward over the handlebars and urged the old Triumph along the track that used to be wide enough for a bullock dray, but is about the size of a sheep track these days.

Up we charged, up the ridge, ducking our heads below the tree-ferns, swerving to miss the fallen branches, feeling the sting as leaves and creepers whipped our faces. Then down we plunged from the crest, the bike slithering on the wet carpet of rotty leaves, the girl screaming still like a shrill silly whistle trying to drown the organ thunder of the machine.

At last we reached the place where you have to stop because the track suddenly does a five-metre vertical drop down a rockface that ends in the creek – that's one of the remnants of the Big Slide.

The girl was off before I could turn the ignition off. I let the engine die, and hopped off myself. It was almost scarey, the sudden silence, and us two standing in the forest darkness, staring at each other's faces.

She was almost white with anger, or maybe fear, and that seemed to bring out the scratch on her cheek. I could just feel her thinking: 'He's going to say *"Fork it or walk it"*', and it felt good for a moment, having that power over her. I thought of my old man, and how he'd be if the logging was stopped, and it seemed like paying her back a bit for all the trouble.

And then her eyes got to me again, they really are this greeny-green, and when she nearly cries they look so good.

'What's your name?' I said.

'Jade.' She tossed her hair back.

My mum's got a pair of earrings that she calls her 'Jades', and they're exactly the colour of this girl's eyes. The name seemed so right, and especially with her being a greenie on top of it, that I burst out laughing.

'What's so funny?'

'Nothing.'

Then she started laughing too. 'For a minute, I almost thought you were going to rape me,' she said.

I laughed all the more. I don't know why it seemed funny, it just did.

'What's your name?'

'Col. Colum.' That was funny too, the other kind of funny, me giving her my full name. I got off my bike. 'Come for a walk,' I said.

I dived off to the left of the rockface, down a steep bank, and let myself ski on the wet humus right to the bottom. She slipped and slid on her thin-soled city gumboots, and ended up coming down on her bum. We started laughing again, or maybe we were still laughing, and it seemed normal to haul her up, and then to keep on holding her hand as we crossed the creek, and then to still keep on holding it as I led her.

Led her . . . where?

I wasn't really admitting where I was going, but deep-down I knew.

Grandad used to say: 'It's a long road, to the palace, and a hard one.' Of course, it was that, when I was seven, but I think he wasn't talking about the actual way you had to walk, but more about something inside you.

And even the actual way was hard, for Jade.

I won't decribe how to get there because I don't want anyone going there (even you, even though Kathy now knows where it is and those others.) But it's up and down over country that all looks the same to someone who doesn't know it. I've told you about the Big Slide, but I don't think I've said that Grandad sometimes used to call the whole area we lived in the 'Moving Country'. It all moved about so much, see, it was all still so alive and fresh and wet, it was like it hadn't decided yet quite where and how it wanted to be. The farmers' fences shifted and toppled because the land under them slid around, and all the houses in Cornwall had wonky foundations. And when you were in the forest, you could feel the ridges twisting and changing direction, so you'd start out on one and think you were following it, then you'd get onto another one, and be lost.

That was why no one ever went in there, unless they had a reason. And that was why my palace was safe.

I could see that Jade was totally bushed, and getting scared again.

'You sure you know where we're going?' she started panting.

I didn't answer. Because by then we'd got to the special secret bit of the palace road, and I wanted her well and truly muddled. Just to make sure, I made her shut her eyes and turn in a circle three times, then I kept my hands over her eyes and pushed her through the little opening into the middle of a great hollowed-out, mountain ash stump.

I took my hands away, and let her feel the tree. It's like a kid's cubby in there – not that it's small, but it's kind of cosy, with the darkness lit by the patches of sky you see way beyond the clematis ceiling. She thought that was what I wanted to show her, and started to gush: 'It's lovely! Just like one of the ents in Tolkien!' (Whatever that means.)

But I pulled back the big bit of bark I keep against the other entrance, and made her get down on her hands and knees and start crawling behind me.

There's a tunnel, see, through the ring of blackberry and prickly coprosma, and it goes about thirty or forty metres. That was Grandad's way in – it's the only way in – and I sometimes cleared it through again with Mum's secateurs, but Grandad and I kept it so that if you didn't know about the stump, you wouldn't ever find the tunnel.

It was why I'd still felt a bit safe, even after Grandad told Kathy Dolan about the Settlement. I was pretty sure that no one could get in there, without me to show them. And of course there was no way I'd take Kathy in.

... Writing this now, I've got the Walkman on, and I'm listening to this tape by this Vivaldi guy, and in a funny way it is like she said, like the forest. Or maybe it's just the herbs doing it to me, making me feel just like I did that day after I crawled in.

After the dark of the tree and tunnel, you come suddenly out into light, and stand up, and then there's a funny moment when the blood rushes to your head, and your eyes see in bright flashes while they get used to the new day, and then the herbs spin around you, almost crushing you with all the different smells that are sweet and spicy on top of the normal lovely forest smell of wet earth and mulchy leaf. Then you hear the creek rushing and jostling as the two arms meet, and the birds of course, and the wind way above you in the canopy.

I'm not saying this well, but I know Jade felt it too as she came in.

Then after a few seconds, the standing and seeing and smelling and hearing all become separate again, and you get the next surprise.

'It's lovely,' Jade said, 'but what is it?'

She started running through the old orchard, feeling the moss and lichen on the trees, gazing up into the autumn heaviness of apples and pears and quinces, and as she ran she trampled the camomile and brushed against the peppermint geranium and the applemint, and she seemed to make a stream of scents flow behind her, as I followed.

Now she was at the door of the palace, and I really liked her for stopping under the roof of the old verandah, and saying, almost whispering: 'Is it all right to go in?'

I turned the handle on the big door, and as I watched her step in I had this really funny thought about the first Sam, and wondered how he'd felt when he took his Lady in for the first time.

Did he feel kind of proud, like I did? Proud of her and proud of himself and proud of the place?

Jade ran around in little circles, gasping and saying: 'Oh Col! Oh Col!'

Maybe I'd better describe it better, so you know all of what she saw.

Well, as you come out of the tunnel you're nearly at the place where the two arms of the creek meet. There's a little stone ford there, that Grandad and I built, and you cross that. In front of you there's the orchard, and the buildings up behind the fruit trees. The palace itself looks down to the creek junction, but all the buildings are higher than the creek of course, so they couldn't be flooded.

The palace has a verandah running across the long front and down the two sides. There's the huge front door, and then two more shuttered doors at the front and a couple more down the sides.

When you come in the front door, you're suddenly in this big room, as big as four normal-sized rooms stuck together and opened up. The floor is made of river stones, big smooth flat ones, cemented in with a clay mortar. The walls are packed mud, a creamy buttery colour. The ceiling is wooden slats of hand-split timber, kind of dark golden. And up above that, though of course you don't see it from the inside, there's a roof of wooden shingles.

Opposite the main door there's a fireplace, like a cave, where you could roast a whole sheep, no worries. But this fire-cave kind of humps in leftwards, and to the right of it there's another cave, for the cook to sit in, I suppose, and his helpers. It's so big, two people could easily sleep in it. (Grandad and I often have.)

And in the space of the room there's a huge round table, that's the smoothed-off butt of a great mountain ash. To give you an idea of its size, around it there are forty seats that are ordinary stumps, and between each seat there's plenty of elbow-room. (In case you're wondering how Sam got the table through the door, the answer's easy: he built around the table.)

You can see why I knew it was a palace, when Grandad first took me there. It made me think of this funny old film I'd seen on TV, called *Camelot,* that's about King Arthur and his knights, and I used to imagine Sam sitting in the middle of his round table, surrounded by the blokes who went to stay there and have parties while he waited for his Lady.

I don't think I've made it sound anything like as good as it is, but still, Jade was rapt. She kept sitting at different places at the table, like Goldilocks, then she sat inside the fireplace, and was a cavewoman, with her long black hair falling down so I couldn't see her face.

That made me think of something, I don't know what, but have you ever had your insides kind of shift and you've thought, *'This has happened before'?*

Like everything, in an instant as you're seeing it, seems like a picture that you've once seen, and you for a moment are kind of frozen outside it, looking in at it?

Well, I sometimes get that, but this time, I didn't, quite. There was something wrong inside the frame. And that was worse.

'Come on,' I said, to get away from the feeling.

Out the back from the big room, on one side, there are the two long guest rooms, where you can still see the framework of some of the bunks, and the wooden hooks where the blokes hung their clothes.

'So people actually *lived* here!' Jade exclaimed.

Despite how much I liked her, sometimes she was so dumb.

Then I showed her the two little rooms on the other side, that Grandad called the scullery and the still-room. That's where they used to get the food ready, and Sam used to make this strong cidery-drink called scrumpy out of the apples. He made a kind of apple-whisky too (Grandad reckoned), and wine from the blackberries and elderflowers.

Jade worked the old pump handle in the scullery, and gasped again when real water came out. And in the still-room she climbed inside one of the old broken scrumpy barrels and sniffed the ghost of a smell of groggy apples.

'Oh Col,' she said. 'It's heaven.'

'There's more,' I said, and led her out the back.

Most of the other buildings are pretty fallen down, because the rot's got into the timber, and Grandad and I only really had time to keep working on the palace and Sam's cottage, but I took her on a tour of the chookshed and the pigsty, the cow-bails and the stables and the horse yards and the bullock yard, and of course the old mill.

That's really just a kind of skeleton now, but you can still see where the mighty corner-posts were, and where the heavy roof-beams have fallen in. There's no equipment, of course because when the blokes moved to Cornwall, after the Big Slide, they took everything they could shift with them.

She looked less keen on all that, just kind of glanced quickly at the different shapes of the fences and tumble-down sheds and said stuff like: 'It must've been really pretty.' And when we got to the mill she wouldn't go in in case of snakes.

'Well, what do you expect from someone from the city,' I kind of consoled myself, and then something made me remember that crazy plan of Kathy's mate, to bring city tourists to Cornwall, and how I'd felt kind of cold in the gut, just at the thought. 'No worries,' I laughed at my fears.

'There's no way they'd ever want to come in the forest.'

'What's so funny?'

I looked at her gumboots, and started again. (Did I say before, as well as the soles on them being *smooth,* and the uppers being *short,* these boots were *green.* I mean, she was . . . everything was . . . her inside and her outside . . . her name and her politics and her eyes and her boots and her whole way of being . . . was . . .)

'Nothing.'

She loved Sam's place though. It's another old ash stump, like the cubby stump that guards the tunnel, but Sam had roofed this one and turned it into a two-room cottage, with its own chimney and a little round table, some shelves and a dresser and a wooden bed-base. It looked all neat and clean and homey, because sometimes I stayed there, so there was even an old foam mattress and a couple of blankets, a slightly broken blue flower vase and two enamel plates and mugs, a billy, and my special stockpile: a few tins of spaghetti and soup and sardines, a tin of biscuits, tea and sugar and powdered milk, and half a half-bottle of Loch Lomond whisky.

We had a swig each, and I mixed some milk powder and water in a bowl for Mog. *'Miaow . . .* 'I called, but there was no sign of her. Probably scared of Jade, I thought, or out hunting. Or searching the forest for a feral tom. She was more than half-wild herself.

'Mog, Mog . . .' I called again, and she slid out of a shadow (she's black), but wouldn't come any further.

'Whose cat is it?' Jade asked. 'Is it yours?'

'No.' I didn't have a cat. Once, when I was little, I took home a kitten, one from the palace, but the old man wouldn't let me keep it. 'We're not having any useless bludgers around here,' he said, then he drowned it in a bucket.

'She just belongs to the place,' I told Jade. Or the place belonged to her, I thought. Grandad reckoned there was always a cat here, and she was always called Mog. When Sam came, by himself, he brought the first one, and by the time of the Wet Winter, there was her daughter, or maybe granddaughter. She wouldn't leave, when all the people did, but stayed on, to guard the palace (Grandad told me when I was little.) And she had a daughter, who had a daughter, who had a daughter, who had a daughter, who . . . I gave her a quick look, but she seemed pretty skinny.

'Come on.' I grabbed the billy and a bit of food, and left Mog to her milk.

It was early afternoon by now, and the sun came warm and golden down into the Settlement as of course it never does in the forest. We were quiet, for a while, as we walked back through the orchard, sampling apples, then suddenly Jade turned towards me and hugged me and whispered, 'Thank you.'

I kissed her then, on her scratch, on her closed eyes, and still without opening them she asked: 'But what is it?'

And so I took her to the door again and pushed aside the climbing roses and showed her the final part of my secret.

The sign has broken off at one side, but you can still read the dark curly words that are poker-worked into the smooth, pale wood.

'*The Palace,*' she read.

I led her away then, down to the creek, and made a fire, and we had a smoke and another swig of whisky as we waited for the tomato soup to boil. She chattered on, about her family again I think, and the night in the cell, and whether tomato soup had dead animals in it, but by now the poshness in her voice didn't make me feel outside her, and I could listen to her like I did the creek, just letting the flow run over me as if I were a stone.

After we ate, she took her clothes off suddenly, and jumped into the deep hole behind the ford.

I'd never seen a girl without her clothes on before, but the way she did it, kind of as if it was an obvious thing to do, I didn't even stare. Just stripped off too, and jumped in, and we splashed around like a couple of little kids. The sun was hot and yellow all around, but we were inside this rushing pale-green coldness.

We got out, and lay beside the fire to dry, and I can remember thinking 'Soon, Colum,' but I was so happy, I wanted everything to happen very slowly, so it would last forever. She seemed to fall asleep, her wet hair against my arm, and then the whisky and the smoke and the sun must've got to me too, for the next thing I remember, there was this dream.

I was me, but I was Sam, and I was someone too that seemed older in time than Sam, that was part of the forest. I was cutting a tree with my little silver knife, making it fall with a crack and a swish, for the knife was magical of course. But as the tree fell, I was it too, and I heard a fearful kind of pulsing in my brain, as I fell, and I saw the earth rushing up to meet me. The falling went on and on, down and down, and the whirling sound got louder and louder, and now I knew it was a chainsaw, and I looked down and saw me still cutting down the tree that was me.

Louder and louder the sound got, closer and closer as I fell, and then I heard a scream that sounded like a woman's, splitting out from my heart, and I woke to see Jade hurling on her clothes and Kathy and Garry getting out of the noise that wasn't a chainsaw, but a helicopter that had just landed on the open bit of creek-flat where the waters meet.

Now you'll maybe understand why I didn't fall out of bed with gratefulness when Kathy Dolan sent me a present.

I'll stop for a while now, because it's nearly time for tea, and besides, I can see them wheeling Nick back and I want to know how he went.

▷ ▷ ▷ ————————————

Nick came back a bit tired, but grinning at me. 'No worries,' he said. 'The doctor, he says, "Easy job!" He says, "Old Nick, he's fit as a . . ." ' He slapped himself on the chest while he searched for the word.

'Fiddle?' I suggested. I was good at sayings, because of Mum.

'Yes, fiddle,' Nick agreed, then looked a bit fazed. 'But what is it means, this "fiddle"?'

'You know,' I said. 'Violin.' I mimed playing one, and made a screechy noise. I guess I felt like mucking around a bit, after the detective and thinking about Kathy and then writing down about me and Jade. Plus I was real happy that Nick's op is going to be OK.

'Ah,' Nick said, 'like the lyra.' And he played a lyra for a while. 'But why does it fit, this what-you-say.?'

I had to admit, he had me beat.

'Funny language, English language,' Nick said.

Then we got onto music, and I let him have a listen of my (Kathy's) Walkman. The Vivaldi was still in it, and Nick conducted it for a while.

'Is good,' he said, pulling the ear-plugs out, 'for English

music. But I get you better music, Greek music. You know ----------?' He said a Greek name I can't remember.

I said I thought I'd heard of him.

'You know, *Zorba the Greek?'* And Nick hummed that till I remembered it. I'd once seen the film on TV, with Anthony Quinn and the other bloke dancing on the beach. Now I thought about it, Nick reminded me a bit of Anthony Quinn, as well as of Grandad. And the funny thing about the dancing was, it wasn't poofy, in the same way that Jade taking her clothes off wasn't sexy.

Nick had been going on, while I was thinking. 'You know, Koo-koo-eh, what I tell you?' Then he said bits of it again, and from what I could work out it seemed that this Zorba bloke, the one who wrote the music, was in this Greek Communist thing.

'Good one,' I said as my tea came.

'Yes, very good man,' Nick agreed. 'Very good fighter, very brave man. You know, they put him in prison, when the Hoonta is in power.'

'Come again,' I said through my cauliflower.

'The Hoonta. The fascist. Not the same fascist as I tell you last time. Well, same, but new faces. 1967. The . . . how you say . . . the Colonels. When they in power.'

'Ah. Got you.' (I didn't, but still.)

'And they torture him. And he is very sick man. And everybody outside, all his comrades all over the world, they want to know how he is, and he cannot get a message out. Finally, after long time, this postcard is how you say, snuggles out, and you know what it is?'

'Nup.' I was trying to work out if the white stuff tonight was chook or fish.

'It is music, see, for this little song, this happy little song, and I sing it for you.'

He sang, and I will say it was real nice, sort of bouncy. The words were the same all the time, repeated, like a little kid will sing the same thing over and over till it doesn't have any sense any more. They sort of sounded like: *'Ein entaxei, ein entaxei, ein entaxei . . .'*

'And you know what is it means, this words?'

'No, tell me.' I was interested now, and besides, whatever the white was, I'd finished eating it.

'It is: *"It's OK, it's OK, it's OK . . ."* See?' And Nick sang it again, but in English this time, and after a bit I joined in too.

Nick suddenly broke off, and gave me a long look. 'But you know what is it *means,* this *"It's OK"*?'

'Huh?' I thought. 'What can "It's OK" mean but . . . well . . . "It's OK"?'

'Is *earonia,*' Nick said. 'How you say? When you write something, but the peoples who reads it sees more than the words, what they say on their face?' Nick's hand was kind of opening and closing, clutching at the air, as if he'd catch the word somehow. *'Earonial!'* he repeated loudly, like you talk to foreigners. 'You have this word too.'

Something clicked, and I was suddenly back in one of Squirt's Lit lessons. 'Irony!' I translated.

'Kala!' Nick said. 'Good! And so, this "It's OK", it is – how you say?'

'Ironic?'

'I-ron-ic, eh, for a bloke in gaol, and he is being torture, to send a happy little song to say "It's OK". So it means "Is not OK", eh? The gaol is not OK, but also the Hoonta, the fascists, the whole . . . everything . . . is not OK. And because of the Hoonta, the Greek peoples is not allow to talk free, and say the Hoonta is bad, or we are put in gaol too. And so many peoples, they take to sing this song, and they sing "It's OK, it's OK, it's OK," but they give a secret kind of wink to each other, and they mean "Is not OK" . . . OK?'

'OK,' I said. I thought I got it, but then Nick went and explained it more.

'But also too, ' Nick said, 'this song, it sort of mean "It *is* OK", because the peoples know when they sing it that they're unite together to hate the fascist, and so one day the fascist will be kick out, and it *will* be OK.'

Nick looked kind of exhausted from all the explaining, and I was reeling.

'Were they?' I asked. 'Kicked out, I mean?'

Nick just rolled up his eyes in a way I've learned means 'of course', then he added: 'I told you – *Ein entaxei, ein entaxei, ein entaxei . . .'*

I took it up: *'It's OK, it's OK, it's OK . . .'*

Then we swapped languages for the second verse, and did a duet in Greek for the third, and English for the fourth . . . till Baby Nurse came and Nick got into trouble for not eating up his nice tea like a good boy, and we both got roused on for making too much noise, and the shop trolley rattled up and I bought the evening paper.

I'll keep it though, to send me to sleep later, and go on a bit with this.

▷ ▷ ▷ ———————————

So Kathy and Garry got out, and there were three blokes still in the helicopter – the pilot, and I suppose the Channel 2 News blokes whose copter it was. (The name was on the side.) I had my clothes on too in a second, and I kicked the fire out, grabbed Jade's hand, and hauled her across the creek.

Kathy was yelling: 'Col! Colum! Wait! I'm sorry! I didn't mean . . .'

But we were down the tunnel, crawling like prisoners in a war-escape movie, and after a while I couldn't hear anything but Jade's little cries as the blackberries got her.

When we were out of the tree stump, I looked at my watch. 5.30. Then I looked at her. I felt strange with her now, sort of shy and embarrassed, as if Kathy seeing us lying there naked had made us dirty. And I felt sort of responsible too, as if I should apologise for the dreadful thing that had happened at my place.

But Jade started giggling. 'What on earth was that all about!' she said. 'Who was that girl, what were they doing?'

I said nothing.

'Aerial perves!' she giggled.

I realised that of course Jade didn't understand that no one ever came to the palace, she just didn't see the terribleness of what had happened. (Did she even realise it was my place? I wonder now.)

'But why did you grab me, and drag me out? I know those Channel 2 News guys, they've been covering our camp. Maybe we could've conned them into giving us a lift back. Hey, we could've had a ride in a helicopter!'

I turned away and started into the forest. 'You can go back if you want to.'

She looked quickly at the blackberries, then stumbled fast after me. 'C. . .o. . .l. . .' She dragged it out real long, pleading. 'Don't leave me.'

I realised she didn't have clue where she was, and she was scared.

'You'll come back to camp, won't you, and have some tea with us?' She put her hand in mine, so trusting, like a little kid might, that I felt again all the sort of softness she brought out in me.

'Sure.' Sure I'd go and eat with the enemy. After all, I'd been betraying my side all day.

Besides, the dream was with me still, the picture of me cutting myself down, and I felt as if I didn't know what my side was any more.

I hauled her back through the forest to the bike, then zipped along the old track, down the Farm Road, then down the new track to the greenies' camp. It was pretty dark by the time we got there.

Just before we walked into the circle of light and noise and boiling billies, she stopped, and put her arms round me, and kissed me. Then just as suddenly she let me go and pushed ahead, so that she walked in alone, and me behind her.

'Shit Jade, where the hell've you been? I've been getting worried.' It was the fattish older girl, Sharnda. 'I thought maybe that bloke . . .' And then she saw me. 'Oh, hi!'

Jade was busy with the cooking fire, as if she was part of the camp and I was a stranger who'd just come in by himself. She seemed embarrassed.

'Hi . . .' I felt awkward, and wanted to go, but I wanted to stay with Jade. I looked at the tents, and wondered which one was hers, and if maybe I'd get another chance if I hung around. 'I'm Col,' I said.

'You're from the town,' Sharnda said.

'Sort of.' I felt real defensive, as if she thought I was a spy or something.

'He's on our side,' Jade cut in quickly, but without looking up.

'Good on you! . . . Col, was it?' Sharnda grinned. 'Here, have a beer.' She passed me a slightly warm can. 'We get a bit jumpy, because the cops reckoned some town bloke came here last night, and we don't want any trouble. But it's great to find that one of the locals is with us. Come and meet everyone. Hey, Jade, introduce your friend.'

Jade joined her to take me over to the campfire, but the way we walked I could've been Sharnda's mate – or no one's. And then suddenly it seemed I was everyone's.

'Col . . . this is Mike, Mike Marchant . . . and Jim, who you met this morning, and Rob and Sally, and Dave and Tes and Al and Suzie and . . .' (It was Sharnda talking of course. Jade was looking shy, or something.)

I gazed and grinned at all the faces in the flickering light. It still wasn't quite night, but it was dark enough for everything to seem strange. I thought of those movies where an explorer walks in on a camp of cannibals. Apart from Mike Marchant and Jim the lawyer, most of them had funny hair, and they all had badges on, and there must've been about forty of them, and none of it was what I was used to. They were all saying 'Hi', real enthusiastic.

'. . . But you'll work out the names later,' Sharnda finished.

'Yeah, just have a seat, mate,' Mike Marchant said, and he moved up to make a space for me on his log. He stuck his hand out. 'In case you didn't get the name, I'm Mike.'

'I know,' I mumbled, then felt silly.

'Yeah, everyone knows Mike,' said the bloke with the guitar, who turned out to be called Dave. Then he started singing, quiet and maybe a bit sarcastic:

"Old Mike Marchant had a camp, ee-I-ee-I-oh.
And in that camp he had a tent, ee-I-ee-I-oh.
With a little girl here and a little girl . . ."

'Cut it out, Dave.' Mike was quiet too, but real heavy. I noticed the girl called Suzie get up and go over to help Sharnda and Jade. (They'd gone back to the cooking fire.)

Then Mike started talking to Jim and a couple of other blokes about his campaign for that city by-election, and how the troops in the city were getting on with the leaflet-ing and the graffiti-ing.

'What're you going to do,' asked a bloke with long straggly hair, 'if we're not out of here in time for the election?'

Mike laughed. 'We'll be out, mate, no worries. We'll have this won in a few more days. The way I hear it, the boys in the Labor Party back-room are really putting the pressure on Buckley to stop the logging here. They can't afford to lose Hadley.' He turned to me, like Squirt does when he thinks I don't know my arse from my elbow. 'Buckley's the Minister for Conservation, Forests and Tourism.'

'I know,' I lied.

'They'd still have a majority of one,' Dave cut in.

'One?' Mike mocked, though whether he was laughing at Dave or the Labor Party wasn't clear. 'They wouldn't risk it.'

But Jim was sucking on a dead pipe, and looking a bit worried. 'They just might, you know. They can call a full election in the New Year, so that's only nine months or so to hang on, and they might just risk it. You've really got the Premier's back up, you know.' He laughed. 'He reckons he won't be . . .'

Mike laughed too. 'Yeah, don't tell me: "I *won't be threatened, I won't be blackmailed, by any bloody middle-class trendy.*" But you'll see. It's the middle-class trendies who vote in Hadley, and he'll be singing a different song when we get closer to the 30th.'

Writing this down now I just checked the date on the evening paper. (There's another airline crash all over the front page.) It's the 27th today. And no different song from the Premier. So it looks like Mike Marchant was wrong. Not that it matters now, for this year, because of the rain.

At the time, I was thinking how the old man, and Bluey Waters, and his son Big Jim, and Mr Robinson, and all the other loggers and millworkers, and Scott and us too, were just like pawns in a chess game that was being played by Mike and the Premier. To Mike Marchant, we were the enemy, but he never saw us as real people. And the Premier too, though he reckoned he had to save us our jobs, didn't care about us as people. It would just mean he broke another election pledge, if we were thrown out of work. But it sounded like he'd be willing to sacrifice us, like chess players sacrificed their pieces sometimes, if he got scared enough about losing this Hadley place. The whole thing was being decided by a bunch of greenies, and a bunch of back-room boys (whatever they were), and not one of them thought: 'If the logging stops, how will Mr Ferris pay the mortgage, how will Mrs Ferris pay off the HP on the lounge, how will young Col ever get a job, how long will the Ferrises last before they're all at each other's throats, like they were in the bad winter, three years ago? And with Mr and Mrs F and Col all fighting, how long will it be before the old feller just gives up the ghost?'

It made me sick. But the other thought, of the logging going on and on till in a couple more years they'd logged their way right up to the palace, that made me sick too.

I got up and went over to the cooking fire. 'Want a hand?'

'Thanks, Col. As you can see, it's pretty sexist round here. The women cook while the men talk politics.' That was Sharnda of course. Jade was chopping cabbage into a big enamel dish. She gave me a quick smile, but she was watching the scene over at the other fire. The Suzie girl had gone back when I came over, and she'd taken my seat.

'What're you making?' I just wanted to try to get back to the closeness we'd had before.

'Coleslaw. *Bloody* coleslaw.' I saw she'd cut herself, and her thumb was still bleeding slowly through a bit of Kleenex.

'Here, I'll do it.' I took the knife from her, and squatted down.

Just then there was a sound as if a woundy bullock was stampeding through the undergrowth towards me. It seems silly now to say it scared me, but at the time I felt this sudden danger warning grab me. Maybe it was the old E.S.P.

I swung round, on my feet now, tense, ready to spring, and this great dark shape almost fell through the bushes onto me. The firelight jumped high, and I saw the flash of the knife I still held in my hand. Something of the dream, and Sam's knife, flashed through me too. And then the darkness stumbled sideways, and there was a crash, and a thump, and a clanking, rolling sound, and Doctor Brian MacBride was sitting in the coleslaw dish and cans of beer were scattering all around him.

'Thank Christ I didn't buy bottles!' he said. Then, still sitting, he passed me a can. 'At least it's cold. The name's Brian.'

'Hi, sorry, I'm Colum.' Maybe it was his accent, brought the full name out of me.

'Colum, eh? Now that's a good Irish name. And would your people be coming from there then?'

'My mum's dad,' I said.

He moved himself out of the dish and warmed his feet at the fire, opened a tinny and it spurted down into the flames. There was a hiss, and a jet of steam.

'Stop pissing in the lentils, Brian,' Sharnda said. 'And move your fat arse out of the serving area. Hey you bludging bastards!' She clanked at a tin plate. 'Bring your dishes, it's ready!'

I won't describe tea. Even though there were no dead animals in it, it was so good it'd make me hungry. I got given a spare dish, and I sat next to Jade at the campfire while I ate. Mike Marchant got Brian to sit next to him this time. They were over the other side. Suzie was with Sharnda and Dave. I worked out, just watching and listening, that everyone except Sharnda crawled up Brian's arse, and thought him and the World Heritage Commission was really something. Even Mike Marchant was all: 'And what do *you* think, Brian?'

'Pity about the coleslaw,' I said to Jade, and she was kind of with me again.

'Would've been lousy anyway,' she grinned. 'I can't cook. Mum won't ever let me.'

I could feel her arm kind of bumping against me every time she put her spoon in her mouth, and I wondered if she meant it to.

Then there was washing up, with everyone doing their own in turn in a greasy dish, and Brian gave me another can.

Back to the campfire, and Dave started playing, and a girl got out a flute. That was nice, just music and quiet, then they started singing greenie songs and I felt left out, even though I was still with Jade. A few people wandered off to their tents, the ones that were couples I mean, and I wondered again about if Jade would let me stay.

'Which is your tent?' I asked, real casual.

'That little red one. Why?'

Before I could think of an answer, Mike Marchant said: 'But how about you, Brian, we haven't had a song from you yet.'

'I'm fine, mate, I'm going grand.' Brian seemed to be more busy drinking than anyone else. (Except maybe me.)

'Oh go on, Brian,' everyone reckoned, real crawl-up-his-arse stuff, and Dave waited for him to start something.

And then his voice just burst out, like his darkness had burst out earlier:

> *A hungry feeling came o'er me stealing,*
> *And the seagulls were wheeling o'er the prison wall.*
> *And the old triangle goes jingle-jangle.*
> *All along the banks of the Royal Canal . . .*

Remember how I said when I first saw him on TV that he reminded me of a picture of Brendan Behan? Well, this was one of Behan's songs he was singing. I knew it because Mum sometimes sang it, and she'd told me the story of it too: how

Behan had made it up while he was in prison for fighting against the English.

(Writing that, I think now of the Zorba bloke's song and how they both came about. The way things are going, I'm going to have plenty to sing when I get to gaol. Joke. Ha ha Colum.)

Anyway, Brian sang. His voice probably wasn't very good, but it had lots of noise and belief in it. He belted out the second verse, about the screws calling, and then his voice took on a softer, really longing sound as he did the one about wanting to be all among the women in the female prison. Then it was back to the chorus, and I got sort of cold tingles as that weird tune went out into the silence of the forest.

And the old triangle goes jingle-jangle.
All along the banks of the Royal Canal . . .

I hadn't realised, but by the end I'd joined in, singing softer and higher than him, like I think you call it a descant. I used to sing a lot with Mum, but my voice had broken round about the time of the fight with Scott and getting in with the old man, and I hadn't done it since then.

Everyone clapped, and yelled, 'Another, come on.'

'Only if my mate comes and sits with me and keeps me in tune,' Brian said.

He was looking at me, and so were the greenies, and Jade nudged me and looked at me as if it was terrific to be asked to sit with Brian. I wanted her to think me good, and so I had to leave Jade, and Mike Marchant got up too and took my bit of log beside her, and I took his seat with Brian.

'Hang on, boyo,' he said, 'we need better than beer if we're to make fools of ourselves.' He dived into his black coat pocket and brought out a bottle of Jameson, screwed the cap off, took a swig, handed it to me, and launched into 'The Wearing of the Green'.

I won't bore you and go right through the concert list (even if I could remember), but I know we did 'The Foggy Dew' and 'Sean South of Garryowen', 'Kevin Barry' and of course 'Danny Boy' and the 'Soldier's Song' and 'Kathleen Mavourneen', and I know it didn't seem long till we were halfway through the bottle. Dave and the flute girl sort of played along quietly with us when they could get the tune, and the others sometimes came in on the choruses. Then Brian ripped into one I'd certainly never heard Mum sing:

I'm the queerest young feller that ever you heard.
Me mother's a Jew and me father's a bird.
With Joseph the joiner I could not agree.
So here's to disciples and High Calvary.
Tra la la, tra la lee . . .
How would you how would you like to be me?

'You don't know it?' he paused after the first verse. 'It's called the 'Ballad of Joking Jesus', and it's by old Jimmy Joyce himself.'

I saw Jade prick up her ears across the campfire. I felt really dumb again, with all these people who went to university and that. 'Yeah, I've heard of him,' I said. Jade looked away from me, and she seemed to try to catch Mike's eye, but he was talking to Suzie who'd moved over there.

Then Brian started from the beginning again, and I couldn't do anything but listen.

I can remember lots (I seem to pick up songs real fast), but I won't tell you any of the rest of the verses. You should get a hold of it but, some time. Specially if you used to be Catholic, like me.

A couple more swigs. A cigarette to get the voice nice and rough. Then Brian reckoned, 'And here's a special one for you Aussies.'

Of course it was 'And The Band Played Waltzing Matilda', a real sad one about war. Now Jade was looking really miserable into the fire, her eyes those wet pools again. We sung on, and I watched her across the flames sitting by herself on the log (Mike and Suzie had gone now), and she looked kind of small and lonely, and I thought about how much I liked her. I mean, I really did like her, as well as wanting to fuck her.

'I'd better be going,' I said when the song ended. I looked at my watch, as if time mattered. (12.45, I remember.)

'Come on,' said Sharnda, 'one more.'

But I could see Brian had done his dash, and was ready to get on with just the drinking. He passed the bottle to me, and Dave and the flute girl wandered off, and most of the rest of the greenies sort of dribbled away. I kept doing E.S.P. *'Stay, stay'* talk at Jade, but I didn't know if I could hold her right through a session with Brian so I started to shift.

'You off, boyo?'

'Yeah mate.' (Not if I can help it. I looked at the little red tent.)

He let his arm go from round my shoulders, and I let go of him too. I suppose we had been like Mike Marchant said in that dumb interview 'in each others' arms', but that says nothing about how we'd been in the singing, how we'd sung off each other, and for each other, then against each other, then with each other, around each other, about each other, then under and over and him leading and me leading and then us going together and together till it was one great singing that wasn't either of us but something else pushing out into the blackness of the night.

'Sweet dreams,' he muttered as I went towards the darkness. Then he looked back into the whisky and the fire.

I touched Jade's shoulder and she came with me across the creek to where I'd left the bike.

'Can I stay?' I said. There were black fire smudges on her cheeks, and I kissed them. Then there was wetness that I tasted, running down like tears.

'No, Col, no,' she said, and leant away from me.

Then, you know how I've described her moods changing, well suddenly she burst out laughing. 'Not tonight, Josephine,' she said.

And then I snapped too. Her voice was posh again, I wasn't good enough for her, and I couldn't even understand her.

'What the fuck do you mean?'

She was kind of giggling, and I wondered if she'd had a smoke maybe while I was hitting the piss with Brian. 'Nothing. It's just something Napoleon is meant to have said to Josephine, before a big battle, or something. You know who Napoleon was, don't you?'

'I think I've heard of him,' I said. Putting on what Squirt calls the macho veneer.

'Oh Col,' she giggled, 'I love you.'

'What the fuck does that mean?'

She stopped laughing, and leant back against a tree as if she was tired or something. 'Not tonight,' she said.

'Tomorrow?' I asked.

'Yeah,' she looked alive again for a moment, as if I'd sent her off on a new track. 'Tomorrow is another day.' She kissed me very calmly on the cheek. 'Come for tea again.'

She headed back towards the campsite, then turned as she had that first day to apologise about the rabbit.

'I do actually like you, Col,' she said. 'Thanks for today.'

'See you tomorrow,' I said, but she was gone.

▷ ▷ ▷ ———————————————

One o'clock, Thursday morning. Listening to the tape Kathy made of the juke-box music, while I write. A real hotch-potch, as Mum says. (The End of the Road juke-box is famous for being way out of date.) Now it's 'Why Do Fools Fall In Love?'

I think that's how I felt when I was riding home through the forest. All sort of high and low and happy and sad.

I was cold, I remember.

No, I didn't have my new Fair Isle jumper, because Mum was finishing sewing it together as I walked in the back door. She shot a kind of nervous look at me, as if there was something up, but I didn't know anything except *Jade Jade Jade* and maybe tomorrow night.

I remember thinking it was late for Mum, but she was like that with a jumper, if she'd just finished it. She had to iron the pieces (the board was out), and get it sewn and all done, like. She'd sometimes said she'd like to knit 'professionally'.

'Just try this on in a sec, will you dear,' she said, 'and see how it looks.'

Then the old man burst out through the bedroom door in his pyjamas, his face dark.

'You're late!' he said.

I nodded. Since when had being late been a sin in this family?

'Don't just nod your head. Answer when you're spoken to!'

'Yeah!' I said. 'Yeah, I'm late, yeah, I'll answer, get off my back.'

I seem to have written this before. But yeah, it was the same old thing as Thursday night, but more so. The old man didn't seem so strong but, in his blue-striped pyjamas. Plus I had a skin full of booze, and for the first time I realised I was nearly as tall as him.

'I'm going to bed,' I said, and he just stood there while I walked into the sleep-out and did.

▷ ▷ ▷ ——————————

And that's what I'm going to do now. But while I do, I'll leave you again with something to be going on with. I just opened tonight's paper past the airline crash, and here's what's on page two.

P.S. You wouldn't credit this. Now the juke-box tape is playing the *Zorba* song. There's a bit of talking first, from that scene where Anthony Quinn and the other bloke are on this empty beach together. Remember? Quinn is all whiskery and dirty and strong and alive, and the other bloke is a weak guy, and he wants to be like Zorba (Quinn) but he doesn't know how. And the talking before the song goes:

The Other Bloke: 'Teach me to dance, will you?'
Anthony Quinn: 'Did you say . . . dance?'
He pauses for a moment, then says: 'Go on, my boy.'

And now the music starts, real slow, and kind of pulling you into it, so if you (I mean I) didn't have your (my) legs in plaster, you'd be into it, doing it now, getting faster, stepping, pausing, hopping, and now it takes off, and me with it.

End of P.S. I think I'll just get into this music and sleep. You can read the paper.

▷ ▷ ▷ ——————————

The Examiner
Wednesday 27 March

ONE-LEGGED VC DIES

LABOR PARTY IN DIRE STRAITS

The sudden death this morning due to a heart attack of the long-standing member for the state seat of Ridgeway,

Mr John (Jacka) James, could well sound the death knell for the state Labor Government.

The Labor Party is already troubled by the possibility of losing the swinging seat of Hadley in the by-election to be held this Saturday, 30 March.

If Hadley is lost, Labor's majority in the state Lower House will be reduced to one seat. And if this happens, the government will certainly lose power after the Ridgeway by-election, for the Labor Party's possession of that seat has long been one of the greatest curiosities of the political scene in this state.

The seat of Ridgeway is a country one, covering the fertile mixed-farming area around Wobbiac, in the north of the state.

It forms part of the federal seat of Chesterfield, which always returns the National Party candidate by a large majority.

On a state level, however, the voters have unfalteringly supported Mr James since he first stood for the seat in 1947.

The reason lies solely in Mr James' personal popularity.

In 1940, when a young private, he was awarded the Victoria Cross for venturing alone into enemy ranks and destroying a crucial machine-gun nest, single-handed.

He was later captured by the Japanese and sent to the Changi Prisoner of War Camp, where he initiated one of the most daring escape attempts from that hole of hell.

After its failure and his subsequent re-capture, he was brutally tortured, with the result that for the rest of his life he has borne the scars of his torment.

Later, he was sent by the Japanese to work on the dreaded Burma-Thailand railroad, where he lost a leg when an attempt to blow up the enemy Staff Tent with stolen gelignite misfired.

At the war's end, he returned to Australia and his own area a hero, and his popularity was increased by his quick smile and cheerful demeanour despite his obvious physical disabilities.

Prior to the war, Mr James had been a potato picker, an occupation he could not continue because of his artificial leg.

In 1947, though he was only 28, he announced his

decision to stand for Parliament because, he maintained, the Returned Serviceman wasn't being given a fair go.

When asked what party he would stand for, he replied, 'I don't care really. If there was a Diggers' Party, I'd stand for that. As there isn't, I might go for Labor. That's what my old Dad voted.'

Stand he did, and in the 1947 state election he was returned with a rousing majority.

It was clearly a sympathy vote, given as a mark of respect and affection to a local boy who had helped save the country from the downward thrust of the Japanese.

That sympathy, respect and affection has continued throughout the years, with the result that on some occasions Mr James has been elected unopposed.

The Ridgeway residents, however, make it clear that they vote not for Labor but for 'old Jacka'.

Even the secretary of the tiny local ALP branch admits: 'If it wasn't for Jacka, Labor wouldn't even be able to win a chook raffle around here'.

So with their beloved Jacka gone, the Ridgeway voters will certainly vote at a state level as they vote at a federal level – for the National Party.

And if Labor has already failed to hold the swinging seat of Hadley in Saturday's by-election, a National Party victory in Ridgeway will mean that the balance of power will be Liberal/National Party coalition 50, Labor Party 49.

The question is, will this threat cause the Labor Party to rethink its strategy in relation to the Hadley by-election?

The Independent Green candidate, Mr Michael Marchant, has promised to direct his supporters to allocate their preferences to Labor if the Labor Party breaks the government's contract with Cornwall Milling Inc., the company that controls logging and milling in the Settlement Creek area.

With the Green preferences going to Labor, Labor would have a good chance of retaining Hadley – and hence power, even after the National Party's sure win in Ridgeway.

But the Premier has previously announced that the Labor Party will win Hadley alone, and that he will not be threatened or blackmailed by what he calls the lunatic conservationist fringe.

In an interview today, the Premier was looking distinctly worried, but he repeated his promise that the Cornwall mill would not be closed unless an alternative industry could be established in the area.

With only two days remaining before the by-election, the question is: how quickly can the government find a viable alternative industry?

The Minister for Conservation, Forests and Tourism, Mr Cyril Buckley, was today not available for comment.

However, a representative of his department, Mr Garry Lazlo, said: 'We're looking into something. But we have to convince the Premier. And besides, it's a race against time.'

It certainly is. With the return to the city of Mike Marchant and his supporters, the Green campaign in Hadley has been going from strength to strength. Every telegraph pole bears a tree sticker, and each day street theatre, busking and non-competitive games take place in the shopping mall and parks.

The popular folk-rock band, the Ents, are staging a free concert in the area's football stadium on Friday night to support the 'Save The Settlement Creek Trees' cause.

It is at this concert that Mr Marchant will make his final announcement guiding his supporters as to how to direct their preferences.

What will his advice be?

Only time will tell.

Page 4: Mr John James, obituary
Page 7: Memorial Service arrangements
Page 12: Historical Feature, Changi, Hell-Hole of the Pacific.

▷ ▷ ▷ ———————————

4 a.m., Thursday, 28 March. Just woke from a dream. Have to write it out of me.

It begins with the falling that I've been falling all these nights, which is why I write, all night, to stop it, that's normal, nothing to write home about. (Joke, Colum. Ha ha. Where's your home, son, to write to?)

(Yeah, who *do* you write to? To you. Well, who do you do?)

Anyway. Yeah. The falling. The always falling that is me

falling to me. Me the tree and me cutting it, me at the top and me at the bottom, and then the scream that rings in my heart like a woman. That is me.

But this time he catches me, and takes me to the beach.

It is pebbly and wide, grey, white, going on forever. I am the other bloke trying to be like him, and he is Brian.

'Teach me to dance, will you?' I say.

'Did you say dance?' he reckons. 'Go on, my boyo.'

And so we sing, I mean dance, together through the white ward, because now he's Nick, his arms in his pyjamas holding me, and the beach is here, but Nick isn't any more, but the old man is, in his striped blue pyjamas, and then he's someone else, and this time there aren't pyjamas, and I'm trying to tell him I love him, and then the falling falling again.

And now I walk through a door, the ward door up there, and I'm not here with my legs trapped in white, I'm walking. But the door leads into a tunnel like the barrel of a gun and I crawl and crawl through the darkness, no way out, the blackberries scraping at my eyes, but now I look out into the clearing of the palace and Jade and Kathy are not wearing any clothes and in each other's arms.

They're so beautiful because this kind of long fine fur grows out of their bodies, Jade's black and Kathy's red, with white skin shining behind it.

I feel I'm wrong, just to be me, and bolt back.

Falling falling down the tunnel this time, like something's dropped on me, and then it's 4 a.m., Thursday 28 March, or actually a bit later now that I've written it down, and all I've got to show for it is a couple of pages and a headache and a bit of come on my pyjamas.

Shit, this is embarrassing. I didn't realise when I started that writing's like taking your clothes off in front of a stranger. At least, this sort of writing is, because I'm trying to get down all the truth. I hope you're a bloke, and then maybe you'll understand. But now I've got this far, I might as well tell you this strange thing about sex in hospital.

I haven't been able to get off by myself while I've been here. I've gone back like a little kid to waking up and knowing it's happened. That's why I hate the nurses washing me. They take my pyjamas away and give me clean ones. I try to stop it in the normal way, by making it happen. I think of Jade, swimming with her, even Baby Nurse, even Kathy Dolan, but I'm dead as my legs.

And after dreams like the last one, dancing on the beach, I get scared and wonder if I'm a poofter. Deep down.

I think of gaol, and getting raped.

Stop it.

Since I've been here and the dreams, I always come in the falling.

That's the scream, that is a woman, that is me.

I wonder who she is.

▷ ▷ ▷ ———————————

Thursday morning. They let me sleep in past breakfast, so I feel a bit better now, but hungry. I should've said yes to the fruit cake.

Listening to Kathy's tape, the first thing on side one has got into my brain.

It's this woman's voice that sings:

What should I write? What can I say?
How can I tell you how much I miss you?

The weather here has been as nice as it can be.
Although it doesn't really matter much to me.
For all the fun I'll have while you're so far away,
It might as well rain until September . . .

I don't need sunny skies for things I have to do,
Cos I stay home the whole day long and think of you.
As far as I'm concerned each days a rainy day.
So it might as well rain until September . . .

It doesn't matter whether skies are grey or blue.
It's raining in my heart cos I can't be with you.
I'm only living for the day you're home to stay.
So it might as well rain until September.

September . . . September . . .
Oh it might as well rain until September . . .

I don't know why I just wrote that out. Maybe because every day when I start this, I don't know how to start. And maybe that's because as I go on and on with the tale, I get closer to the bit I don't want to do.

It's funny though, that song makes me kind of homesick. It's probably because it's about rain, and I think of home and how it's pissing down, there. (Mum rang again a minute ago, and as usual we discussed the weather.) I think how the earth will be cold and wet down there now till about September, and September maybe seems important too because that's six months from now, and it's then that they reckon my legs will be properly right again. (I wonder if they have whatummy-therapy in gaol.) And September makes me think of the palace at that time, when it's better than gold as Grandad says, with the daffodils all out. It's like a great glowing carpet, right through the orchard.

Stop it.

Get on with the story. Where was I?

Oh yeah. Saturday night, I got home late and had a bit of a row with the old man and I went to bed.

▷ ▷ ▷ ———————————

Sunday morning, I woke up late. I was a bit seedy from the night before, so I said I didn't want any breakfast. The old man was off somewhere, and Mum was pretty quiet, watching a little line of ants going up and down the wall next to the stove.

'The blokes will have to get a move on, if they're to get all the logs they need for the winter,' she said.

'It'll be right, Mum,' I said. 'The ants are probably just going to church or something.' Then I realised.

I mean, Mum always went, but for her to miss Mass in Lent, that was impossible. Lent was like kind of spring cleaning, Mum always said, when you got your soul all spic and span for Easter.

'*Spring* cleaning!' I mocked once, when I was giving it up. 'Typical! The church doesn't even know what time of the year it is!

But Mum jumped down my throat. 'Yes son, spring, and I agree it's all topsy turvy here in Australia, but that's the fault of the hemisphere or whatever you call it, and not of the church. In Europe, where Easter started, it *is* in the springtime, so when Christ rises, He does it when the plants are coming back to life after their winter sleep, and so the people can see the proof, all around them.'

I can remember at the time I thought of the palace, and how

the bulbs of the daffodils lie dark inside the earth, and then spring (sorry) up after winter, and I did kind of see how that could make it all seem more believable. Well, a little. (Though not to me.) But course I kept up the argument.

'Easter didn't start in *Europe.* Jesus was an Israeli, or whatever you're meant to call them.' We'd just started having Squirt, and I could hear him saying: 'They're not *Jews,* Colum . . .' Of course, now I think of that ballad of Brian's:

'I'm the queerest young fellow that ever you heard.
Me mother's a Jew and me father's a bird . . .'

Mum snapped. 'It did so. And that's the end of it.'

It was the end too of our talking about religion. So I never told her, a year or so later, this story of Squirt's, that made her seem kind of right. Squirt said how when Christianity started up in Greece, like in 1 A.D. or whenever it was, the Christians took over the old heathen festivals, and they held Easter in the spring, because that's when the heathens used to have fertility festivals, and make sacrifices and stuff to get the plants to grow and the sheep to have lambs and even the women to have babies. There were some really gory things they did, so Christ's death kind of fitted in with the sacrifices, but I never really got the connection because Scott and Danny and Terry were in the class then, and we all started carrying on to Helen and Monica about 'Wait till springtime, baby,' and that sort of stuff.

. . . Where was I? I get carried away sometimes. But I was really just trying to explain how it seemed absolutely impossible for Mum to miss Mass that Sunday morning.

'How come you're home?'

'Oh I don't know,' she sighed, 'I guess I just didn't feel like it.' She was looking at me a bit funny, as if she expected me to remember something or think something or something, but I was too crook to think much.

I had a shower, packed my football things into my sports bag. Mum gave me the new Fair Isle, to wear after the game. I said it was real nice and everything, though I still always felt a bit funny about Mum's knitting – no one else wore fancy jumpers, and I thought it was maybe a bit poofy. Then I said gooday to Grandad, and headed out the front way.

It was an Away match that day, the first match of the season, at Mulvers Hill. The bus left at midday from outside Woolcotts' store, and as I waited for it, mucking around with Scott and Danny and Terry and Sean, this white Alfa pulled up.

A middle-aged bloke got out to get some petrol, and I noticed a girl in the passenger seat, waving at me. Scott was whistling under his breath at her, and the other blokes were reckoning who was she? I pretended I didn't know her, because it was (I suddenly realised) that Suzie girl.

Then 'Hi, Col!' she yelled, and looked like she might get out, so I went over to her.

'You off?' I said. I could see a pack and sleeping bag in the back seat.

She suddenly looked real bad-tempered. 'Yeah, my fucking father saw me get arrested on TV, so he's fucking turned up to get me. Reckoned he'll cut off my allowance if I don't go home. I'm not meant to get arrested, because I'm doing law. Fucking shit.'

The bloke came back.

'See you later,' I said.

'Yeah, see you!'

Scott and them were on at me about who was she? (Thank Christ they didn't recognise her as a greenie.) 'Oh, just some chick from Morlong,' I said. And then luckily the bus pulled up, and we all piled in (except for Squirt who always drove himself) and that was the end of it.

I won't go into all the details about the game. To make it brief, we lost, and we should've won because Mulvers Hill's a pissy team. I missed a couple of easy marks, and handed them one of their goals on a plate, and whenever I ran I felt my head like a great rock I had to carry. The A-grade team lost too, and I think we all felt it was like a bad omen. I mean, it was bad luck to lose the first game of the season, but more than that it was like the final thing after the week of greenies, and it seemed to make everyone feel dismal about what would happen with the greenies on Monday – and afterwards.

In the bus coming home I heard blokes talking about what they'd do if the mill closed down, where they'd move, what sort of work they might look for, whether they'd be able to sell their houses in Cornwall, even whether their wives might have to go to work or how their kids would get on at a new school with none of their mates . . . It was the first time I'd ever heard anyone talk as if the logging might actually stop, and it was really depressing. I can remember looking around the bus and thinking: 'We're just a big bunch of losers.'

We'd got some tinnies at Mulvers Hill, and after a while the dismalness changed to a kind of bottled-up anger. As we passed the padlocked track to the new coup, Big Jim Waters reckoned we should stop the bus and all go in and just punch the shit out of the greenies, and I reckon if it hadn't been that there was a free barbecue on at the pub and everyone was starving, the blokes might've done it.

I think now: if they had've gone in, what would I have done? On the Saturday night, Jade had said: 'Tomorrow is another day', and as far as I was concerned, it'd turned out to be kind of true. I don't know if you play football, but if you do you know how being in the team makes you part of the other blokes. And so coming home that Sunday night I thought like the other blokes in the bus, and not like I had when I'd sat around the fire with the greenies.

Here we go again. Two-bob-each-way Colum.

But the blokes talking as if the mill might close, and everyone have to leave Cornwall and go to different places, had suddenly made me feel lonely and kind of frightened. What if the old man and Mum and Grandad and I had to move somewhere, and it was somewhere that Scott and them didn't move to, and I had to go all through the trouble of finding a new gang to hang around with? What if I had to be alone again?

So what would I have done if the bus had stopped?

To show you how mixed up I was, before Jim said that about stopping, I'd been wondering if I could ask the driver to drop me off there, so I could go in to the camp and have tea, like I'd told Jade I would.

Then when Jim suggested it, I knew I couldn't, because all the blokes would know I was going to see the greenies.

Anyway, we went on to the pub – I guess it was about half-past six by then – and I thought I'd go in and have a couple of beers (bugger Kathy Dolan!) and then sneak out to the camp.

When I walked in, I wondered what the hell was happening. There were green streamers all over the pub, and green balloons, and Mrs Dolan and old Dom Dolan and Mrs Dolan's Mum were wearing green ribbon rosettes, and other people in the pub had green crepe paper round their necks and green party hats, and blow me down if amongst the other people there wasn't my own Mum, who never went to the pub. But the final thing to take the cake was Kathy Dolan, who was running around collecting glasses, all dressed up like a lady leprechaun or something in a full green skirt and puffy-sleeved white blouse, green jerkin and white stockings and black shoes with buckles, and a little green cap on her red hair.

'Happy Saint Patrick's Day, Col!' Dom yelled and passed me one of a long line of beers he had on the bar counter.

Kathy was looking at me, kind of wary, and her face was a bit red but that was probably the heat. And then *I* went red, thinking how she'd seen me and Jade, and then that brought back all the fuming.

'Nice gear you've got on,' I said.

'Shut your mouth,' Kathy snarled. 'Bloody Dad threatened to kick me out if I didn't wear it . . . Here!' She thrust the leaning tower of glasses into my hands and I remembered Sunday night was the night of my job, and there was no way now I could sneak out to the forest till after the pub shut.

▷ ▷ ▷ ———————————

Hurrah! No more bedpans. The Chinese lady doctor just came, with a couple of blue men, and they brought me a wheelchair. They put me in it and showed me how it worked, and then one of the Blue Men took me down to the toilets and showed me the special one with a hoist-thing in it, so I can lift myself out of the wheelchair and onto the seat, then back into the chair again.

They reckon I still have to be in bed most of the time, but I can get up for a couple of hours a day, go down to the telly end of the ward at night, or out to the verandah and get some air.

I'm so happy. Or nearly so happy. But as the old man says: 'You get nothing for nothing.'

The bad side of it is that I've been moved to a different bed, right at the end of the ward, because this new bed has its own hoist-thing so I can get myself out and into my chair.

You probably would've laughed, seeing me say goodbye to Nick. It was as if I was moving to the other end of the earth.

'I'll come and visit,' I said. 'And promise you'll come up and see me.'

He seemed real kind of touched that I didn't want to go. 'You good boy,' he said. 'You and me, we comrades, no matter how far we are, three metre, thirty metre . . .' He waved his arms to show a bigger and bigger distance. 'Three-hundred-million metre, we still together, always now, we struggle and fight together.' He took my hand and held it hard, like you do when you're a little kid and you're swearing a promise. 'Entaxei?' he asked.

'Entaxei,' I agreed. That's the Greek for OK, like in that Zorba bloke's song.

I can see him down there, joking with one of the Blue Women as she gives him his lunch. For a second I'm almost jealous that he's laughing with someone else. My bed looks really lonely, down there, all empty. You probably think it's funny how I'm going on, but I feel as if he's the only mate I've got in the world.

Despite him sending the weed, I don't think things are really going to be OK with Scottie.

But here's my own lunch too.

▷ ▷ ▷ ———————————

I think every bloke in Cornwall must've been in the pub that night, except for Helen Tayler's old man. A heap of women like my mum who never went were there too. Plus the twenty or so coppers who were staying at the pub, and a few reporters who were in town already for the morning. The beer was on the house, and if you went out to the beer garden you could get a paper plate heaped high with meat they had roasting on a spit there and hot spuds and salad. Scott and them came back with tucker and reckoned I should get into it, but firstly Kathy Dolan was serving out there, and secondly I was flat out collecting the empties and drinking the odd full one.

And of course I was having a yarn to this and that person as I scooted around. At one stage, I remember, fairly early on, I picked up from the table where Mum and Mrs Robbo and Mrs Bail were sitting, and Mrs Bail said: 'Oh, you finished the sweater, Colleen, it *is* nice I must say.'

Mum was on her feet then, fiddling at how the jumper fitted on my corners and saying: 'You're sure the blue's OK?'

'It's come out a treat,' said Mrs Robbo. 'You know, you should do it professional-like, I reckon, open up one of them little craftie shops, like what I'd like to do with my sewing.'

Mum looked dreamy, but she said, 'Yeah, but who'd buy a jumper like this, in Cornwall?'

A voice behind me cut in, real earnest: 'I would, Mrs Ferris.'

I swung around and saw Wee Willie Wilkinson. He's a bit of a joke as a copper, a short, plump, baby-faced bloke with fair wispy hair, but you couldn't help liking him. (The dobber!)

Mum looked a bit amused. 'Would you, Willie?'

'I would too, Mrs Ferris, honest I would.' Now he too was poking at the pattern. 'I like this bit, see, where it almost looks like little reindeers. I had a jumper like this when I was a kid . . .'

'Well, if you're that keen, Willie, I'll make you one.'

'Would you, Mrs Ferris? I'd be happy to pay, you know.'

'Just give me the price of the wool. Lord knows, I'm always looking for someone to knit for.'

I got away then. Mum was already measuring him up with her eye, and getting into the knitty-gritty, so to speak, of whether a brown background would suit him best or navy blue like mine . . .

I may have mentioned that the Dolans hadn't had the pub for long. This was their first Saint Patrick's Day there, which was why none of us had known what to expect. Anyway, I suppose we were all thinking the streamers and free piss and food were pretty OK, when blow me down if at maybe half-past eight or so there wasn't a blast of noise like a strangled cat, and into the pub walked a little old guy in a suit with a green vest, tuning up a fiddle. Behind him were two more little old men who could have been his twins, and one of them had a piano accordion and the other had a banjo and a bodhran. They turned out to be a group called The Reelers, that old Dom had hired from the next big town past Morlong. It also turned out that even his family hadn't known about this bit of the celebration. I saw Kathy stare, and heard Mrs D say to her mum: 'God almighty! We'll be paying for this till next St Pat's Day.'

Well if the party didn't start then! I've said that normally my mum was the only Irish person in Cornwall apart from the Dolans, and of course they were actually born in Australia too, but if the Martians came and staged a spree in Cornwall then I reckon everyone in town would suddenly remember a great-grandad or something that had had antennas.

The Reelers played, and the tables were pushed back against the walls, and to give you an idea of things I'll say that I even saw the old man doing a kind of a jig with Mum. Then after a good long bit old Dom called for quiet, and made a speech welcoming everyone and thanking everyone for being such good customers and making him and his family feel at home here in Cornwall.

'In fact,' he said, 'I've never been one for stopping in the one place for long . . .'

'That's for sure,' I heard Mrs D mutter.

'But I'll say now that I like it so much here, that I've decided that Cornwall will do me for good.'

'Pull the other leg, Dad,' Kathy yelled out.

Dom turned to her and grinned. 'You save your whistle, girlie. You'll be needing all the breath you've got. Because I'd now like to announce that the Reelers will play a few jigs, and they will be accompanied by a performance of traditional dancing, done by none other than your smiling barmaid, Kathy Dolan!'

Kathy went white. 'Dad!'

But Dom wasn't having any of it. 'Come on, girlie, I didn't pay out all that money on dancing classes for you, just to keep your figure trim.' He turned proudly to the drinkers. 'She's won prizes for it, you know. She's a real treat to watch, my girlie here.'

Kathy was heading for the residential stairs but the Reelers were already getting into the tune and the old blokes were all yelling 'Come on, Kathy-love, show us your stuff!' and the women were shouting 'Don't be shy love!' and Dom literally grabbed her around the waist and lifted her into the empty bit of floor, and Kathy gave in.

I suppose it was good, if you go for that sort of thing. Very tricky, and real fast.

Scott and us stood in the corner with Jan Henderson and laughed, but everyone else was clapping along or banging the tables in time with the beat, and Kathy really did keep it up, I'll say that for her. After the first tune, the band went straight into another, and then another, and by the third there was sweat pouring off the lot of them.

In the end both she and the band collapsed in puddles, Dom called for me to turn on the juke-box, Kathy raced upstairs, the Reelers had a drink, Scott danced with Jan, then Danny danced with Jan, then Terry danced with Jan, then Sean, then me. That might give you some idea of how Jan Henderson was the only girl in town who wasn't engaged or married to someone, apart from Helen Tayler and Monica

Ward (who of course weren't there), and Kathy Dolan, who you wouldn't dance with anyway. And besides, now she was dancing with that Garry bloke. (She'd changed into jeans and a T-shirt. It was so hot I got down to my sweat-shirt, and tied my Fair Isle round my waist.)

'Bloody poof,' Scott muttered, and pushed me hard into Garry. I didn't mind. Seeing him and Kathy together brought back how they'd helicoptered into Jade and me being at the palace.

'Watch it!' Kathy muttered at Scott. (She hates him, for some reason.) Garry grinned at me, as if to say: 'Sorry for interrupting your fuck, sport.'

I danced close to Jan, I don't know why, maybe to kind of say: 'Well anyway, I've got something else going tonight.' Meaning them to think Jan, but in my head thinking *Jade Jade Jade.* I looked at the clock, 10.30, the pub would have to close in a while and I'd be able to get out. Time was going slow, but somehow too I didn't completely mind the delay. I felt at home, here with my mates, not how I felt with the greenies. I looked at Jan, heard her Cornwall voice singing along to 'Jailhouse Rock' (more ESP, eh?) and I remember thinking: 'You're having yourself on, Col, to think a posh bitch like Jade would have you as her bloke. Jan's more your style. I suppose it'll be my turn to be her boyfriend soon, now that Terry and Danny have finished with her and Scottie's getting sick of her. Only Sean to go.'

And maybe too, about the delay, maybe I was scared about what I'd do, when I got out to the forest and Jade. I'd never done it, and I was scared I'd do something stupid.

Then Squirt cut in on me to show how democratic he is, dancing with the town slut, and Dom called for me to run around after the glasses, the Reelers came back on, I had another beer . . .

Maybe I should say here that I think I was pretty pissed by then. I hadn't eaten anything all day, and I can remember the pub floor seeming a bit wonky and voices seeming real loud in my ear one minute, and all drifty the next. Faces swum in and out too.

Then all of a sudden, Dom was yelling, 'Time's up, sorry, ladies and gents!' It was half-past eleven, and normally when the pub shuts Dom lets the hard core stay on as long as they like, old Golden Gloves doesn't mind, he's there himself half the time, bludging the odd one. But this night (Dom whispered to me) they had to put on a bit of a show for the city inspector.

'Come on!' Dom yelled. 'It's a working day tomorrow.'

Snarls and yells. 'If the greenies fucking let us!' And so on. Suddenly the happiness turned to anger, and then the anger kind of focussed on the coppers, and blokes were muttering how all these out-of-town bastards should just piss off back to the city and let the locals get rid of the greenies.

'Hop out to the bottle-oh, would you Col,' Mrs Dolan said, 'and see if there's anyone wants takeaways.'

The bottle shop is at the other end of the pub, past the residential entrance, so I missed seeing the blue that broke out between some of us, led by Big Jim Waters and Mr Robbo, and half a dozen city cops. Of course, Scott was right in it, defending his old man, and Terry and Danny, sticking up for Scottie. Sean was out with me, buying a few cold ones.

I just realised I said 'us' there. 'Some of us.'

A funny thing about writing seems to be, when I go into the tale, I seem to go back into the bit of Colum that was there when the thing I'm writing about happened.

So when I was telling you about Saturday and being with Jade, I was in the greenie bit of me, and now when I'm talking about that Sunday night I'm getting more and more into normal old Col, one of the boys.

Sometimes I even feel that Colum's not real at all. He's just a made-up character, as untrue as the idle prince, say, in that fairytale poem.

But maybe I just like to pretend that, because I don't like to face up to what he did that night. I don't like to think he was me.

Quit stalling, and get on with it.

(This is it.)

▷ ▷ ▷ ————————————

Maybe it was the football that started it, then the talk on the bus, then the booze. Or maybe it was the fuming that had been building up and up in me since the Thursday night, when I'd gone home and had my first row with the old man. Maybe that anger got muddled up with the feeling I had when Kathy and the Garry bloke landed into my palace. And maybe that feeling, of having something stolen from me, was caught up with the feeling that the greenies had come to steal my hope of a job and my friendships and my whole way of life. And maybe it was all something to do with how I'd felt when I'd looked into the rabbit's head, and seen the tunnel, no way out, like I was inside the barrel of a gun.

I don't know.

But I do know that by closing-time on Sunday I was tight as a fist with the pressure of it all. I was also dead-set, one of the boys.

I could hear a bit of the rumpus as I served Sean. *'Bastards!'* I said, meaning anyone who wasn't one of us. I served a couple of other people, while Sean had his head out the door and gave me a running commentary on who was flying in and out of the main door . . .

'Scottie . . . his old man . . . now there's a cop, that big fat one . . . It's OK, Scottie's on top . . .'

I would've been down and into it myself, if I hadn't had to mind the till.

Then a voice said: 'Excuse me will you, boyo?' and a large dark shape pushed in the door past Sean and it was Brian, three-quarters pissed already by the look of him, and asking for a bottle of Jameson and two packets of Blue Winfield.

I served him with my head down, thought he might be too pissed to recognise me, but as I rung up the till, he said: 'And a happy Saint Patrick's Day to you, me golden boyo.'

Scott and Danny and Terry were pushing in now, looking a bit wrecked and yelling at Sean to fucking get a move on, and I remember Sean taking in me and Brian and looking at me funnily.

I thrust Brian's change at him. Luckily then Mrs D appeared through the back door and said I could knock off now, and the sooner I got my drunken mates off her premises the better. Brian reeled back past Scott and them as I grabbed a bottle of the fifteen-dollar-special Scotch instead of my wages, and then I was out in the night.

Scott was watching as Brian squashed into a Vee-Double-You and wrestled with his seatbelt. Scott seemed to have gone real cool all of a sudden, his eyes narrow, thinking slits.

'That's that fucking greenie I saw on TV,' he said softly. 'He was out the camp the other day.'

I heard Golden Gloves yelling: 'Go on you kids, I've saved you once already tonight from a kip in the cells, get on home . . .'

'Come on!' Scott yelled at us, and led the way round the corner to his place, where we all jumped into the Jet.

Saved by the bell!

Well not quite, but at least a couple of things happened when I got to that point, to put off this bit I don't want to get to. (But don't worry, I really am heading towards the end. In my story now it's nearly midnight of Saint Patrick's night, Sunday, 17 March, and by about half-past nine on the Monday morning it'll all be over.)

But when I wrote that last bit it was about 5.30, Thursday, 28 March. I could see the old black lady leaving Nick, and I gave them both a wave. Then Baby Nurse came up to me with a phone message from the Lawyer scrawled on a bit of paper. It said:

'Where the hell's your statement?'

The shop trolley came, and I blew the last of Sally's dough on a packet of Drum, two packets of papers, matches, a couple of Mars Bars. (No sign still of this emergency cheque. I don't want it, but still, it'd make me feel a bit more comfortable.)

I wheeled out to the verandah that runs along the window-side of the ward. (I'm over that side too now, now that I don't need it so much.)

Rolled a Drum and watched the city. It's a still night here, not cold. The sunset was different from home, it sort of hung in this heavy yellow-mauve-grey sky that pressed down on me like the top of a sandwich. I was in the middle, and the bottom slice was all these roads with cars whizzing crazy like Mum's ants. I felt squashed, and I know I couldn't ever live here. Got depressed again, thinking how I can't go home.

Then tea. It was these weird pale-pink sausages, that had been split down the middle and the gap filled with something squiggly and white and soft. (Sort of made your imagination go to extremes.) Then stewed something and custard.

I can see the seven o'clock ABC News is on the set down the

other end of the ward now, but the News is usually too political for me so I'm writing this and listening to Midnight Oil and eating Mars Bars.

The weather's on! I'll wheel down and catch it. See you later!

▷ ▷ ▷ ———————————————

Shit, shit, fucking shit!

But that doesn't say it either.

So fumed up I can hardly write, but writing this might at least be a way to get it out of me. I can't even talk to Nick about it, I'd have to explain so much of what's gone before that he wouldn't understand. (Plus the great-grandson and co. are streaming in all around him.)

To cut it short, after the weather (still pouring at home, not that it matters now anyway) *This is Australia* came on. I wasn't going to watch it, but that lady introducer that wears bow-ties said: 'Blah blah blah . . . Cornwall . . .'

Then the scene changed to Kathy Dolan and that Garry bloke picking a couple of apples.

There was a man's voice now, talking over the picture, saying stuff like: 'An exciting discovery was made recently in the Cornwall area by Garry Lazlo, of the Department of Conservation, Forests and Tourism, and a young local girl, Katherine Dolan, with the help of our ABC News Cruiser team.'

Close-up of Kathy Dolan's face, eating an apple.

'Katherine, who is researching the local history of the area, heard a rumour of an old timber-milling settlement buried somewhere in the heart of the forest, a place where no one had set foot for well over a century.'

Close-up of the Garry bloke, eating an apple.

'She alerted Garry, who in turn recruited the aid of our News Cruiser helicopter to search for the forgotten place.'

Aerial shot of treetops, then the Settlement.

'After a low-level reconnaissance of the forest, we suddenly saw a clearing at the junction of two creeks, and what appeared to be some buildings.

'Once on the ground, however, the discovery turned out to be far greater than Katherine and Garry's wildest dreams.'

Picture of Garry and Kathy running to the door of the palace, then Garry barging straight in. Full picture of the palace, the verandahs, with Kathy kind of hanging about.

'One of the buildings, constructed of packed mud and mountainash timber, is still much as it would have been in the middle of the last century.'

Picture of Kathy and Garry inside in the great room, running around the table, squeaking.

'Inside too, things are still just as they would have been before this settlement came to an end. Katherine explains what she knows of the history . . .'

Close-up, Kathy sitting in the fireplace, saying something like: 'Evidently there was this big landslide, one winter, and they couldn't get the logs out any more and so they all had to just pack up and move to Cornwall. It's really sad, really.'

As the camera kind of lingered on the scene, I thought of that feeling I'd had, when Jade had sat in the fireplace, and I'd felt there was something wrong inside the picture that she made. And I knew that somehow I must've been having one of the ESP things, or whatever they are, because the Kathy picture now was right. But wrong, *wrong*, WRONG! She'd no right to be there.

The reporter carried on: 'But though the people of this place moved away, there is still a ghostly sense that they inhabit it. Water still runs clear and refreshing from what appears to be the kitchen tap . . .'

Picture of Kathy in the scullery, drinking from her hand. (I think of Jade, and how she'd done that too. The whole thing was as if Jade had just been some kind of play rehearsal for Kathy.)

Picture of Kathy outside, sniffing at the pineapple sage.

'. . . And the herbs that grow wild all over this fairytale wilderness, pay tribute to the unknown women who must have planted them . . .'

('Ha, ha you gig,' I thought, because of course it was Sam. No woman was there until the Lady. And she was the only one, ever.)

Picture of Kathy and Garry poking at some of the old sheds and that.

'The tumble-down ruins of hen-houses and pigsties, cow bails and yards, bear witness to the thriving community which must have once flourished here . . .'

Picture of Kathy and Garry gasping at the great beams of the fallen-down mill.

'And at last our two explorers came to the reason for the

existence of this pioneering settlement, the ruins of the mill where the men milled the mighty trees that in those far-off days stretched for thousands of hectares all over this area.'

'It is a somewhat different story today. In the decades that have passed since this first mill was founded, more and more of the virgin forest has been cut down. Today, a view from the air shows the inroads that man's depradations have made.'

Aerial picture moving over the forest. Seeing the scars through the green, scar upon scar, the tracks and the mess left from the last few years' logging, and the piddley scrub in the places that are meant to be regenerating, then the few areas where the blokes haven't got to yet, like a sort of curtain round the palace, but a curtain that could be ripped apart as easily as my death curtains when the Night Sister comes, well, I feel sick even writing down.

'Now, only a small proportion of this mighty hardwood forest remains. It is because of this, of course, that conservationists have recently been active in the area, risking arrest in order to highlight their demand that logging here must cease immediately.'

Picture of the Friday's demo, with Jade and Sharnda and Suzie and Mike Marchant and Dave being picked up by cops and carried over the creek, singing 'We Shall Not Be Moved'.

Then picture of (oh shit, stop it stop it!) *'One young activist was even prepared to risk his life . . .'*

The bulldozer swinging into the tree that is me. Stop it.

Go on.

After that, it was almost good to see Kathy and Garry, back on the verandah.

'The scene here at the old milling settlement, however, seems far removed from such political rough-and-tumble. Yet could this discovery help save the forest? I put this question to Garry Lazlo, from the Department of Conservation, Forests and Tourism.'

Close-up of Garry, looking (as my mum says) like the cat that's swallowed the cream. He told the camera: 'I'm speaking quite off my own bat, because of course the Minister doesn't even know about this yet, but I reckon this place just has to be at least put in the care of the National Trust. It's clearly part of Australia's heritage, of the world's heritage, if you like. In Australia, we don't have Stonehenge or the Parthenon. We do have great Aboriginal sites, going back sixty thousand years or so, but as far as white people are concerned all we have is somewhere like this. It's like a living museum – much better than those fake olden-days villages at Ballarat and Old Sydney Town. I reckon, speaking personally of course, that this place must be saved, and the forest around it. And the way to do it is through tourism.'

Picture of inside the big room of the palace again. The bloke's voice went on.

'Looking around this place forgotten by man and time, it is indeed like a living museum. This building where Garry and Katherine sit is in such good repair that one almost feels that the ghosts of the old settlers must still flit around here, replacing the odd post and shingle.

'The whole place makes you feel as if it was only a moment ago that the inhabitants packed their goods and chattels, and moved out.'

The picture moved through the door, into the sleeping quarters.

'At the back, there are two long rooms which clearly functioned as dormitories.'

Picture of front of the palace again, with Kathy on the verandah.

'So what is this building, with its great accommodation areas, its vast hall? The answer wasn't too hard to find.'

Picture of Kathy picking a rose.

'When Katherine went to pick one of the climbing roses that trail up these old verandah posts, she revealed a sign – half broken, it is true, but a sign that leaves no doubt about the building's function.'

Picture of the sign with Kathy pointing excitedly at it.

In case you couldn't read, the bloke explained: 'Yes, the sign says "The Palace".'

Close-up of Kathy, almost stammering: 'The Palace . . . Hotel. It must've been The Palace Hotel!'

Wider picture again. Bloke's voice: 'Yes, this building was clearly that most vital of Australian institutions – the local hotel. And, one might ask, what more fitting memorial to our ancestors could we have, than a humble pub . . .?'

Picture of inside the vast hall again, making the table and the benches look lonely somehow.

And over this Slim Dusty singing 'The Pub With No Beer'.

▷ ▷ ▷ ————————————

Of course, I had to make the reporter's words up – I don't pretend I remember everything exactly, though I do seem to pick up songs the first time I hear them – but that's how it went.

Sitting here now, after writing it, I don't feel any better.

That stuff about the pub at the end, I could almost have stomached it if it wasn't for that. (That, and the me-tree picture.)

If I say this, you'll think me a complete dunce, but what the shit?

You see, I never knew till then what my palace had been.

Maybe because I knew it as a palace from Grandad's stories, that's what it kind of stayed for me, even after I didn't any longer really believe in the prince and that. I simply never asked myself what it really was. It was just where old Sam's blokes lived, and where they ate and drank the food and scrumpy he made for them. I never saw him as running a pub, and charging them money. I guess I sort of saw him as a prince of hospitality, turning on the works like a lord. But now he's just a money-grubbing

▷ ▷ ▷ ——————————————

Got interrupted there by the Night Sister running up saying: 'Phone for you, Colin, at my desk, hurry, long distance, strictly speaking it's too late for calls, but just this once.'

I thought it must be Mum again. ('What's up?' I panicked. 'Has Grandad died?') I hoisted myself out, wheeled down to the desk, picked up the phone.

'Hi? Mum?'

Silence. Then, 'It's me,' said Kathy Dolan's voice.

Silence.

'I suppose you saw. I didn't mean it. I didn't know they. I . . . sorry.'

I hung up.

As I sat there, feeling all the fuming coming back, the phone rang again. I picked it up, knowing it'd be her, knowing this time what I'd say.

The long-distance pips, sound of coins falling.

'Get fucked!' I said.

'Col?' said a voice as if it wasn't expecting to be me.

I hung up. Then I knew it'd been the old man.

Sitting now, wondering what he would've said, what I

would've said, what he would've said next. If I hadn't have thought it was Kathy Dolan. If I had've known it was him. What would I have said?

Sitting now, I can't stand this, not even a good joke, Colum.

Ten-thirty now, the big lights are off but I can see that Nick's asleep down near my old bed. I could do with a shot of aeroplane fuel.

Nothing for it but to go out to the verandah and have a smoke.

▷ ▷ ▷ ————————————

Sitting stoned on Scottie's dope, I fight the night but cannot.

Stop it.

Now.

Start.

The flight through the fog-trees. (I meant to write 'fight' there.)

Later there was flying. Through the air but downwards. You know how when you're sleeping sometimes, and your stomach lifts and drops you? Well, it was like that.

But before the flying, there was the fight.

After we followed Brian through forest.

(That's right Col, start at the beginning and work through to the end.)

But before that. Begin back at Scott's. We all jumped into the Jet. No we didn't. Sean didn't. I remember now. He went home. But Scott, Terry, Danny, me. Then Brian's Vee-Double-You was heading down the Farm Road, Terry rolling a smoke, Scott cruising along slowly letting Brian get well ahead, no need to chase like a movie, know where he's heading. I can see our headlights peering out into the fog like wobbly eyes. Nothing to see. But we know what's there. Here in the Jet there's fog in my head, not green, but white, grey, pass around the Scotch, the smoke, with my mates I am, that's me, but maybe soon I'll go and see Jade, be a different Colum.

(Who?)

(Where?)

Then there. Parked our car near Brian's, outside the padlocked chain. Set off up the track after him. I could hear him, moving like a woundy bullock. But I was quiet, knew how to walk.

The fog was thick as smoke. Something, anyway. You (we) couldn't see two metres in front of us. I was in front. We didn't want to lose each other, so we held hands. Sort of a string of us, like those girls' paper dolls. Dark and thin inside the whiteness. We could've been blackfellers, I thought, hunting an enemy. Someone had sung us wrong, he'd put a curse on our jobs, and so we were after him to kill him, because his blood would take the pain away.

(But why were we following him? No one had said. Just were. Like a dare. Scare. Like you play hidings as a kid. Or Murder In The Dark. Stop.)

He started to sing, the old witch-doctor. A song of his people.

> *'A hungry feeling came o'er me stealing,*
> *And the seagulls were wheeling o'er the prison wall . . .'*

His voice came at me through the fog, but I couldn't catch him. And it was my job, I was at the front. I knew the forest.

It was my place.

Palace/place. I've never seen that before. How it connects. Does it?

Off on another web.

Did you ever see that Jap film called *Macbeth*? Squirt showed it to us because Macbeth is written by one of the guys on our classroom wall (though none of them looks Asian, but still). I went because he said the same film guy made *The Magnificent Seven*, so I went, but it was nothing like that.

Still, it wasn't bad but. At the beginning (I only stayed for the beginning, then I walked out) this big Jap called Macbeth is the prince see. He wears black leather, and he gets lost in this fog, and so lost he loses his mates, and scared, and that. It's his own forest, but for the first time he doesn't know where he is in it, and he's off the track, and that frightens him.

Because things get worse, because he's holding hands with his mates, and Scott lets go, or he lets go of Scott, or something, and suddenly he's by himself again, like he used to be when he was a little kid and no one would play with him. Scott used to bang the suitcase like an enemy, pounding all around. Singing to mock him.

So he wanders in the fog-trees, a prince without a tribe.

Now it's cobwebs that he fights through, running panting

from tree to tree he tries to cut the webs with his silver knife, but it's white and sticky, this land, doesn't want him.

Now there's a witch, Macbeth bumps into her, coming round the corner of a tree, and she's saying something Japanese that means she's putting a curse that Macbeth will lose his land, and then he won't be a prince any more.

I walked out after that, so I can't tell you what happened. But Kathy said (that was in the time I went with Kathy) the trees all got up at the end and bulldozed the baddies down. Whoever the baddies were. *The Magnificant Seven* was a good Western, but.

Don't know what any of that's got to do with all this. But still.

Try again, Col. Run it fast down from the middle.

. . . See, it was the singing and the footsteps all around me, I could hear him going *'Jingle jangle'* and sometimes bits of yells from Scott and them. Did I say we were off the track by now of course? The trees bumping into me, the dead rotty smell where I fell, like it's scarey as a kid when you played hide and seek, have you ever felt something coming to get you?

So then I ran round a corner and as I did the other way there bumped this piece of darkness right into me I screamed into another scream that is coming from the black thing that I am hitting hitting at its face to stop it yelling coming at me we're rolling on the smell of rot oh Dad someone save me.

Now it's OK all right here's my mates I roll away and I lie and see some feet kicking at the struggling shape and there's blood on his face and I don't like that so I run and run and run and run like Mum used to play with me about this little piggy that went wee wee wee wee all the way home.

But when I got there, the piggy wasn't. No Max-Max-scratch-scratch, all gone. Oh God.

▷ ▷ ▷ ———————————

Friday morning early. The Night Sister reckons she found me leaning over the balcony. I think she thinks I was going to jump. Was I? I remember writing out there, and then the falling falling, not asleep but wanting the falling to start to stop it. I don't want to read what I said. She made me have a sleeping tablet.

'I don't take . . .' I said.

She sniffed the air and looked.

I shut up.

Then slept a bit I suppose but now I can't.

She's just brought me a cup of tea.

I've decided. I'll just write that thing for the lawyer, and then I'll put all this writing away for good.

Good.

Just noticed on the calendar in my homework diary. It's Good Friday. So what's so good?

MY STATEMENT

On the night of Sunday, 17 March, I picked up glasses at the hotel till closing time.

Then I went down the recreation reserve by myself (alone) and got drunk.

I realised I'd lost my new Fair Isle jumper, or maybe someone stole it.

A bit after dawn I went for a walk into the forest to clear my head.

I ended up at the greenies' camp.

I climbed up a tree, just for fun (or maybe I was drunk still).

I went to sleep up there, and the next thing I knew the tree came down and I had broken legs and I was arrested.

That is the truth.

Yours sincerely,

Samuel Colum Ferris

I've never had heroin, but if it's anything like writing, I don't ever want to. An hour ago I'd given this up, and now here I am, back on it again.

Hi!

Why?

Cause it gives me a Hi!

Another bad one, Col. (I can see you going: 'Path-*et*-ic!')

Seriously though, it does make me feel good. No, but better. More better-er, anyway. A little. It's a bit like having a spew, when you're crook. Or Grandad, coughing up the phlegm in the mornings. Horrible for other people, maybe, but nice for you. (That's me.)

Plus deep-down I think I have this superstitious feeling that when I get to the end of this tale, something's going to happen. Like it might all turn out to be a bad dream, and I'll wake up, safe in my little sleep-out, or maybe in Sam's cottage.

This morning I've got this real sense of *hurry, hurry,* like I've got to get it done today.

(Yeah? So why don't you get on with it?)

▷ ▷ ▷ ————————————

Running home after Brian, it was a long way, but didn't seem like it.

I came in the back gate. In my head there was this thought about how I'd get twenty cents from the coin jar on the fridge. (I still only had my ten cents on me. Funny to think that if I hadn't have bought that Chiko Roll, Brian mightn't be dying, and I wouldn't be maybe up for Manslaughter.) Anyway, I was going to go up the phone booth, ring up the cop shop like one of those anonymous bombers, and say there was a wounded man in the forest, go get him. (I reckoned Scott and them would've had time to get away by now.)

But in the yard, I felt an emptiness. Max didn't snuffle and grunt from his night-pen. I went and checked: no pig.

I pelted into the sleep-out, then slammed through the kitchen screen-door, yelling, 'Mum, Mum, Maxie's gone!'

I guess if I'd have been thinking, I wouldn't have expected her to be up, but she was, sitting staring into the fire-box of the stove.

'Yes, Col,' she said. 'I wondered when you'd realise.' I remembered her watching me, since the night before.

Then, like the night before too, the old man burst out of the bedroom, but this time he had his pants on, and I knew he also had been waiting.

A picture came into my head of Scott coming in from the beer garden with his plate. A spit turned inside me. 'You killed him!' I yelled.

The old man shrugged. Looking back, and trying to give him the benefit of the doubt, I suppose he might have looked as if he wished he hadn't. But all he said was, 'He was fully grown.'

Then Max was me, or I was Max.

'You don't just *kill* someone,' I said, 'because they've *grown up*!'

'Colum . . .' Mum murmured.

'Don't you yell at me!' the old man yelled. 'I've had just about of you lately! Coming in at all hours, treating your home like a boarding house!'

'Home!'

'Dear . . .' Mum said, though which dear she meant wasn't clear.

'If that's your attitude, you can . . .'

'Don't worry, I'll get out before you can kill me too!'

(More E.S.P., eh? Maybe.)

I slammed back towards the screen-door, but he was right behind me, we both kind of fell through together, and then us both swinging, fighting, like I'd never done since that day with Scott. I remember the small space, no room to fight between the bed and cardtable, and then he lifted me one and I was up in the air, shooting through the fibro with a crack.

Landing on my bum in the yard, I saw this shape shaped like me in my wall.

Grandad's voice was somewhere, Mum's too, behind a picture of the old man framed in fibro.

'Col . . .' said someone, but Col was on his bike, screaming back into the fogtrees.

▷ ▷ ▷ ————————————

Break it there a minute.

Break it there.

Max.

▷ ▷ ▷ ————————————

10 a.m. The mail's just come. A big parcel from Mum, with a fruit cake in a tin and my bank book and an Easter card. (Not like you might imagine, with a bunny on it or something, saying 'Have a Happy . . .', but a Catholic one, with Jesus dying on the cross and blood-tears that cling to his face like the dark red sap that makes crystals down the bark of a mountain ash in springtime. It's got that same text, that's on the kitchen wall, about Him Dying to Save Us All. On the back in tiny printing there's a kind of sermon, about how we should follow in His

footsteps and make our own lives a living sacrifice. Maybe you see now where I get some of my weird ideas from.) Still, inside it mum had put a normal letter.'

Dear Col,
I couldn't stand the ants any more with their circles all the time reminding me of how bad this winter's going to be, with your Dad as restless, so decided to irradicate them and look what I found down beside the stove! Thought it might come in handy, though there's nothing in it. Would you like me to send you a postal order? I should of thought of it before. Hope the cake's OK and not a bit dry in the middle. The oven seems faster now I've cleaned. Though now I sometimes think I miss my ants. Silly, isn't it? Dear, I do know how you feel about Max. But please don't hold it against your father. I know, when I came to live in the country, I found it hard the way animals are raised up and then killed, but really, you must of known all along it would happen sometime. After all, a fully grown boar isn't a pet like a cat, is it? Can you remember, when you were little, bringing home a kitty you'd found in the forest? And we (Dad, really) wouldn't let you keep it? Didn't want any useless animal, he said, but see that's his country way. Animals have to give you something, in his book, like eggs and bacon. I'm sorry. Maybe, if you'd of had a cat, you wouldn't of put so much into poor old Maxie. Still. Bygones are bygones.

Kathy was round yesterday, just a visit, no history or anything. She said to say hello. Sean's taken on your Sunday nights at the pub. Grandad is missing you very much, I think, as are we all of course. He's quite over the hills and far away at the moment, rambled on to me last night all about some prince and how he had to abbdicate or whatever the word is and give up his palace, took me a while to work out he'd been watching that Edward (is it?) and Mrs Simpson show they've been re-running on the ABC. (When will they put on some nice new programmes?) That nice Mr Lazlo came too with Kathy and talked to Dad and Grandad, I don't know what about, by that stage I was teaching Kathy to cast on. Such good manners he has, but then those people do, don't they? I think Kathy's a bit keen on him, poor kid. I know they do sometimes get married, but they wouldn't ever be able to have children or anything would they? Anyway, he's too old for her. I'm knitting him a pullover, after the one for Wee Willie. (He's decided on brown. Mr Lazlo's having green. He insists I call him Garry.) Nice to have something to do anyway, to get my mind off of things.

Rain's eased up a bit today, not that it matters now, the track's too bad for the men to get in there. Oh well, that's all that comes to mind. Would you like some bedsocks, or anything? Hope the cake comes in handy. Dad and Grandad and I send our love,
love,
Mum

The other thing in the mail was the cheque from the Emergency Fund, sixty bucks for two weeks, with a note from Sally.

Dear Colin,
Here it is at last! You'll need a bank book to cash it, so if you haven't found it yet you'll have to open a new account. There's a Commonwealth across the road from the hospital (just down from the hotel). They tell me you're mobile now! Hope that's cheered you up!

More good news! I've managed to reserve you a place at the Church of England Young Men's Hostel, for when you come out. You're very lucky, it's only two to a room and breakfast provided. (No dinner, but there are plenty of restaurants nearby.) Nice and handy to the hospital, and a nice crowd of kids there. Quite a few are students, as the uni's so close, and I know you'll soon find your feet (so to speak!) and make friends.

Anyway, hope this has all cheered you up. (Things are never so bad as they seem, are they?) I'll drop in and see you son.
Best wishes,
Sally Browning
P.S. Just checked your file and noticed you're down as Roman Catholic. Does that matter? About the C of E, I mean? The evening prayer meetings are optional (and anyway, we all have the same God, don't we?) Afraid St Vincent de Paul is booked out. So many Catholics!

I had some cake and took a wedge down to Nick but he had

his eyes shut and his fists clenched again to fight the fascist, so I just left it on his table and came back.

I'll get a bit more done, then off to the bank.

▷ ▷ ▷ ————————————

Where am I?

Yeah . . . I rode back up the Farm Road, then up the bank onto the old palace track, along that till I was about on a line from the clearing, then left the bike and crisscrossed down by foot into the greenies' camp.

You probably don't believe this, but I'd forgotten about Brian. I mean, something in me must've known, because I avoided the new track, but in my head there was just this whole red-blackness that was everything, and nothing. Brian, Max, the old man, that was what I was running from, and I was the rabbit heading down the tunnel, down and down into greater darkness, and something in me kept crying *Jade Jade*, like when I was a little kid and I used to run from Scott, but in me then it would be *Mum Mum*. And I'd get home and she'd hold me, and make them go. Over the hills and far away.

Will you believe this too?

I don't know.

I find it pretty far-fetched myself, but in this running to Jade, I wasn't thinking of a fuck. It was just her liking it, at the palace, and the fact that I'd taken her there, the first person. I'd never even done that when I was going with Kathy Dolan, those couple of months. Way back. But her lying next to me, like a friend. That was why I ran to Jade, yelling as I came into the clearing: *'Jade, Jade!'*

Kicking over billies, clattering like Brian had, right up to the little red tent I ran, yelling: 'JADE!'

But the tent was empty as Maxie's pen, and it all closed in on me (I should be stoned to write this bit too, because the world was coming in at me like it can get when you're out of it. But I wasn't out of it but in it, in the clearing as Jade stepped hauling a black jumper down her naked skin as she stepped out of another tent and Mike Marchant behind her.

So I went up the tree. That was me.

▷ ▷ ▷ ————————————

In the dreams
something screams
leaves from a frightened forest gleam

(My poem for today).

12.00 midday, Friday, 29 March. Time is getting like a clock. If it'd wind down, it might stop.

Sitting in my wheelchair with my folder and a cappuchino and a lamington and two dim sims at this cafeteria-papershop place that's part of the hospital, across the road from the bank. Just posted the statement to the lawyer and cashed my cheque. The most money I've ever had all at once. That, and being out in the world for the first time, makes me feel like a prince. Maybe. Who knows how princes feel? But every time I read this poem Kathy sent me, I think I understand it more. I'll tell you my latest bit:

The hours in the hourglass
are stilled to fine fear, and the wood
to empty burning. Tom the hind
walks in his sleep in pools of blood.

Sometimes I feel like a little kid, who's only got one toy to play with, so he makes it be everything. That's how this poem is to me. It's funny how it always fits.

Easier somehow to cross the road to the pub and write outside the white beach. Feel a gig in my pyjamas and dressing-gown, but who cares? I don't know anyone in this city (this world).

Now.

I'm up the pole. No I'm not, really. It's the old man that's that. But that's what he'd say. Or something worse. Last night (was it?) when he slammed me through the sleep-out wall he called me every name under the sun.

(Sun: hey come and warm me. It's cold up here! Where's my new jumper?)

'You're no son of mine,' he yelled.

As if that would make me cry. *'Sticks and stones can break my bones but names can never hurt me.'* Mum taught me that when I was little, when I ran back to her. When Scott and them called me things. And Mum was wrong. Names do hurt. The one she gave me, that wasn't nice. When everybody else is called Scott and Sean and Danny and Terry, to have a name like mine. I'm Colum.

Not really, really I'm Sam. But it's like I wasn't good enough, to have that name. So I'm Colum.

It sort of fits better, now I'm up here. Like a tree. No, I'm not a tree, I'm me.

A tree's what I'm up. Way over the top, living out on a limb, where I've been for I think a long time now. (When was the beginning?)

It's swayey up here, and green, I've got to hold me on when I fall asleep, or sometimes when I think I'm awake and my mind wanders round, I need some ropes then too.

Since I went through the hole in the wall, my head's let the sway in.

I can see the rest of them getting up, like something on television, crawling out of the tents, Mike listening to the radio, Dave fanning up the fire, Sharnda putting the billies on, and Jade's looking up at me, her hand over her eyes to shut the sun out.

That's what the old man said. 'No son of mine.' And shut me out.

As if I'd want to be.

I never did.

Jade's yelling something to me now, but I can't hear.

I don't want to, that's why I came up here.

(Where?)

(Why?)

Just to run.

When you've got to the bottom of the tunnel, up's the only way to go.

Scrabbling.

Scribbling.

Probably.

Time goes so strange up here, all green and black and

dappled, sometimes sways around my head.

I need ropes, to try to tie down what's been happening.

Go up to the bar to get another beer for old time's sake as you might say (or maybe you mightn't) and the headlines of the afternoon paper are in the wire racks across the road, outside the cafe place.

PREMIER GIVES IN
SETTLEMENT TREES SAVED

I'll buy one in a minute. Just drink this drink. It all seems outside (inside) me.

So up the pole.

Go again Col.

Breaking fast like a tree, I've got to do it quick now.

Anyway, I'm here. This is me, see. Down on the ground, the greenies. Time goes, till enough has. Cops and blokes come. Not the city inspector in charge, but old Golden Gloves.

(I know now – who told me? – that the city inspector was off with Brian, who Wee Willie had heard moaning off the track, lying in a coma.)

(What's that, when it's at home?)

(What's home, when it shuts me out?)

No home, no sun, cold up here . . .

'No son of mine', the old man thought (I was in his head), swinging the dozer.

But before that.

Where am I?

Yes, Golden Gloves.

He's in charge this morning, see, so this time there's no 'Would you mind stepping this way please, Sir?' No carrying the greenies gentle.

Golden Gloves just yells across the creek: 'Yous bludgers had better move your arses if yous know what's good for you!'

The greenies sit down, link arms, start to sing.

'We shall not be moved . . .'

They are, but, quick smart, for Golden Gloves never gives the order to the cops, he just gives a slight nod (I can see it all from up here) to the old man who like me sits above the rest, and then I hear the thrum of the engine and the old man drives the dozer steadily, slowly across the creek.

Screaming now, the greenies scatter sideways, but Big Jim Waters leads the blokes in behind the dozer, they're catching greenies as they run. 'Link arms!' yells Mike Marchant, but the only arms linking are the arms of the blokes around the greenies as they catch and bash them, and on it comes, the noise that is my old man, pounding the earth like a woundy bullock, making the world seem to tremble even up here where the green sways me like a leaf.

Then I see Jade, she jumps out right into the coming of the dozer, yelling something I can't hear, Jade pointing high at me, the old man looking up suddenly and for a second it is like the moment with the rabbit and we can see into each other's brains.

Then he's down inside himself again, swinging the wheel, away from Jade, swinging swinging too hard too fast too much swinging moving dozing coming hard now fast no stopping now starting now *now!* And now the falling down the tree that is me, I hear a screaming in the dream.

That will not stop.

▷ ▷ ▷ ———————————

The Examiner
Friday 29 March

PREMIER GIVES IN SETTLEMENT TREES SAVED

In a press conference called this morning the Premier announced that the government intends to break its contract with Cornwall Milling Incorporated, the company which controls logging and milling in the Cornwall area.

'There shall be no more logging of the Settlement Creek forest,' he announced.

The Minister for Conservation, Forests and Tourism, Mr Cyril Buckley, who was present at the press conference, added that his department will be endorsing a proposal made by the Save The Trees Society that the Settlement Creek forest be declared part of the World Heritage. This would mean its preservation for all time.

The reason for the Premier's sudden announcement is clear.

Tomorrow the voters of the state seat of Hadley will go to the polls in the by-election caused by the retirement of the sitting Labor member, Ms Anne Greaves.

In recent weeks Mr Michael Marchant, leading conservationist activist and Independent Green candidate for Hadley has been urging his many supporters to lodge an informal protest vote unless the government saves the Settlement Creek forest – in which case, he has promised, he will direct his preferences to the Labor Party.

Most political observers believe that it will be the Green vote that decides the outcome of the Hadley by-election. If Labor lacks Mike Marchant's preferences, the Liberal Party will almost certainly win.

While this situation has been causing concern in Labor Party circles since the opening of the Hadley campaign, and especially with the growing popularity of Mr Marchant after the logger's brutal attack upon the greenies at the Settlement Creek site, the Labor Party's worry reached crisis point after the sudden death on Wednesday of the Labor member for the country seat of Ridgeway, Mr John (Jacka) James.

As the Labor Party is certain to lose Ridgeway in that forthcoming by-election, it became vital for it to retain Hadley.

If both seats were lost, the Labor Party would be out of power.

Today's sudden announcement by the Premier of a complete halt to logging at Settlement Creek is clearly a last-ditch stand to win the Green preferences, in the hope that this will save them the seat and thus the balance of power.

Only a few days ago, however, the Premier announced in reply to Mike Marchant's ultimatum that he would not be threatened or blackmailed.

When questioned this morning about his apparent about-face, he stressed that he had not given in to what he calls the lunatic fringe.

'I said before that I would not halt logging if it meant the loss of all the jobs in the Cornwall area. And I hold by that statement.

'The situation however has changed. After reading a report compiled by a research officer of Mr Buckley's department, and seeing last night's *This Is Australia*, I suddenly saw a way whereby my government can honour both its election promises, and halt the logging in this area without a loss of jobs.'

(Last night's A.B.C. programme *This Is Australia* featured the discovery of a ghost town buried in the Settlement Creek forest, an intact living museum of the old pioneering days that is quite unique in this country.)

The Premier continued: 'I can't give you all the details at this point in time, but I can say that the Minister for Conservation, Forests and Tourism intends to establish a tourist industry in the little timber town of Cornwall, which will provide many more jobs than the number lost through the end to logging.

'I have been in touch this morning with Cornwall Milling Incorporated, and have made them certain offers, which they find agreeable.'

The Minister for Conservation, Forests and Tourism, Mr Buckley, also declared his enthusiasm for the plan.

'We've just got one little hiccup to straighten out,' he said, 'and then we'll be in like Flynn.'

The one remaining question is: will this proposal satisfy the greenies?

Mike Marchant is expected to make his pronouncement tonight at the free Ents Concert at the E.G. Whitlam Stadium, in the heart of Hadley.

Meanwhile, at Labor Party headquarters, all fingers are crossed.

Page 9: Churches Combine for Anti-Poll Protest Vigil

▷ ▷ ▷ ———————————

Back in the ward.

Why do I keep looking at my watch?

As if I know I've only got about another hour of this in me. Then I'll have to.

Stop it.

Find out where. How. He is.

(When it ends, will something other start? That's my only hope.)

(Please God, I'm not a Catholic now, but make it nice next.)

(If you had one wish in the world, what would you wish for?)

(If you were me, I mean.)

(Sweet dreams.)

I go back to the poem and find it saying now the sort of hope I hang on to:

for, as the themes knit and unfold,
somewhere far on, where all is changed,
beyond all twists of grief and fear,
we look to glimpse that land again

Just a little bit more to tell you.

I'll do it as if I'm someone else. (I often think I am).

▷ ▷ ▷ ———————————

When the tree came down, it went backwards, into the forest, so it didn't hit anyone. Col lay on the ground, and there was this pain. The face of the old man had its mouth open, yelling something Col's screaming wouldn't let him hear.

'Go away, just go away!' Col yelled, and in the end he did.

The next bits come back now.

Longtime waiting. No one would pick Col up, scared to move him.

A sound of thunder and Col started to laugh. 'It's stopped,' his mouth said. Land safe till the next time. All this pain for nothing. Squirt was right. It's (I'm) irrelevant. And the ants saved it, after all. (Or maybe my red rabbit?)

Then pictures floated in and out of other heads.

Wee Willie and the city inspector. Things like Brian's name and 'arrest' and 'assault' and 'possibly manslaughter'.

'Do you understand?' asked the policeman.

'Yes?'

Rain splashed like tears down his face.

Then after more long time of waiting, Col heard a noise like a helicopter. 'I must be dreaming,' he thought, because that's what helicopters do, they come and wake you up.

But this time they put him in it. There was a needle in his arm. Someone sleeping next to him.

'Brian,' Col thought. It was good to have a mate to sing with.

But this time the helicopter just made him sleep more. And when he woke up he was in the white beach, alone and here.

▷ ▷ ▷ ——————————

In the ward, alone and here, I'm lonely now I'm finished.

'Start at the beginning and go to the end,' said the Lawyer.

That's where I am, but why aren't I?

And where is Brian?

Afternoon visitors spill in the door, someone coming to my bed, neat hair, suit, smile, man, deadshit, briefcase, who?

(You?)

▷ ▷ ▷ ——————————

The Argus
Saturday 30 March

BIZARRE TWIST TO MACBRIDE BASHING

Since Monday, 18 March Dr Brian MacBride of the World Heritage Commission has been lying in a coma in a private room in Queen Mary Hospital.

The victim of an alleged brutal bashing, he was found early that morning, as he lay a short distance off the track that led to the controversial new logging coup at Settlement Creek, where conservationist forces (including Dr MacBride) were camped.

While his immediate suffering was caused by lesions to the scalp and concussion, the greatest risk to his life was caused by some hours of exposure to the elements, which resulted in pneumonia.

Until yesterday, he has been in a coma, and all

news of his condition and even his whereabouts were concealed from the press.

Shortly after midday however the Medical Superintendant of Queen Mary Hospital, Dr Felicity Chan, released the news that Dr MacBride was now out of his coma and on the way to recovery.

One of the most bizarre aspects of this senseless attack upon the United Nations advocate for forests is the fact that the young greenie activist, Colin Ferris, charged with the assualt, has been in a public ward of the same hospital.

JERRY DENNING reports.

When I entered the white-tiled portals of the Queen Mary Hospital yesterday afternoon, I little thought that I would soon be meeting the hospital's most illustrious patient, Dr Brian MacBride, let alone witnessing a strange reunion.

My intention was simply to talk to the controversial young conservationist, Colin Ferris, who was rushed to the hospital in the Morlong Air Ambulance on Monday, 18 March, suffering from injuries to his legs that he sustained when falling from a tree in which he had been engaged in the greenie activity of 'tree-sitting'.

One of the many strange aspects of this case is that Colin would normally have been taken to Morlong District Hospital, but as the Air Ambulance was in the vicinity to collect Dr MacBride it seems that Colin was included in the ride, and brought to the same hospital.

Another strange aspect is the fact that it was Colin's father, Mr Sam Ferris, a logger, who drove the bulldozer into the tree in which Colin was 'sitting'.

And yet another puzzle is why anyone so committed to the cause of saving trees that he should risk his life to block a bulldozer, should attack a spokesperson for his own side, as Colin is alleged to have done.

It was questions such as these that engaged me as I entered the ward.

The hospital had placed a ban on interviews with Dr

MacBride, but what would Colin's reaction to the news of his recovery be?

The pretty student nurse at the door pointed him out to me.

I saw a young man with medium-length dark curly hair and a somewhat serious expression sitting in a wheelchair at the other end of the ward, busy with a folder on his knees.

'He's always writing,' said the nurse. 'He's doing HSC.'

As I approached him I felt as if he were sizing me up. I remembered an experience in the little timber town of Cornwall, near Settlement Creek, where I first went just before the violent confrontation between loggers and greenies.

On that occasion, the local youths – all of them unemployed – were initially suspicious, but after a couple of beers we established a firm mateship.

Colin was looking at me in the same wary way, and I reminded myself that this was no sophisticated city conservationist, but a frontier-town boy, albeit an unusual one.

Would I be able to win his confidence too?

I was suddenly conscious of the 'Doze In A Greenie' sticker that one of Colin's contemporaries had plastered across my briefcase, and which I had neglected to remove.

When I saw Colin's awareness of it, it seemed an unfortunate beginning for a talk with a greenie who had indeed been 'dozed in', and who, Dr Felicity Chan had told me, may always limp as a result.

I quickly introduced myself, and to get over the difficulty I remarked on the coincidence of him and Dr MacBride being in the same hospital.

'Where?' the young man demanded, appearing to be suddenly strangely tense.

Not thinking, I named a room number in the private wing.

At that, our interview appeared to be concluded.

The young man's wheelchair could well have been time's winged chariot.

An old Greek woman and other startled visitors

scattered as Colin took off through the ward, out the door, and across the corridor to the lift.

I hurried after him, but had to wait for the next 'down' lift.

In the hospital's main foyer, the receptionist was reeling from an inquiry as to where the private wing was.

Hurrying on there myself down the passage-ways of this labyrinthine old structure that is the teaching hospital of the nearby university, something made me think of Colin as a young Theseus, following Ariadne's thread to the den of the Minotaur.

I thought too of how in the legend it was Daedalus of course who had constructed that maze, the same Daedalus who had caused the destruction of his son Icarus, just as Colin's father caused young Colin to fall.

Strange thoughts? No doubt. Perhaps they were set off by an old Greek patient in Colin's ward, whom I had heard yelling after the fleeing youth in his native tongue.

In truth, any thoughts as I ran were better than my fears that by giving Colin the whereabouts of the World Heritage Commissioner, I had inadvertently set the scene for the relapse of that patient.

The actual scene, however, when I arrived in Room 3 was perhaps even stranger than my imaginings.

Colin and Dr MacBride were both weeping and laughing and hugging each other, while a visitor with a notebook sat nonplussed at the bedside, and two nurses scurried around trying to sort out the upheaval.

When a modicum of quiet was restored, Dr MacBride refused to allow the duty sister to evict his visitors. Though obviously weak, the patient declared: 'Let's be sorting this thing out once and for all.'

It then turned out that the other visitor was Detective Inspector George Tomkins, who had been allowed in to question Dr MacBride about his alleged assault.

It also transpired that Inspector Tomkins had questioned Colin earlier in the week about the discovery of a piece of clothing of Colin's in the forest near the comatose body of Dr MacBride.

'So you know this boy?' the Inspector inquired of Dr MacBride.

'Am I knowing my own self?' replied Dr MacBride in his lilting brogue.

As the Inspector went on to ask if Dr MacBride could identify Colin as one of his assailants, I observed a strange tension flow between the two patients.

Then the Irishman turned a cold eye upon the policeman. 'You can take yourself and your little black book away,' he announced. 'As far as I'm concerned, I had a few too many drinks in honour of St Patrick's Day, and if I chose to fall down in the forest and knock my head and get pneumonia, then that's what happened, and I'll thank you kindly to be believing me.'

Somewhat more than nonplussed now, Inspector Tomkins asked Dr MacBride if he were declaring that no assault had occurred.

'Yes and I am, and that's the devil's own truth of it,' the fiery Irishman pronounced.

At that point the hospital's medical superintendent, Dr Felicity Chan, arrived to ask us all to leave the room.

'Come back tomorrow boyo!' Dr MacBride yelled after the departing youth in the wheelchair.

Back in the foyer, Detective Inspector Tomkins still looked sceptical to say the least, but there was little he could do but retire.

'You're still up for Offensive Behaviour,' he muttered at Colin. 'Plus Trespass.'

But Colin was whizzing his chair in circles, and I doubt if he even heard.

With the announcement by the Premier yesterday of the halt to logging in the Settlement Creek area, and the dropping of what could even have been a manslaughter charge against him in different circumstances, Colin Ferris has a lot to celebrate.

Does the Labor Party too have reason to cheer?

At last night's free concert by the folk-rock group the Ents, which attracted a crowd of 15,000, many of them Hadley voters, Mike Marchant urged his supporters not to vote Informal, but to give their preferences to Labor.

Will this turn the tide for the Labor Government? Will it hold Hadley, and thus the balance of power?

By tonight, the result of the by-election will be clear.

Page 1: Hadley Goes To The Polls.
Page 7: Mike Marchant: The Man Behind The Charisma.
Page 18: Weekend Feature: Settlement Creek, Ghost Town of The Living Past.

▷ ▷ ▷ ———————————————

Saturday lunch time.

Slept last night and slept and slept and slept.

Nothing in the sleep but being asleep.

Just woke up a minute ago, then Baby Nurse came down with the paper and I read the bit I've just put in for you.

'Quite famous, aren't we,' she mocked.

I'm so happy, I gave her a piece of fruit cake.

'Bad for my figure,' she munched.

Only wrong thing at the moment is that Nick's off at his op, so I can't tell him about any of this. After wheeling around in the foyer yesterday afternoon, I had my tea, then I had to be by myself to sort out how fast things had been happening. So I went out and sat on the balcony and listened to the Ents concert floating over from the stadium. I hadn't realised that *this* is in Hadley. I mean, when they said in the papers an inner-city seat and all that, I didn't even know where the hospital was. The nurses are going out in dribs and drabs today to vote. Not that I care really, it's just politics. The way I look at it, they're all just in it for themselves. There's a bit on that T.S. Eliot tape Kathy sent me, that I've been listening to a bit, where he says:

Something something is the worst treason,
to do the right thing for the wrong reason.

Like the premier saving jobs, then saving trees. You look at him on the TV and you know he doesn't know what it is to have HP on the lounge, or to walk in the forest. It's all just keeping power.

That's how I look at it, anyway.

. . . Afternoon visiting's starting. Think I'll just scoot down and see Brian. Today they let me put on a jumper that Mum sent me in her first parcel, so despite my pyjama bottoms (split up the sides because of the casts) I feel more like a human.

Well.

'Blow me down with a feather,' as Mum says.

Sitting now at the cafeteria-shop place, 6.15 pm and I'm having fish and chips for my tea because I don't want white stuff. (This is yellow stuff). They'll be shitty about where I am, but what can they do? Throw me in gaol? Ha! It's only since last night when I sat on the balcony making myself believe I don't have to go there, that I realise I don't have to go there.

Since I thought the story was over, even more has been happening. Have to write like a steam train to keep you up to date. (Do steam trains write? Well, you know what I mean.)

So, what this afternoon?

Well, firstly, Brian.

I snuck in, he hasn't got the tube in his arm any more, and he's looking good.

I was still a bit scared of course, I know he knows I did it. I guess I wanted to talk to him by himself and try to explain and say thanks for saving me and I'm sorry (I've even wondered if I haven't been writing out this tale for him), but he was all 'My boyo' and just wanting a yarn.

To show you how he's back to his old self, at the end he asked me if I could snick off to the pub and buy him a bottle.

'Not that I'm necessarily wanting to drink it you're understanding, boyo, but I just feel more at home if there's one around.'

I said sure, and also told him about Nick and how when Nick's over his anaesthetic and everything tomorrow I'll bring Nick down to meet him, with a shot of the old aeroplane fuel.

Those two will get on great guns.

I suddenly realised today that it's not just Grandad but Brian too that Nick reminds me of. In their different ways, they've all got this whole way of looking at things. I don't know what I mean, but I mean they're all the opposite of people like Mike Marchant, who just has one thing and limelights out on that, and different too from the premier (not that I know him) because to him it's all bargaining this off against that.

I'm getting off the track.

(Isn't that funny? Peculiar, not ha-ha. Till last night, writing a sentence like that would have brought back the fog-trees, but not now.)

Anyway. Fish and chips. A bottle of Jameson in my lap, that I bought out of my new money and will take to Brian tomorrow. The Irish tape playing for the first time in my ears.

But what I'm really trying to tell you is who was in the pub.

Jade.

Flicking back her hair as she lined up a shot, I saw her at the pool table as I sat in my chair at the bottle shop. She sunk the black ball, then turned round and saw me too through the window.

Looked like I was a ghost, then a monster, then she was Jade and she raced in the bottle-oh door and almost hugged me, then settled on 'Hello'.

I can't hate her.

I did for a minute and said no, I wouldn't come in and have a drink, and she went, 'Go on, oh Col, go on, don't be a shit', and other Jade-stuff till of course I did.

Partly I think I was stunned, thinking everything was getting too coincidental (I think you call it) like something in this book by Charles Dickens that Squirt made us read last year, where this long-lost convict turned up again in the end and everything tied up almost too neat like one of Mum's Fair Isle patterns or the themes (I'm not sure what they are) knitting in that bit of the poem. But anyway, it was easy when I worked out that while there's a huge city, and I don't know any of it, I seem to be in this middle bit that's called the seat of Hadley, and that's where the university is too, and this pub is where the uni students drink, and that's why Jade and Sharnda and Dave and Suzie and Mike Marchant and all of them were drinking there tonight after handing out leaflets all day at the polling booths.

So feeling maybe as confused as the long-lost convict must've when he got back into the story, I had a beer and let them rave. Geez, city people can rave.

Get this! Mike slapped me on the back, and said how my old man bulldozing me had probably been what he called (I think) 'the clincher' as far as getting heaps of voters to go Green in Hadley.

I felt pretty uncomfortable.

'Plus poor old Brian getting bashed,' he added.

I wheeled away.

'Did he win?' I asked Sharnda.

She looked as if I was strange. 'It isn't announced yet. And of course he lost. But we won yesterday. The forest's saved.'

I quite like Sharnda. She squinted at me through her cigarette smoke and said: 'That's what you wanted, isn't it?'

Is it?

I try to imagine a group of tourists gaping through my green land, or I think of city people spilling into the palace, chip packets amongst the daffodils and voices yelling, and I think I'd rather have the whole fucking lot go down.

If it isn't just mine, I'd rather it was no one's.

Then Jade brought me a beer.

She said, 'Come here.'

I'd noticed Mike Marchant wasn't with her tonight, or even with Suzie, he was getting off on himself. So 'Oh yeah,' I thought, but I followed her into the corner past the pool table where the mirrors were.

'You once showed me your secret,' she said. 'This is mine.' I realised she was pissed. 'Look.' She dabbed her fingers at her eyes, and suddenly they weren't this unbelievable green any more, but ordinary and blue-grey. 'Coloured contact lenses,' she said. She looked at me bleary, like someone who can't see. 'Plus I made up my name. It's really Emma.' She started laughing, till I did too.

Sitting with my fish and chips, I think that's probably why I like her. She makes you have to laugh.

The news is on the TV in the cafeteria now, and Labor's won Hadley by so much, thanks to the Green preferences, that they won't even have to count the postal vote. So the government will stay in power and I'll go back to face the Night Sister.

▷ ▷ ▷ ————————————

No no no no
the fascist finally won

▷ ▷ ▷ ————————————

Late Sunday morning. After I freaked out completely over Nick, the Night Sister made me have a couple of sleeping tablets so I've just woken up. Baby Nurse told me I'd missed out on the hot-cross buns. Stiff. My head's got this slow heaviness in it, though whether it's from the crying or the sleepers I don't know.

I won't try to explain the crying. Nick was my mate.

But maybe it'd be good (for me, I don't care about you this morning) if I try to write down/work out why I feel so guilty.

It's not just because I didn't go and say, 'Good luck!' Truly, he'd made me think that the op was going to be so easy that I didn't know I had to do that. (The Night Sister told me that all along he knew he only had about a fifty per cent chance. As if that made it better.) But I do feel that since I've had my chair and my window bed and my fruit cake I've had like a new life and haven't needed him so much. Plus the last couple of days I was too busy with finishing my tale and finding Brian and realising I'm not going to gaol to even visit him.

But still, all that isn't why I feel somehow as if his death is my fault.

It's just that I have this kind of superstitious feeling (I don't know what you call it) that so much was bad, that there had to be like a sacrifice to make it good again.

. . . That's all muddled up, but I can't say it any better because it *is* a muddled-up feeling I have about it all. Maybe if you've ever been a Catholic, you'll understand. (Not that I am one any more, but still.)

. . . I think of how he got his enemy, and how it waited in him for years, and I try to tell myself: he died for his country.

Or for the peoples, as he used to say.

But I do still see Nick as somehow my fault.

I can't help it.

▷ ▷ ▷ ————————————

Sunday night, just after tea. Sitting out on the balcony, trying to sort out today. Everything still keeps happening more and more.

I guess I should be used to strange visitors by now, but when Garry Lazlo turned up this afternoon, well, it really seemed the limit.

Hadn't he stuck his nose in enough?

But to rub it in, like, here he was, with a big bunch of pink roses. 'Trust a poof,' I thought.

'G'day,' he said, and dumped them in my lap.

Before I could throw them back, Baby Nurse was there, sniffing at them and raving. 'I'll get you a vase.'

'What're you doing here?' I said.

Garry grinned. 'Just fixing up a hiccup.'

'Huh?' I thought. (He wasn't hicking or anything.)

I was about to tell him to piss off, but he cut in: 'Would it be all right, Nurse, if I took Col out for some fresh air in the gardens?'

'Oh of course, by all means, gush gush!' went Baby Nurse.

And before I could say anything, Garry was whizzing me down the ward and into the lift, and then we were out in the sunshine. Along a path and down another till we ended up in this little kind of private patch, hidden behind a big holly hedge. Garry parked me and flung himself down on the lawn.

He squinted up at me, and around his mouth there was a kind of smirk as if he found the look on my face funny. 'Don't worry,' he said. 'I'm not going to rape you.'

Of course, I hadn't really thought he was, but him saying it, made me red or something.

'What do you want?' I reckoned.

He grinned more then, and went for his pocket. 'Just thought you might feel like a smoke.'

Well. I didn't say no. In fact, I didn't say anything for quite a while, and neither did he. It was as good as Scott's stuff. In fact, it was just like Scott's stuff.

'Where's it come from?' I asked.

'Kathy Dolan.'

The sun seemed all gold around me, warming the whiteness out of my legs. Even Nick seemed less dead.

But as the old man says, 'You get nothing for nothing.'

Still without saying anything, Garry felt in his pocket again. I thought he was going to make another smoke, but he handed me this folded piece of paper. I opened it up, and it was a photocopy of some torn old document, with a kind of rough map and tiny old-fashioned writing that I mostly couldn't understand.

There were some words I got, such as 'Samuel Ferris' and '1854' and 'fifteen (15) acres at the Settlement Creek junction, at the agreed price of One Pound per acre'.

Garry cut in: 'It's a title deed to the land the old pub's on. It means that Samuel Ferris bought it.'

'Yeah,' I thought. 'So what?' It had nothing to do with me. Kathy Dolan was the one who liked dirty old pieces of history. He should show it to her. 'Where'd you find it?' Not that I cared.

It was Garry that went a bit red then. 'In that trunk under your bed.'

I let the brake off and started heading. Talk about the outer limit! 'Those are *my* papers!' (Not that I ever read them, but they weren't there for him to read either.)

I was halfway up the path when Garry grabbed the chair and shoved it deep into a boggy bit so I couldn't move.

'Just listen will you, you little prick,' he shouted. 'Don't you get it? That bit of forest, it's not state land like all the rest, it was Sam's!'

'So?' Sam was dead. Long ago.

'So? So cop this. Amongst the papers you've never even looked at, there was a copy of Sam's will, leaving everything to the second Sam. And there was that Sam's will too, and it left everything to the third Sam.'

See what I mean about feeling like I've got into some kind of old book? You know, where a lost will and missing heir turn up at the end, and everything's OK?

'So Grandad owns the Settlement.'

I was just getting real happy, thinking how I could tell him to tell the government to stuff their tourist thing, when Garry looked at me kind of sideways. 'Well . . . not exactly,' he said. 'He owns it, but what with his mind being like it is, the courts wouldn't think he was fit to decide what happens to it.'

I started to swear and stuff, but Garry yabbered on with his legal crap, something about how before Grandad had his stroke, he signed some paper giving the old man the right to act for him.

Of course I just fumed more. The old man had never been to the Settlement. (Grandad always reckoned there were the Doing Ferrises and the Dreaming Ferrises, and the old man was the Doing kind, so Grandad had never even told him about the palace.)

Then Garry told me to put a sock in it again, and anyway, get this! He reckoned that he'd talked to the old man, and the old man said as far as he's concerned, the land's mine, and whatever I decide to do with it, that'll be it.

His voice went on, blah blah, about how the old man will

have to sign the papers, because I'm not twenty-one, and then how he had to tell me that the government couldn't afford to buy the Settlement from me, because it's priceless and stuff, but I didn't want to hear about money. What was the point? I'd never sell the palace.

Suddenly the world seemed almost too warm and bright. I started to laugh. It was funny ha-ha and funny peculiar all rolled into one. And funny more besides. After all these years of saying the palace is mine, now it really is. I can even build a bloody barb-wire fence around it if I like, and stick up No Trespass signs. That'll keep Kathy Dolan out. And everyone else. And now I don't have to worry about what I'll do when my legs are better. I'll go back and live at the palace. It won't matter about people at Cornwall calling me a greenie, because I'll have my own place. And I won't need a job or anything. I can just grow my food and hunt a bit, live happily ever after, like a prince.

The next thought was nice too. That was to do with the old man giving it to me. Maybe he didn't hate me after all. It's good, not having to hate him back.

But Garry made me feel alone, because he wouldn't join into my laughing. He just watched me, very serious inside his eyes.

'So that's it, is it?' he said. 'The Settlement's yours, and yours alone?'

'Yep.'

Garry got up and left me with the bit of paper.

'Thanks,' I said. 'See you later.'

'No,' Garry said.

'No what?'

'I don't expect you'll ever see me again.'

Maybe it was the dope still working, but that made me sad and a bit panicky. 'But when you come down to Cornwall. To set up the tourist thing.' I almost felt like saying he could stay at the palace, but I'd just promised myself never to let anyone in there. 'We could have a drink at the pub or something.'

Garry looked at me as if I was thick. 'I won't be coming to Cornwall. There won't be any tourist thing.'

When he was nearly out of sight he turned back to me. 'Did you know . . .' Garry seemed to go off on a web of his own, 'there was someone once who got hiccups, and couldn't stop?'

Despite it not having anything to do with anything, I asked, 'What happened?'

Garry shrugged. 'In the end they died.'

'What does that mean?'

'Work it out for yourself.'

He disappeared around the corner of the holly hedge, leaving me to get my chair out of the bog.

I can't take a trick, as Mum says.

Just popped down to see Brian and give him his whisky, and there's a lady in his bed.

Not with him, I don't mean that.

Instead of.

So I went to the main desk to see where they'd moved him, and you'd think I was a KGB agent or something, the way they carried on. It's all hush hush and a Big Secret, where he is, because it seems all these reporters were turning up to talk to him, so they've taken him to another hospital and I can't have his address, even though I said I had to send him something. Nothing for it I suppose but to drink it myself.

I've got this kind of feeling I'll never see him again.

Like Nick. Like Garry.

People keep on dropping out of my life.

Getting on for midnight. (Getting on for pissed again.) I've just got it!

You probably think I'm thick or something (I probably am) but I was flicking through this folder kind of staring at all the words I've collected this last couple of weeks, and I saw that bit in Friday's paper, where that Minister reckoned there was just a hiccup to be straightened out before the tourism could happen.

Just a hick!

That's me.

And if I keep on hicking (kicking), then everyone'll have to move from Cornwall and the town will die. Or maybe the logging will start again, and then it'll be the forest that I kill.

It's like how I used to feel about weekends: I could be part of the town and play sport for it, or I could be part of the forest and look after the palace. But it's worse. Much worse.

I wish it was me that could die.

Go down a nice dark tunnel of a grave, never come up. Sleep without dreaming. It was nice that first day, in the blackberry bush, when I thought I was dead. Free and floaty. But in real life I'm alive in the tunnel all I know is that I can't let people into the palace.

Just see them dropping chip packets amongst the daffodils, carving their names into the big round table. Shouting through the green stillness.

Remembering something once Grandad said, about how it's the job of the prince to keep the land.

He did. I'm sure he did.

But now something makes me think of Nick, and how he said – that long night when he talked and talked – how he said that princes are bad.

'Not in the fairytales,' I argued.

Nick shrugged. (I can see him now, lifting his eyes up, spreading out his hands.) 'I don't know, this fairytales. But in true life . . .'

That's the point, I suppose, about growing up. You have to believe in things as they are. Like it was a cop-out, to think that Nick's death could kind of pay to save us all. I was closer to the truth in the falling, when I thought that it was *my* blood that was needed.

And maybe some deaths work slow like Nick's, living like an enemy inside you, with no bright gush that makes people stop and see you, but just a slow trickle like the sap that clings like the blood-tears down a mountain ash in springtime.

Jumping around a bit now, I'm just putting down ideas as I think of them, but thinking of Nick's made me remember some old Greek legend or something that Squirt told us, about how in the springtime, way back in B.C., they used to kill the king, to give new life to the people and the land.

See you later!

▷ ▷ ▷ ————————————

I looked him up in the phone book, lucky he's got a weird name.

'Hello?' He sounded a bit out of it. There was loud music playing.

'Say *Boo*,' I said.

'BOO!' he said.
I felt the hiccup go away.
I said, 'OK.'
'Happy Easter,' said Garry.
Then the Night Sister came, dark as thunder.
After we got over what was I doing using her phone, *and* still up, blah blah blah, she suddenly reached in her drawer and said: 'Here. I'd forgotten till now. That old Greek man, that friends of yours, I was talking to him the night before his op and he said to give you this.'
I'm listening to it now.
Maybe you think I'm happy, and that it's all kind of resolved, but it's not. I'll never go back to Cornwall, except maybe to visit Mum and Grandad (while the old man's at work), and I know I'll never ever be able to bear to go back to the palace.
Still. I guess for everyone else, and for the forest, all's well that ends well, as Mum says.
I feel Nick's hand holding mine, and I hear him saying: 'Three metre . . . thirty metre . . . three hundred million metre . . . We still together, always now, we struggle and fight, struggle and fight . . .'
'Ein entaxei,' I sing.
So does Nick.

▷ ▷ ▷ ————————————

Saturday Grand Final Day (night).
It's months since I've written in this. I'd thought the story was over, but maybe they never are.
This morning, there was a knock on the door just before lunchtime. Not that Saturday lunch is a big deal here. More like breakfast. Garry was in his dressing-gown. Rick (that's his boyfriend) was in the shower. I was dressed but burning the toast. So Garry answered it.
It was the old man.
First time I'd seen him since that falling.
He held something in his outstretched hands.
'G'day . . .' he said, kind of into the air (as if I was still up the tree).
'Come up for the Grand Final,' he apologised to Garry, 'and thought Col might like to have this. To kind of make him

more at home away from home, like.' He looked at Garry as if Garry was some real heavy kind of landlord. 'That's if you don't mind.' Then he looked at me because he knew I knew that the kitten was one of Moggie's, and that meant he'd been into the palace.

I don't have a word for it, how that little black squirmer looked, inside the big callousy hands of my old man.

Or how the old man's eyes were scared of me, like those of a kitten in a place it doesn't know.

'Mog,' I said, 'little Mog, new Mog, new Mog, my Mog.'

And I accepted the apology for Max.

Garry had his jeans on now, and Ricky too, and the kettle was boiling and the old man was sitting on one of the kitchen stools and Mog was pissing in the corner and then Garry was putting an old jumper in a cardboard box for Mog to sleep on and Rick was saying it was midday and turning the kettle off and getting four cans out of the fridge and then Garry was insisting that I had to go to the footie with the old man, he'd look after Moggie, wouldn't he, Moggie?

So that was this afternoon. The team we go for lost, but at football there's always plenty to talk about.

As he dropped me back here, the old man said: 'Col, you know that trouble we had with the dozer. Why we were late getting the track in. It was the brakes, see, son? And that part they had made up. Turned out it was a real bodgie job.'

Seeing him swinging swinging still coming his mouth coming coming screaming into the tree that isn't any longer me.

'I know,' I said.

The old man nodded.

We never had to talk much to understand each other.

Sitting now in my room at Garry's place, I think how you probably don't even know I'm here. Whoever/wherever you are. What if you wanted to get in touch with me? (Not that you ever do.)

But anyway, here's where I am. When I was getting out of hospital, Garry offered, and it seemed better than two to a room and no tea at the C. of E., specially as it was going to be permanent.

'You probably know,' he warned, 'I'm gay.'

I remember thinking of the dreams I'd had, about dancing with Garry on the beach.

'I think I might be too,' I said.

Garry looked me up and down, then his mouth took on that smirk again, that he does when he thinks I'm young and stupid. 'No such luck,' he said, and hugged me.

That's how come I came here.

▷ ▷ ▷ ———————————

Grand Final Night

Dear Nick,
Pretty stupid, eh, to write to a dead person, but no stupider than writing pages and pages to someone I don't even know. Anyway, just thought I'd say Hi! and I'm still going pretty entaxei. Where I'm staying now, the pictures on the wall of my room were left by the last person and I've never taken them down. One's of Karl Marx, and there's this quote under his whiskery old face that goes: We recognise our old friend, our old mole, who knows so well how to work underground, suddenly to appear: The Revolution.' Just thought I'd tell you, because it reminds me of this rabbit I used to know. He didn't know how to tunnel out, but now I do.

Have a drink for me, wherever you are.
Love from,
Col

▷ ▷ ▷ ———————————

15 Jane St,
Merton
Sat 28 Sept.

Dear Brian,
Pretty stupid, eh, to write to someone just care of the United Nations but no stupider than writing to a dead person, so hope this gets to you. Anyway, just thought I'd say Hi! and I'm OK. Where I'm staying now, the last person left some pictures on my wall and I've never taken them down. One's of James Joyce, and he stands there with his hands in his pockets

looking as if he could take the world on, and there's this quote underneath him that says: 'Silence, exile and cunning.' Just thought I'd tell you. Thanks again for not dobbing.

Have a drink for me, wherever you are.

Love from,
Col

P.S. The court cases were a while ago. We all got off the Trespass because old Golden Gloves never read the Something Something Act that morning. And I just got a year's Good Behaviour Bond for the Off. Behaviour (tree-sitting) – the judge or whatever he was watched me limp in and reckoned that'd keep me out of the action for a while.

15 Jane St,
Merton
Sat 28 Sept.

Dear Scott,

Pretty stupid, eh, to write just care of a P.O. in W.A., but the old man says that's where you are, so hope this gets to you. Just thought I'd say Hi! and hope you're travelling well. I only found out today about Danny and Terry splitting the same time as you, and them joining the army. I know they've been thinking of it, ever since Solly did. I suppose you know the plan about my mum setting up the craft shop with your mum and Mrs Bail? Can't you just see them, sewing and knitting their fingers off like three old witches? (Nice ones, I mean.) Sean's still just got my pub job, but it seems there'll be heaps of work there soon, when the extensions start. (Did you hear the Dolans have actually bought the pub, and they're staying!) The old man reckons half the blokes from the mill are already flat out doing the new road up from Baytown, and of course there'll still be logging work on the pines. You know how Cornwall Milling got the government concession or something to open a ranch-motel? Well, Helen and Monica are going to be looking after the ponies. About their style!

Don't know what I'll do, now the physio's finished. (They reckon one of my legs might be a bit fucked for good, but here's hoping.)

Been having a great time, bludging on sickness benefit in

the city! Going out to lots of bands in pubs and that with this chick called Jade. (You should see her!) Went to the Grand Final today. (The Wildcats lost.)

Anyway, say Hi! to Jan. I always knew you two would get it together. Have a good time (like I am). And have a smoke for me wherever you are.

Your mate,
Col

P.S. Hope you know, there was no need to split. (Just thought I'd tell you.)

15 Jane St,
Merton
Sat 28 Sept.

Dear Kathy,

Pretty stupid, eh, to write to you after all this time, like a letter from a dead person. But anyway, just thought I'd say Hi! and thanks for the Walkman and the tapes. Hope you're OK. Thanks too for the smoke you sent me. I've worked it out now, why you hated Scottie, that it must've been your stuff he ripped off and you were growing it in the forest. To tell you the truth, that made me feel funny for a minute, to think you'd had your own secret place in the trees, when I'd thought I was some kind of great prince of all that land.

But anyway, that's over now. I've given it up. Not smoking! Just princing!

I've been having a good time, here in the city. There's heaps of books at Garry's place, so I get into them a bit, in the daytime (don't tell Squirt!). Swim a lot too, for my leg. On weekends I've been going to bands in pubs a bit with this girl called Jade. (I'm not going with her or anything. She's rapt in this guy who sings in this group called the Ents, so we just play pool and hang around and that in case he notices her.) City people are still like my mum's ants to me. Not that I'd eradicate them, but they could go back into the wall for all I care. I can't wait to get . . .

▷ ▷ ▷ ———

Knowing now who you are, I ring you up.

But not knowing what to say, I just say: 'HI!' That's how I speak to you.

I can hear the clatter of the glasses, the voices of the town. The jukebox is singing.

'It doesn't matter whether skies are grey or blue.
'It's raining in my heart cos I can't be with you.
I'm only living for the day you're home to stay . . .'

At the end you say, 'See you tomorrow . . .'

I say, 'Yeah!'

▸ Epilogue

'Once upon a time, it was Spring,' said Grandad, 'and a prince walked into his land.'

'How old was he?' I asked.

'Oh . . . as old as his eyes and a little older than his smile.'

'And what did he do?' I said.

'He gave away his land in order to keep it.'

'But why?' I said. I just couldn't understand.

Grandad's answer was always the same, and always strange. 'Because he'd learned the truth of fairytales.'

'So are they,' I asked, 'true?'

Grandad picked up a chip packet that lay amongst the daffodils.

'Of course,' he said. 'If you believe in them.'

Other books in the Plus series

THE TWISTED WINDOW

Lois Duncan

Tracy can *feel* the new boy, Brad, looking at her. He's handsome enough and charming – but there's something about him that's rather sinister. Even so, she could never have known how dangerous he really was, or that she was destined to be part of his twisted plans. A taut and unusual thriller.

BUDDY'S SONG

Nigel Hinton

Buddy's in a bad way. His dad, Terry, is in prison; people are being pretty nasty at school; and his mum is busy with her new job. He feels lonely and confused, until one day he decides to learn how to play an old guitar and quickly discovers why his dad loves rock 'n' roll so much. There's excitement, happiness and a way of expressing feelings in music. And there's the chance to dream – of girls, friends and a happy future. But he finds out that his dad has dreams too – which could go out of control and threaten what Buddy wants most. A terrific sequel to *Buddy*.

A BUNDLE OF NERVES

Joan Aiken

Joan Aiken shuffles the surface of the everyday and deals out a handful of stories that range from the weird and fantastic to the ghostly and sharply macabre, but all of which are firmly rooted in the plausible. An excellent collection from a compelling writer.

REMEMBRANCE OF THE SUN

Kate Gilmore

In a country embittered by the Shah's oppressive regime, romance must take second place to revolution, and Shaheen is prepared to sacrifice his musical talents, his plans for a college education in America, his love for Jill, and, if necessary, his life. Set in the turmoil of Iran before the revolution, this is at once a touching romance and a fascinating account of two young people from very different backgrounds torn between love and political ideals.

I CAN'T STAND LOSING

Gene Kemp

Patrick Gates is trying very hard to be positive but living at 17 Constance Place makes it pretty difficult. The Gates family are, in Patrick's own words, a bunch of no-hopers, excepting himself and Mum who somehow keep them all going. Then comes the memorable day when Mum packs her bags and says she's off to Greenham Common . . .

MADAME DOUBTFIRE

Anne Fine

Lydia, Christopher and Natalie are used to domestic turmoil and have been torn between their warring parents ever since the divorce. But all that changes when their mother takes on a most unusual cleaning lady. Despite her extraordinary appearance, Madame Doubtfire turns out to be a talented and efficient housekeeper and for a short time at least the arrangement is a resounding success. But as the children soon discover, there's more to Madame Doubtfire than domestic talents . . .

DEAD BIRDS SINGING

Marc Talbert

Mother gasped and slammed on the brakes. Matt was jerked further into the folds of the back seat. 'Oh my God!

Someone else's stupidity and a split second of madness changes Matt's life for ever. Kindness and concern from his friends keeps him going but does nothing to cure the bitterness in his heart. Can he forgive? Should he forgive?

THE SHADOW IN THE NORTH

Philip Pullman

A elderly woman loses her money on an investment; a music-hall conjuror is pursued by thugs; and a clairvoyant in a trance mentions the names of the richest man in Europe and his mysterious company. Seemingly unconnected events set Sally Lockhart of the trail on an evil far more awful than she ever imagined.

MY SISTER SIF

Ruth Park

Erika's seventeen-year-old sister Sif has always been unhappy in Sydney and longs for the remote Pacific island where the girls were born. And so Erika plots their escape. On their return to the island paradise, however, Sif falls in love with Henry, a young marine biologist and reveals her family's fantastic secret. But their love is tragically threatened by the pressures of an encroaching world on the seas around the island and the creatures living in them.

IT ALL BEGAN WITH *JANE EYRE*

Sheila Greenwald

For Franny Dillman, reading is life. Her idea of heaven is an afternoon with *Jane Eyre* and a bag of crisps. But when she develops an unhealthy obsession for Mr Rochester, Franny's mother takes fright and supplies Franny with some 'modern teenage fiction'. And so the trouble begins.

URN BURIAL

Robert Westall

When Ralph discovers the mysterious creature buried beneath the ancient cairns high up on the fells he realizes instinctively that he has discovered something that possesses enormous and terrifying powers. He is frightened – but why can he not leave the creature and its strange tomb alone? He soon finds that the earth has become a new battleground for an old conflict of races far superior to man.

THE TRUE STORY OF SPIT MACPHEE

James Aldridge

Home to Spit MacPhee is a crazily painted converted boiler on the riverside, shared with his equally colourful and eccentric grandfather Fyfe. Barefoot, boisterous and brave, Spit is an independent spirit and aims to stay that way. However, the threat to this freedom will take more than Spit's ready fists to repel. His future lies between a passionate battle of will – and law – between two women for whom the salvation of Spit MacPhee means very different things.

IF WINTER COMES

Lynn Hall

In the wake of an international crisis, America is threatened with nuclear attack. Suddenly, life for Meredith and her boyfriend Barry in Lombard, Illinois, seems about to be abruptly ended, In the course of dramatic weekend the two young people attempt to come to terms with themselves and their families in the knowledge that Monday may not arrive!

MOSES BEECH

Ian Strachan

Peter is on the run from his layabout father, and Moses Beech offers him shelter in his isolated cottage. They get on well, but for how long can Moses's unhurried way of life survive this sudden intrusion? The answer comes all too soon – and tragically. Winner of the first Observer/Rank Organization fiction prize.

THE SEVENTH RAVEN

Peter Dickinson

A modern thriller, mixing high tension and social comedy in a powerful brew. Doll, just 17, is watching the cast of children stream into the old church when she hears a gunshot – and a few moments later she and the children are hostages of a gang of terrorists. Suddenly this year's opera has turned into a different kind of drama altogether.

THE WRITING ON THE WALL

Lynne Reid Banks

Kev is a bad influence – or at least that's the opinion of Tracy's dad – so she isn't surprised when her parents won't let her go on holiday with him alone. But Tracy is determined to have some fun before she has to settle down in a boring job like her sister. So she finds a good way of getting round her dad – at least, it seems a good way at the time . . .